SUBURBAN SOULS
BOOK TWO

Anonymous

A STAR BOOK

published by
the Paperback Division of
W. H. ALLEN & Co. PLC

A Star Book
Published in 1982
by the Paperback Division of
W. H. Allen & Co. PLC
44 Hill Street, London, W1X 8LB
Reprinted 1983
Reprinted 1986

Printed and bound in Great Britain by
Anchor Brendon Ltd, Tiptree, Essex

ISBN 0 352 31176 2

1

GLORY. Look into my face. You must believe me in spite
of everything.

· ·

STORM. What are you saying?
GLORY. I love you, I have always loved you, and you love
me—you know you do, you love me still.
STORM. For God's sake. Glory.
GLORY. Kiss me, John.

HALL CAINE.

ERIC ARVEL TO JACKY.

Sonis-sur-Marne, March 31st. 1899.

My dear Jacky,

Many thanks for all the papers you have sent me. I went to see
your uncle last Sunday week, and came away with a bad attack of
influenza, which I do not seem to be able to get rid of. I was in bed
three days last week and I feel as if I could put in the same time again.
Raoul is at home for his Easter holidays. If Wednesday suits you,
would you come down and taste the *cuisine* of "our boss." Raoul is
obliged to return on Thursday morning.

If you like Tuesday better than Wednesday—"tip me the griffin."

With every good wish for you and yours, believe me to remain,

Yours very truly,
ERIC ARVEL.

I was far from being cured of my grip, and ought not to have accepted this invitation, but I was dying to see my lying Lily. So I sent a postcard, on which I had printed my own photograph, with my cordial acceptation.

I felt very shaky on the morning of April 5th. and a peculiar accident happened to me, that troubled me still more.

I got into a fiacre to drive to the Eastern station, and the horse bolted in the Rue Lafayette, dashing on to the pavement, and breaking the shafts. I jumped out and looked at my watch. I had just time to catch my train. I called another cab, and I had not been in it five minutes, when this second horse bolted also, and shying at a handcart, which stood by the curb, went headlong into a shop-front, and stopped suddenly, pitching me forward, while the coachman flew bodily off his box, one of the front wheels passing over his ancle and hurting him seriously, if not dangerously. Luckily for me, directly I saw the horse become uncontrollable, I had let down all the windows of my closed conveyance, and as I fell forward, I heard the crush of glass down below in the hollow frames. No harm came to Jacky. I thought I bore a charmed life that day. I jumped out again and was confronted at once by some gentlemen who had witnessed my first accident. They defied me to get into another fiacre, but I did so, and caught my train with not a minute to spare.

Why I mention these strange narrow escapes—two bolting horses in ten minutes—is because they shook my nerves to a fearful extent, and I forgot all the calm resolutions I had made to myself. I had arranged not to mention my enquiry at Brussels, but to be quite cool and collected, and play the part of a lovesick, ignorant fool, sympathizing with a martyr. In my half-feverish state, under the effects of the influenza, these accidents made me quite unfit to struggle against the Arvels, or carry out my schemes with a view to the ulterior publication of my adventure as a novel, as I should have wished.

APRIL 5, 1899.

When I arrived, the father was alone in the garden cleaning the bicycles of Lily and his wife, and grumbling about the way they had neglected them during the winter. "If I object to their carelessness, they say that I ought to look after them." Then he complained of Lily, who had been ill all the time in Brussels, where he had taken her on a little trip, he said. She would go out to a theatre every night, and never got up until noon. He had a bad corn and was evidently worried, haggard, sick and tired of everything. He was especially bitter against Lily's brother. Raoul wouldn't get up early. Raoul did not offer to help him to clean the bicycles. Raoul never opened his bedroom window when he got up. Raoul—he repeated an old story, I had heard from the women—once asked his mother in his presence to leave the house for ever. I enquired when that took place.

"Four years ago," he said, moodily.

"Then what does it matter, what a sixteen-year-old lad has said? He is not your flesh and blood."

I told him that I had brought up a boy, the nephew of my mistress, and that the lad had an awful temper. I went on to say that if children behaved honestly to the world, worked and got their own living, as Raoul did at the London wine firm, never got punished once at the regiment, don't thieve, drink, or get into debt, we ought to be satisfied and we do not want them to hang round our necks and pretend to love us. If children turn out to be respectable, that is about all we can expect. After this and a little more desultory talk, I went up to the house and saw the mother who told me to go upstairs and find Lily.

I saw her with Raoul in the best bedroom. She looked only tolerably well and was highly powdered.

I gave her the sixth volume of "Justine," where I had marked two paragraphs in pencil; one "Lily," and the other "Jacky," with the date: April, 1899 (see Appendix D); the first volume of "Gynecocracy," a most clever and obscene work on the subjection of man to woman; and the scarce novel Césarée (see Appendix E). The latter work I had told her about the last time I had seen her. I also had the Eau de Cologne for Raoul, more perfumes for Madame Arvel, and the quinine wine of my own manufacture for Lily, with papers and magazines for Papa; the arrears of a month.

Lily greeted me very coyly and strangely. She could not look me in the face and I think she had told Raoul to stop with her for a few moments.

I threw the books on the bed before her brother, and after the usual greetings, she kissed me in front of him, and gave him the volumes, which were fastened up in tissue paper, to go and hide for her.

When he had left the room I put the ring on her finger. She seemed highly pleased, and kissed me again very nicely, to my surprise showing me two others that were on her hand.

One was a sapphire, surrounded by brilliants, that Mr. Arvel had bought her in Brussels, and the other was a little pearl with a few roses. This last she refused to tell me who had given it to her, and I did not insist, as I really did not care, and I am pleased to say that I felt only friendly pleasure as I pressed my lips to hers, and I was very cool towards her.

I may declare at once that from this day forward I was able to sit at her side and feel the warmth of her body if she pressed against me, without that electric, instantaneous erection that I had always had in former days.

I praised the beauty of both her new rings, and said that mine was nothing beside them; but I can assure the reader that my gift was handsomer than any she had on her fingers, and she wore a lot of trumpery circlets on both her hands.

Lily said that Papa was in an awful temper, and that the house was topsy-turvy with quarrels, principally through his hatred of Raoul.

"You put him in this terrible state. It is all through you."

She did not reply. I looked round and saw that the door of communication between her mother's bedroom and hers had been put back in its place. She saw the direction of my glance and then I fastened my eyes on hers. She guessed the reason of my mute questioning gaze, and as if replying to the question that was in my mind, said:

"Yes, the door is closed now!"

More proofs of her connection with Papa. When she was only a child-toy for Arvel, Mamma let her come in and out of her bedroom, but now she was his second wife, so to speak, her mother in her first wrath, vexed by the pleasure trip, had caused the door to be fitted up, saying:

"You can have her if you like, since it is no use crying over spilt milk, but she shall not come into our sleeping apartment. Go and see her in her room, since it is to be so, and do all you desire with her, but do not let me see it. When you played with her just a little, under my eyes, before enjoying me, I did not mind, but at present, as you have her completely, it must not be in my presence."

It might also have meant that the connection of the three being no longer innocent; their guilty conscience smote them and they had put up this apparent barrier for servants and visitors, as there was nothing to prevent them opening it in the night; but Mamma would soon get used to these Mormon-like manners, and all three would pass the greater part of the night in one bed again. It was only a matter of time, and money from Papa.

Mademoiselle said she would go and show her Pa my ring, and so we went together.

"She has begged one of you too," grumbled he, "I could not get her out of the jeweller's shop, until she tore the sapphire out of me. You are a fool to listen to her."

Lily had bought a false ring for Raoul, out of her own money. She said: "Pa was furious."

We went in to lunch, and her mother feigned to be a little vexed that I had given the ring, but I think she was pleased all the same. Papa grumbled and quarrelled all the time of the meal. I showed my photographs and they were a great success. Raoul took them all.

Lily opened her eyes, when she saw the one where she was reclining on her brother's breast, and handed it over to Papa, saying:

"Why this is obscene, Pa!"

He took it, looked gloomily at it, and said nothing.

I talked about the Brussels trip and elicited that they had been nowhere and seen nothing. The shops, the streets, and theatres and music-halls, but not a museum, nor had they visited Antwerp, as I had recommended.

After lunch, I went and sat with the father, who still talked about Lily's laziness and Raoul's nonchalance. Apropos of nothing, he told me a story of how, when Lily was at Myrio's, a young chap, a bookkeeper there, came and asked to marry her. He said he answered:

"Yes. Lily will have a thousand pounds when her mother dies, but if you really want to marry her, no dangling about, but an early date for the marriage must be fixed at once. No doubt the chap only wanted to poke her (sic), as he never returned."

Why did he tell me all this? Did he think I was going to ask for her hand?

He spoke again against his stepson, and I explained that I asked for no gratitude from the boy I had brought up.

"What I have done is for my own conscience, not for the youth. I only want him to be able to get his own living, and he can then turn his back on me if he likes. I have done my duty."

I told him that the lad was the son of an officer or a priest, no one knew exactly, and then he suddenly burst into a great fit of anger, and to my amazement launched out into a long diatribe against all wearers of epaulettes. How he had changed in so short a time! And he showed great concern for the martyr Dreyfus, as he called him now, and from this day forward always spoke against the sword-dragging idols he had formerly revered. I immediately concluded that an officer had behaved badly to Lilian; having seduced and abandoned her? Probably the good-looking fellow who came to fetch the dog. And never more did Lily talk of officers, she who had always spoken about handsome military men.

The ladies now appeared, and asked Papa to come out for a walk, or all go on bicycles. He refused, alleging his corn, and we four: Mamma, Raoul, Lily and I, went for a ride to a neighbouring forest, leaving Papa seated in an arbour, in his garden all alone.

Lily and her mother asked me what I had got so excited about. They had heard my voice in the house, a most unusual thing for me. I replied that I had been explaining about bringing up children and had been taking Raoul's part by telling Mr. Arvel about my protégé. They were quite surprised, and I repeated my story.

"You never told me you had a boy to whom you were a father!" said Lily, astonished that I had never spoken of him before.

"I do not like to boast," was all I answered.

The mother walked with me in the forest, and told me long stories about the bad temper and jealousy of her husband. How good the children were. How he did naught but find fault, was tight-fisted, envious of everybody far and near, and above all, hated Raoul. I said it was very strange, but if he was jealous, it may have jarred upon him to find Lily perhaps a little too free in her manners with her brother? Mamma answered indignantly that if the children could not play together without restrictions, during the brief time that Raoul was on leave, they might as well be dead. I said it was very mysterious, and I put it down to illness or influenza. We now separated and I talked to Lily.

She, remembering my supposed desire to be a "slave," cut a twig in the forest and began to try and play her part,—poor girl—evidently wishing to curry favour with me, but I had lost all control over myself, trembling with the fever of my cold and quite unnerved, so I wrenched the impromptu whip from her hand, and before she guessed what I was about to do, I cut her severely across the shoulders.

She ran from me out of my reach, shrieking in pain, and came back to me rubbing her shoulders ruefully. Her eyes met mine and she was silent.

"Et allez donc!" I said.

"C'est pas mon père!" she retorted defiantly.

Raoul had approached us, and heard this last short colloquy. He did not speak, but smiled with the peculiar sardonic leer and scornful twist of his lips. As I had always thought, he was cognizant of his sister's secret of shame.

I must break off here to explain that the dramatic success of the year in Paris was an amusing farce, called La Dame de chez Maxim, which has since been played all over the world, and the catch-phrase of the cocotte-heroine is: Et allez donc! T'es pas mon père!—"Go on with you! You aren't my father!" This is about the best translation I can make of this colloquial French sentence, originating from the vocabulary of the *gamins* of the streets, who, when reproved for bad language, etc., by a stranger, call out this phrase, meaning that they do not care for their interlocutor, as he has no parental authority over them, nor can they feel shame before him.

Lily had used it well, guessing my thoughts by the first half I had let slip, and instead of answering: "You aren't my father!" she had said: " 'Tis not my father!" And I had started this vulgar "gag," because I knew the play was being performed in Brussels, and I felt sure she had been with her Papa to see it. I found afterwards that I was quite correct in my surmise.

I quite forgot all my determination to be cool and collected, and trembling with rage and fever, utterly unmanned, I honestly confess it; I told her I was convinced that she had slept with her father, and I did not mind that, as I had advised her to give way, she having gone so far with him, if she saw it served her interests. She was indignant and protested that it was not true.

"Then you are all the more infamous to excite him, lead him on, and not give way after all. You are equally guilty, if not worse. I am vexed with you, because you wrote me a most pitiful letter from Lille the morning after your first night out with him. It was the cry of a violated woman. And it was all lies, for you went on to Brussels and enjoyed yourself freely, although you wrote on returning how you had suffered, and had no pleasure. You are gay and happy and go to theatres and concerts every night."

"Oh! he did not spend much money," interrupted Lily, with an ungrateful sneer. "The theatres are cheap there. The stalls are only two or three francs. He bought me the ring you saw and a few German aprons that I took a fancy to. That's all."

"You never bought anything for me," I replied, "nothing would have pleased me more than that you should have brought me a sixpenny packet of tobacco, just to show you thought of me."

"He never left me a second to myself. I dared not do it. It was all I could do to buy a ring for Raoul for thirty-five francs. But I assure you, you are quite at fault in what you think about Papa and me."

"Nonsense! You pass eight days in one room with him, doing

all your dirt together, dressing and undressing, using the chamber pots before each other and you want me to believe you are a martyr. I went to Brussels and I know everything. Two beds in No. 4 room, with a screen between, on the first floor. The Boomaens brothers from Ghent are convinced that you are only a little whore he brought from Paris, and not his daughter at all, for what father would sleep in one room with his daughter for eight or nine nights?"

"But he is not my father!"

"All the worse. If he was really your father, people might still think his instinctive pudicity could cause him to restrain his passions."

"If Boomaens said this he shall repent it. Besides, Papa quarrelled with him before we left."

That was a lie, as I ascertained a month or two later.

"Don't stir up any mud, is my advice. Your Papa is a monstrous madman. He could have done things cleaner, by putting you in another room, or in another hotel, or something similar, and contenting himself in the daytime only. You are compromised for ever in Brussels as Arvel's little prostitute. You are a liar of the worst kind, with your lost letters and your conduct last winter. I have found out why you would not see me in November and December. You had the 'whites' and God knows what other female troubles."

I saw a look of intense surprise on her dark lowering countenance. She started. I had enough presence of mind to draw back and remember part of my original plan for the day, which was on no account to speak of the supposed virginity, or the menstrual irregularities of January. It would not do to put her too much on the defensive.

"That is nothing," I continued, "but instead of telling me the truth, you profited by your indisposition to try and torture me, instead of telling me honestly to wait until you were better. You have been home nearly a month and have not tried to come to me, who you adore! You are frightened lest I should see the marks on your bottom, where Papa has whipped you."

She did not answer me, but looked vacantly before her.

"He has always been your lover, more or less. He used to feel your backside and then go and have your mother."

Again she was silent. I went on:

"I feel it is all over between us and it will be for the best."

"No! no! Don't say that—don't say all is over between us. Don't say that!"

"Your life is free as far as I am concerned," I continued, "I have never told you a lie, or served you a dirty trick."

"That is true," she said, "you never have."

"You think of nothing else but lies, falsity, and trickery. I will not and cannot put up with such deceit, especially as my eyes are quite open. I may be a fool with you, but I know my own folly, so that I am only half a fool after all. Infidelity I don't care a straw for—there is plenty soap to be had, but I'll have your heart and brain all truthful as well as your body, or nothing at all."

I do not try to describe her tearful eyes, annoyance, denials, and general air of stupefaction. I think I was in a rage. I am certain this was the first time I ever was in a passion with her. I felt strangely weak and ill, and my legs seemed to go from under me—a sure sign of influenza. She begged me not to get into a passion, and seemed frightened of me, as she said that if I loved her, I ought to believe that nothing had taken place.

My answer always was:

"I am not jealous, as you know. I only complain of being made a fool of, by lying grief and mockery of martyrdom."

But she hated Arvel, she said.

"But you led him on. Remember the eve of Shrove Tuesday, when dressed as a Japanese girl, you said you would never marry, but live always with your Papa. You both talked of the story of incest in the day's paper; your hand passed over his privates, outside his pants, and then you spent hours in the photographic dark-room with him, much to your mother's annoyance, and once before me you warmed your hands in his trousers' pockets."

"Why do you talk of that night of Shrovetide? I dressed up for you. All those caresses mean nothing. I never touched his privates. Such tickling touches mean nothing with a father. You do not know what you say when you talk of exciting a father. It is so horribly vile and repugnant to hear you say that. With you I would do anything, but *his* touch revolts me."

And then, with a groan and a kind of half-sob, as if to herself, she exclaimed: "Oh, that eve of Shrove Tuesday!"

"If I am wrong, why did you not get indignant with the carefully-veiled advice in the letter I sent you before you left, when I called you Mademoiselle Bismarck?"

"What letter?" she asked, with an air of affected ignorance.

"Go and look at it! You've got it still. You are a liar—that is all I can say."

"I am not a liar. But I confess appearances are against me. About the double-bedded room, I acted without thought of guilt. Mother knows we occupied one room all the time. A gentleman and his wife, who own some property near Brussels, came and visited us in our room and saw the two beds."

"What must they have thought!"

"There was no concealment on our part. I am innocent. How could I do it? I hate him so!"

"But it was to your interest, maybe?"

"What interest? Show me what good it would do me, if you can."

I made no answer, but only shrugged my shoulders.

"I owe you an explanation, I confess, and I will give it. I must clear myself in your eyes. I love you, Jacky, and you are too cruel to me."

"There is no explanation possible."

"Yes, there is."

"I defy you to give me one!"

"Hush! hush! Don't talk so loudly. Mother will hear us!"

She ran to her mother, being unable to carry on the argument, and we went home in a tramway. As we walked towards the starting point, I noticed that her face was blue, and her lips violet, as she talked eagerly to Raoul. She was telling him that I had spied on her in Belgium. During the ride, Lily was tearful and sulky. I chaffed her unmercifully and bitterly, asking her what was the date of the month.

"Yesterday was April 4, I believe?" With strong emphasis on

the word, "four," alluding of course, to the number of the room at the hotel of Brussels. I added that the figure four had a great influence in my life, and I asked her brother if he had read a novel by Conan Doyle, called, "The Sign of Four."

I made a lot of stupid jokes.

"How gay you are, Mr. S . . . !" said Adèle.

"I play the clown!" I replied. "This is but the forced gaiety of a broken heart, madam, as they say in the dramas. I am only a clown!"

And aside in English, for Lily and Raoul: "A damned old clown!"

Then to the mother: "Laugh and the world laughs with you; weep and you weep alone!"

"That is very pretty, Mr. S . . . , and quite true!"

Then we reached the house. The stepfather was descried on his bicycle! He had been out alone on it.

We had tea, and then I walked about with Raoul and Lily, both of them complaining of their mad stepfather. He had gone to the wine-merchants, when in London, and complained of Raoul to them, saying he was not trustworthy, etc., and one of the partners told Raoul that Arvel had been to them, but that he had taken his statements with a grain of salt. Raoul showed me a recent complimentary letter from his employers. Lily told me that Arvel had advised one of her best clients to go to a rival milliner's.

During this, Arvel went and sulked alone in his arbour. Lily said:

"Now you won't be invited here so often, because you are talking too much to us. He has been spending too much money on his house and garden, and he is miserable and unhappy. When Raoul's time is up in September, I am going to London to start bonnet-building there. Raoul will then earn about £4 a week in the wine business, and I will keep house for him. I shall get all the custom of the ladies of his employers and their families to start me. Papa wants me to stop with him. He will make me his secretary at £2 a week, and get me work for fashion papers. He gave me that article to translate that I sent you. I could not do it, but I did not want to refuse, as he would have sneered, and grumbled, and scolded, and said I knew nothing. So you did it for me. I typed it on the machine and gave it to him. It was beautifully done, but he found fault, saying there were too many French words left in it. When I am in London, you shall come and stop with me."

She said she had wondered how I got the "dream-face" on the lustful letter I had written, and I explained how I had done it. Then, being alone with me a few minutes, she gave me her lame explanation, which she had now had time to forge, and I, worn out and careless, really ill, sick of quarrelling, said nothing to it.

"During the winter, I had been ill, and had kept the house alone while my parents were away on the Riviera. The doctor advised change of air in the spring. So the journey was arranged. The morning we started, Mr. Arvel went away quarrelling with his wife and servants. He was overpoweringly attentive, and to my surprise took seats in a first-class coupé. I was not present (!) when he retained the room at Lille. Nothing strange took place until I got into bed, when he came round the screen, for there was a screen here at Lille the same as at Brussels, and tucked me up. Then he did what he had never done in his life before (!). He kissed me full on the mouth. At that moment, all you had said, Jacky dear, flashed across me, and I had an awful feeling of disgust come over me. He saw that and left me. If I had given way to him, why should I write that letter from Lille?"

"Because you are a woman, and women often cannot help confessing half the truth of what runs in their minds, without knowing why."

"There you are right. I know that weakness of my sex, but I wrote to you, because after feeling his vile hot lips on my mouth, I cried as I thought of my poor mother, who has lived twenty-five years with him, and I sickened at the idea of letting him touch me. And then I thought of you who I love, who had warned me, and who else could I write to, but you, for comfort? I could not write to you from Brussels. He never left me." (In spite of her disgust, she had eight more nights in the double-bedded room at Brussels.) "I could not let my mother's lover touch me, I swear it. Nothing else transpired during the trip, although he might perhaps have got excited at seeing me dress and undress."

How did she know that he got excited?

She protested greatly, and I said I did not care. I was sick and tired of it all.

I trembled with fever and emotion, and once more, I felt my knees give way. She ran from me into the house, glad to have got through her wretched story, and I think she went and talked to her parents, while I stopped in the garden with Raoul in the dark, for night had now come on.

He took me upstairs into the best bedroom to wash my hands before dinner, and Lily reappeared with a lamp, got me out a clean towel, and left me again.

While drying my hands, she came in, and Raoul discreetly left us.

Now she hung round me, begged me to believe her, caressed my hands and face, and made me suck her mouth, her eyes full of tears, saying that she only lived for one man in this world—me!— and that I had driven her mad by my proposal to let her become the cruel mistress, and I her slave. She said she would soon try it. She promised me a long letter of passion, detailing what she would like to do to me, for Saturday morning, and so she changed the subject, and gave me more luscious, tongueing kisses, so that I could not do otherwise than respond to her embraces, and clasp her tightly to me, and I murmured, as I kissed her, speaking with my lips on hers:

"Lily! My Lily! Oh, darling Lily!"

I was now full of lust. But they called me from below to come and dine, and she released me. I left her to go downstairs first, so as not to show that we had been together, and as I went towards the door, my head swam round, I staggered, and had I not caught hold of the top of the banisters, I should have fallen. I looked round and saw Lily standing watching me, the garish flare of a petroleum lamp full on her face, as she held it up to throw a light on the stairway.

If ever I saw a fiendish look of wicked triumph on the features of a living creature, it was then. She thought she had fooled me completely and I shall long recollect how I said to myself: "I am glad I am slightly indisposed. I have the influenza. I have not said so, and they will think I am mad with jealousy, and lovesick as a callow youth. I am glad I stumbled, and that Lily saw me staggering down the stairs."

At this moment, Papa, who was waiting for me to go down to dinner, stepped out of his little library, holding a parcel in his hand. It was my "Romance of Lust," neatly tied up. He thanked me for the loan of it, and said he enjoyed it immensely.

I took it, and now Lilian came down in her turn.

"What is that you are giving to Mr. S . . . ?" She said this in a strange, drawling tone, looking steadfastly at her Papa, the while.

"Only some books," was his reply, and the light died out of his eyes, and the same frowning, dull expression came into his face.

I took the packet, and we all went downstairs, but I thought of the same scene last summer, when Mr. Arvel returned me "The Horn Book," and I knew they had read "The Romance of Lust" together.

I purposely forgot to take away the volumes when I left that evening, just to see what would happen, and always hoping that perhaps it might furnish an incident for my book.

We dined in the workshop in the garden. Everybody was dull. Papa hardly spoke. Lily took cod liver oil before dinner. I could not eat. I told them the two carriage accidents of the morning had upset me, and I thought I had caught cold.

Then the father suddenly, coolly spoke of the Brussels trip, and how Lily had prevented him from sleeping, by clapping her lips together all night, like a baby suckling. The mother joined in the conversation, and plainly showed that she knew of the double-bedded room arrangement. Lily kicked me under the table, and said that anything is better than "snoring." She meant that for me, when I slept with her last summer, as she explained to me after the meal, when we were going to the station.

While this talk was going on, I looked closely at them all. We each spoke in turn, except Raoul, who held his head down, bending over his plate, his lip curled in a devilish grin, and it suddenly dawned upon me that this was all prearranged. Mamma looked defiantly at me, as if to say: "Now, sir, where is the harm you thought you knew of?"

Lily had told Papa before dinner that I had gone to Brussels to spy upon them, and that I knew about the sojourn at the Brussels hostelry. Papa had then said: "Let us talk about it openly at dinner, as if it was the usual thing, and no secret." It was a "bluff," and Papa only made his case worse in my eyes, as he had shown me that they were all in the secret of his amours with Lily; Mamma, and Raoul, the brother. Granny I never saw again. She had now been pensioned off. I suppose she was in the way, and perhaps knew too much, as she was very indiscreet.

After this joking about the double-bedded room, there was an awkward pause, and Lily rose to get a clean plate. She left her seat, walked behind Papa, and I distinctly saw her pass her hand behind his neck, caressingly. I pretended not to see.

After dinner, Lily, Raoul, and myself went for a short walk with the dogs, and during our stroll, Lily, when Raoul forged once ahead, asked me if I was still angry with her. I was worn out and answered indifferently.

"You are vexed with me."

"How can I help it, when I think of what you wrote to me. Oh! that letter from Lille!"

Hypocritically, I looked up at the moon, and imitating Lily, gave a kind of a sigh, which died away with a little moan. She caught my hand and pressed it convulsively.

I told her I had a girl waiting for me on my return to Paris.

"If I do not find her at home, I shall go to a brothel, and choose a thin, dark lass, as much like you as possible, and while I enjoy her, while she caresses me with patient hands, and submissive mouth, I'll call her Lily."

"If you do that, you'll not be a man at all, but simply a beast!"

But she said that coolly and did not seem to care. She had got tired and pale, her features were drawn. The powder, worn off, had not been renewed. She was sallow and careworn, and I felt thankful to be able to say to myself: "She looks ugly."

When we returned to the house, we found that Mamma had kicked out the servant, the only one they had. Papa grumbled. Lily sat down and fell to pieces, as it were.

"I'm not well and we shall have to do the housework to-morrow ourselves."

They were all dull and miserable. I said "good night!" and Raoul and his sister saw me to the station.

They both talked against Mamma's temper now, and how she was a "servant-hater."

I had noticed during lunch that Lily's dog Blackamoor had a nasty wound, a piece an inch long being torn out of his cheek, along the jaw, and I had said at table: "I suppose he has been fighting?" Nobody answered but Lily, who hurriedly replied: "Oh yes, it is nothing!"

She told me now that she was frightened lest I should insist on this topic, or take up the dog and examine it, etc., as the wound really came from a tremendous kick given to the poor brute by her Papa.

She once more alluded to the slavery mania, thinking perhaps to please me. I asked her what she would do to me.

"You must not ask me, as you are my slave. The very fact of you wanting to know would make me refuse to tell you. But I know what I want to do to you and I won't say."

"Not if I beg you most humbly to be good enough to let me know?"

"I will put it in the letter I'm going to send you. You must come and see Mamma and me and have a cup of tea, when she is certain that Papa is going to be in Paris all day. You can come on your bicycle. I will make it right with Mamma and let you know the day. Papa is not to know."

She had made friends with her mother apparently.

I got into the train and leant out of the carriage window to say a last "good-night!"

"He has been very rude to me all day," said Lily to her brother, looking at me.

"Rude, perhaps, but natural!" was my answer, and she nodded assent very prettily, with a kind smile, as the train moved out of the station.

The next few days, circumstances, which I shall not reveal here, added to some old suspicions and recent slips of Arvel's garrulous tongue, led me to discover the true reason of the wretched state of things at the villa.

What he earned as a financial reporter was not enough to pay for all he had been laying out lately, and he had other employment connected with his travels. This had been suddenly cut off, and not only did he feel the loss of these resources, but there was danger in the air. It was worse than a mere pecuniary loss; it was a catastrophe which I shall say no more about, except that the dark cloud passed over, but the money did not return.

I went and reconnoitred the road to Sonis on my bicycle, to get familiar with the route, and on April 8th. I received the following:

LILIAN TO JACKY.

April 7, 1899.

My naughtiest and best,

At last, I have found something! After all my seeking, here is a combination, which I believe will receive your sanction. Here it is: you and I will go to Belfort for the Whitsuntide holidays, if my brother does not get leave, which is highly probable.

I have already said at home here, that if my brother does not come, I should go myself to see him, and Mamma approves of my project.

Naturally, my parents think I go alone, and as to my brother, you will tell him that having heard of my journey, you wished to accompany me, as you wanted to see him, and he will find this quite natural. I will arrange with him.

Now, do not go and raise a lot of objections, for there are none to be made, and if you don't find my idea a wonderful one, I shall know you do not love me any more. What day can you manage to come on a bicycle? Find out when is the next settling day at the Bourse.

I love you,

LILY.

I answered "yes" for the journey to Belfort, as Whitsuntide was May 21st., and things might change by then. I arranged about the bicycle visit in a rather short, cool note addressed to "my naughtiest and worst," and had strange thoughts about Raoul and the collusion of this wonderful family.

Lily did not want to come to Paris to me, to undress before

me in the open daylight. She wanted to ward me off until she could get me into a bed with her in a month's time, and make me believe I had taken her virginity.

I felt that I had no longer any influence over her; she had no strong desire for me, as her Papa's daily caresses with mouth and fingers kept her sufficiently cool to be able to play with me at her own sweet will.

I felt rather amused to think that Lily could offer me nothing of herself until Whitsuntide; and the pleasures of slavery and the passionate letter appertaining thereto, which she had promised me, had dropped out of her erratic mind.

I thought it time to throw a bombshell into the camp, and I sent her the following terrible letter, which was a sort of ultimatum. I did not care if she answered it or not, or how she took it. My only care was to leave the question of her maidenhead and her *fausse couche* of January as much as possible in the background.

When I wrote it and the following letters, I always asked myself how they would look in print. I was now working more for the gallery than myself.

JACKY TO LILIAN.

Paris, Monday, April 10, 1899.

Since I last saw you, Lily dear, I have reflected a lot. I have been thinking of nothing but you, and I write to you this day calmly and deliberately. My health is much better. Sleep has returned to me. And without gall, without acrimony, and without temper, without feverishness, erotic or otherwise, I tell you that I am absolutely decided to break with you entirely, and therefore with all your family as well, unless you treat me with the entire frankness to which I have a right. I have chained myself to you, but I left you your liberty always. I am not jealous, nor in your way. I am greatly excited to think that men desire you. You are my adored little whore. I love you with all the strength of my soul. You are the last love of my life. And that is why I am leaving you.

When you went away on your journey, I did not ask you to write to me. On the contrary. See my letter which you received on the morning of your departure, wherein I called you: "Miss Bismarck." I wrote in the most delicate manner possible.

It has pleased you to invent a fairy tale, so stupid, that when you tell it, it comes on to rain, merely to make me wretched. Please note that I did not ask you for any details, or to tell me anything at all. You have accumulated lies upon lies in your weakness for lying. But even among lies an observer can unravel the truth, for lying women cannot always lie.

What is this idea you have for posing as a martyr before me, who can read your thoughts as if your brain was in the palm of my hand? Why play the black drama of the unfortunate girl persecuted by an infamous father?

I told you this winter that no power on earth can prevent a woman from communicating with the man she loves. I go farther:

NO POWER ON EARTH:

a) could have made you take this journey, if you did not like;

b) could have made you sleep in that room at Lille, if you did not like;

c) could have made him stop out of your bed that night. That is IMPOSSIBLE;

d) could have made you continue your connection in Brussels, if you did not like;

e) could have made you accept the ring he gave you as a reward for your kindness to him, if you did not like.

Your false allegations, your comedy of indignation disgust and sicken me!

The story of the lunch with Fontarcy and Clara—and his lordship, and all of us, are ready to begin again if you say the word—the story of my brother and his refusal to meet the unknown little brunette I proposed to him; all this proves that I am no vulgar, jealous fellow.

Suppose that I am infamously vicious—(you once called me a vicious man in front of your Papa)—perverted, depraved, a sadique, like Mr. Arvel, whether he be satisfied or not (?)—anything you like—but I never laid a trap for you. I have never lied to you up to now. I have showed myself to you as I am. You could have refused me, or driven me from your side.

I will not have your body, if I cannot have all your sensual confidence. I want to know all, down to the slightest detail. That will excite me enormously. If not, all is finished between us for ever. I want to be your accomplice, but not your dupe. Besides, I have never been your dupe for long.

Never more shall you bring tears to my eyes. I'll have no sadness coming from Lily. I will not let you make me suffer morally any more.

Since the month of October, I have found you out three times in flagrant lies; useless and dirty, stupid lies, and all told to me, who loves you, and who you say you love.

And you do love me, I am sure, for nothing forced you to continue your connection with your poor old Jacky.

You know pretty well all about the horrible sadness of my life; the daily sickening torture I undergo; the terrible fatality that pursues me, and 'tis you, my little Lily darling, who offer me as a supreme consolation, a mass of stupid artifice, that the greatest goose of a coquette would not dare to use towards a schoolboy. Such mockery is too much for me to bear.

I shall suffer from this breaking off of our connection, I confess. I do not play at being strong-minded with you.

But I must and will suffer alone. I am free to inflict upon myself what moral torture I like, but I refuse you the right to make me suffer, by lying manœuvres and stories, supported by lame reasoning.

In answer to this letter, I absolutely order you to send me a wire at once, no matter what other letters, etc. may be on the way. In this telegram you must tell me if you consent to the complete breaking-off, or send me a word of tenderness to make me understand that you give way to my reasoning.

If you desire no more of me, of my caresses, of my virility, of my mouth, of my inventions of passion, slavery and other exquisite follies, I want my ring back, and I can manage to get it without putting your honour in danger. In my poor eyes, burnt with the tears you have made me shed, that ring has a sacred character, and I will not allow it to remain on the fingers of a lying woman, such as you are.

I love you, and shall always love you whatever happens. I kiss you over and over again, perhaps for the last time.

JOHN S...

At the same time, I enclosed a sort of commentary of Lily's letters, from the one sent from Lille, down to that ordering the translation of the article on ladies' fashions.

I copied her letters, and the comments were made in red ink.

I do not repeat them here, as they were simply the criticisms that I have given already in the preceding chapter.

I began by saying that I wanted her to be as depraved as she liked, but with frankness with me.

I alluded to the villanous character of the Lille letter, and how I had wept on receiving it, and believed she was a martyr, until I reflected upon the cruelty of her postscript on her return, when she said she was free on that Sunday.

I pictured her drinking champagne with Papa, and I wanted to know why he should be jealous of the brother, when he loved the sister?

I told her I should have married her long ago, had I been rich enough, and I asked her if that infamous letter, written after her "first night," was not a vast mystification. I informed her that certain things had transpired between her and her mother's lover at Nice in 1898, and that they had both conspired in the past winter to cheat Charlotte out of marriage with Raoul. That they had read my bawdy books together.

I alluded to the falsity of one of her letters where she accepts my ring, and says not a word about the one Papa had given her in Brussels. How could you, I went on to say, since you talked of how he worried you with his open manifestations of passion, which do not prevent you accepting jewellery from him. And on April 5th., after speaking against him all day, you caress him furtively at dinner.

I made no copy of this strange document, but I have just discovered the last page in the rough, and so I give it here:

Then comes the article to be translated, and I write the ironical and erotic rubbish about the man who suffers from unsatisfied desire! The whining letter of Lille is forgotten, or is naught but a lie.

And so I depart for Brussels, thinking that Lily, her eyes open at last, had shut her door against him at night. I shall find that they have had two separate rooms when I make my little inquiry. I start off, like the idiot that I am, saying to myself that if everything has taken place as I fancy, the gift of my poor little ring may have a deeper meaning.

(Here I drew a rapid sketch of the famous No. 4 room.)

Why then this false story of martyrdom; why pose as a victim when it is she who causes pain, and wants to make all men suffer, or rather those who cannot save themselves by reasoning or common sense?

At Brussels, I am told of her gaiety; her happy life; she goes out every night and sleeps until noon. Why not? But why this eternal desire to lie?

Then there is the noise of her childish romping with Papa like puppies playing, as they were heard in the hotel; and the state of the bedding, the sly hints of the lookers-on about the little Parisian whore of Mr. Arvel, who pretends she is his daughter, and introduces her to the outgoing lodger, saying: "Ma fille, monsieur!"

All this is nothing to me. I knew it, pointed it all out, and prophesied it long ago; but why always this fearful craving for muddy lies to me, when I am so liberal in my ideas, and to whom Lily has spontaneously said ten times this year: "I love you?"

To my great surprise I got a reply by return of post, she having received my awful letter and "commentary" in the morning. She answered it at once, and I read the following at dinner time:

LILIAN TO JACKY.

Sonis-sur-Marne, April 11, 1899.

Your letter, as mean and as unworthy of you as it is of me, will nevertheless not make me confess a thing, which is even still more infamous than your conduct towards a woman, who has only one reproach to make herself, that she loves you. All the proofs that you seem to have accumulated against me, leave me absolutely full of disgust for the littleness of your principles and your judgments. I believed you had larger ideas, and I supposed that at your age, you had enough knowledge of the world to know that even when appearances are against a person, it does not always result therefore that she be guilty. But enough talk of this sort; all I could tell you would not convince you, since you seek a motive to break with me. Let us note by the way, that the one you have found is simply idiotic and won't hold water.

Certainly I will give you back your ring, but in a thousand fragments. Then you will have to work your brains, as you were obliged to do when you ordered this one, so as to have another made for your half-sister. Choose it of louder taste; this one would be too simple for the daughter of Madame X. It was useless to threaten me with means to make me give it back; do you think I would wear it now? I have no wish for it. But know that your threats do not frighten me. Now: adieu! Remain with the people who love you, and know not how to lie. Cherish such worthy folk, and above all do not neglect your half-sister. She may be useful to you.

                                                                    LILY.

I was delighted at the success of my manœuvre. Her letter, with its allusions to the "accumulations of proofs," and her acknowledgement that "appearances were against a person," were precious, and constituted as near an approach to an avowal as anyone could expect from a perverted female of her class.

It will be noted that she calls herself a "woman." In her letters of the autumn and before, she always spoke of herself as a "young girl."

My mother had married again, and my half-sister by my late stepfather, was now a very handsome young girl. Mr. Arvel knew her, and had seen her often in Paris. So I am almost sure that he was reading all my letters now, and had helped Lily to write the foregoing one.

These allusions to a female member of my family; her vile show of jealousy, shows us how her brain had been warped when young. Incestuous herself, she doubtless believed with a faith cunningly fostered by Papa and Mamma for their own ends, and to stifle eventual remorse, repentance, or disgust in their daughter-prostitute, that promiscuous intercourse was a regular thing in all families.

I recollected too the story of Pa's hot kiss at Lille and compared it with what a woman had done to her, as the reader will note she told me when first we talked freely together. What a trumpery machine is a female's magic lantern of lies and how few are the slides!

JACKY TO LILIAN.

                                                      Paris, April 12, 1899.

Excuse me if I write to you again to-day, but I wish to rectify that part of my letter relating to the ring, which you were good enough to accept from me.

It was wrong on my part to have asked for it back. I ought not to have spoken about it. It was a gift: that was enough. I do not quite remember what I said that seemed to be threats, but in any case, believe me that nothing was farther from my thoughts.

For all words that might have wounded you, concerning my poor little ring, kindly accept my sincere apologies. Sincerely, I ask your pardon.

To show my good faith, only on this head, I beg you, not without a little emotion, to be amiable enough, on the contrary, to keep it always, as a souvenir of the few nice moments we passed together, trying to forget all bad ones.

Do not wear it unless you like; but keep it in a corner of your wardrobe, with the old letters, bits of ribbon, locks of hair, and other trifles that women hide jealously from all eyes. Now and then, the ring will come under your notice, and it will be very pleasant for me to suppose that you will then think of him, who was—not for long—your

JACKY.

Once more: I retract with frank regret all I said about the ring I gave you, which was made for you, which belongs to you, and no one else, and that you, ought—dare I say it?—that I order you, to keep for ever.

LILIAN TO JACKY.

Sonis-sur-Marne, April 13th. 1899.

No, a thousand times no, I'll not keep your ring. If all is to be at an end between us, it has no longer any value for me, and will only be a source of grief and regret. I have been frank with you, but I ought not to have been so. Please let me know, how I can send you the ring, as well as the books I now have of yours.

This Whitsuntide voyage, which seemed to please you, is the reason that caused you to seek a rupture, I am convinced. You dared not refuse me, and yet you did not wish to make this trip, for many reasons that I know as well as you. And I was building so joyously on the idea of passing a few delightful days all alone with you.

Indeed, when I reflect upon your conduct, I detest you.

LILY.

JACKY TO LILIAN.

Paris, April 14, 1899.

My Lily,

You say that my poor little ring would have no value for you and would be a source of grief and regret if all is to be over between us? As I do not wish anything coming from me to give you trouble and woe, I prefer to tell you at once, that nothing is over between us. There now! Are you pleased?

Tell me frankly that you are happy, and that you detest me. Write me at once a very long, very passionate letter, brimming over with love and hate. I understand that you detest me now. I have done all I could for that, it seems. I am "mean, unworthy, infamous; I disgust you by the littleness of my principles and my judgments. I threaten a poor woman, who has only one reproach to make herself—that she loves me—and I seek for enjoyment in incest!"

Chuck nothing more, please. There's no room for the rest! In spite of all these faults, in spite of Jacky being the most crapulous and cynical being; in spite of his having insulted, vilified, and dragged you in the mire; as no other woman has ever been mortified since the world has been a world, you still have the courage to want to travel and remain alone several days with this criminal; this scoundrel; this wretched insulter of women; this incestuous beast?

So be it, your perversity shall be satisfied. I swear to you, little Lily, that you shall take this journey with me, but I will make you cruelly expiate all the wrong you have done me, by the shameful erotic humiliations you will have to submit to, to make me spend, by all the ways I shall order, without troubling about your pleasure, and you shall hate me as much as you like. You will have to work hard all the same. I shall have a whip. You are warned. Don't come unless you decide to be the docile slave of a hard and severe master; as you were last summer my bitch, my slut, my toy.

I feel you love me and that you can't do without me. I won't let you be unhappy. If you only want my love and my caresses to be completely happy, come and I'll take you, sweet little monster.

Besides, why should I deprive myself of the soft pleasure that this connection gives me, because I believe that you like to juggle with my heart, excite my jealousy(?), and get up tricks for me generally! Since I see clearly through all your little manœuvres, your malice and finessing—what matters it to me, after all? Run along, my love, my passion, do as you like. You act on my flesh, and I excite you. Let us forget the rest.

But you are not going to let me long for your dirty little body up to Whitsuntide, I hope? Have you no longer any desire to strip naked before your master? I offer you my mouth, and a bottle of champagne when you choose. I'd like to lunch alone with you. I want to see you and quarrel with you, if you like. To bite your lips, spend in your mouth without the least shame, clutching your head until I hurt you, between my thighs, and saying roughly: "Go on—suck away!" And you would swallow all my disgusting spendings, so hot and thick, that I should spurt into the back of your throat. If you write me a nice long letter, very erotic, very loving and very dirty, I will tell you in my next, how I spent with a little trollop I met at the Eastern station, when I left you on the 5th.

Come quick, or arrange something. Keep me from spending with a lot of females who disgust me.

Shall I be your slave? If you care about it, you will remember that you owe me a long letter, where you said you would tell me how you would spend by the cruelty you would show to me, if I was at your disposal, resolved to obey you for an hour.

Write then. When you go to bed, take some paper and a pencil, and any book you like, to serve as a desk, and write to me at length and voluptuously—in bed.

Sunday, I made a reconnaissance to find a good road from here to your place on my bike. I find I can do it in about an hour. I was within three miles of you.

Take it and suck it.

JACKY.

Please lend me for a few days, that "commentary" I sent you—the extracts of your letters, with the red ink notes. I will give it back to you. I want to look at something.*

I lent an obscene work in four volumes to your Papa: "The Ro-

---

* I wished to make a fair copy of it for my book, and I also wanted to see if she dared to allude to the fearful exposure of her hollow lies. I had the same sort of motive for mentioning "The Romance of Lust." As I expected, she never referred to either of my questions. It amused me very much to set these trifling traps for her and her Papa. About this time, I used the type-written address, that I had saved from

mance of Lust." He made up a parcel to give it back to me. I forgot to take it. Will you open your eyes and see if the packet has not been lost or mislaid? The book is rare and worth a trifle.

The journey that I can easily take with you, has nothing to do with the motive of my breaking-off, I swear it.

Here is the true motive. I explain once more, although I believe I have already made you understand in my letter and the "commentary."

You write from Lille, that you are unhappy. I take that awfully to heart. At the end of the month: you back again, I begin to suspect that you are not unhappy at all, on the contrary, and that your story of martyrdom has only been imagined to torture me by jealousy (?) and malice aforethought. It didn't take, dear, because I'm never jealous. To find out the truth, I go to Brussels, where you have "suffered" from the "task," etc. I arrive and hear you have been going the whole hog.

What am I to believe? You say yourself "that appearances are against me." I won't insist. I only note that you possess a peculiar frame of mind, that I have not yet seen in any woman up to now, and I've known a few. You say to yourself: "I love him, what can I invent to teaze him?" Generally, when a woman loves, she says: "I love him, let me try to please him in every possible shape and way."

Now I know you. I shall finish up by laughing at your wickedness. I know all your tricks! !

JACKY.

LILIAN TO JACKY.

Undated (Received April 17, 1899.)

No sir, you shall not have a long and loving letter from your Lily, since when you felt inclined to be "naughty," you let the first "trollop" you meet, profit by it; a girl picked up I know not where. How clean and how appetising for me!

You are cynical with your ideas, and the cheek you have to tell me of your dirty pranks, me who you love and who loves you so madly,

---

her Pa's letter of January; cutting it off the old envelope and pasting it on another. She never spoke or wrote about this little joke, which must have been noticed at the villa, proving that her parents, or at any rate, Sir Giles Overreach-Arvel, knew what was going on; or pretty near, according to the muddled version that the daughter would give them, as my letters poured in.

so sincerely. I forbid you, do you hear, to tell me of all these horrors. You will make me believe that the love you feel for me is bestial. Please note that I wish also for that love, but as I am very greedy, I want the other love as well. You understand me, do you not, since you read all my thoughts so well?

It is evident that you cannot always burn yourself up with simple desire, but when you let yourself go, keep the news to yourself. I wish to fancy always that you only love me, in thought as well as otherwise. I am as one crazy at the idea of being able to be entirely alone with you for a few days, and above all a few nights.

I do not for a moment wish to make you languish until Whitsuntide, and I ruminate over a host of projects, so as to be able to slip off and lunch, and remain a few moments with you, but it is awfully difficult. Why don't you come down on your bicycle? At least, I should see you, and feel you near me, and then I have to make you expiate all the pain you have made me feel for the last fortnight.

You are not jealous, say you? So much the better for you. I am jealous enough for two, and I am very unhappy now and again, when I think that there are people who see you every day; who form an essential part of your life, whereas I? . . .

Come then next Thursday on your bicycle. It will seem quite natural. You will arrive after lunch, and you will certainly be invited to dinner. Is that settled?

If you have been well disinfected since April 5, I kiss you with a long, long kiss, as I should wish to do in reality.

LILY.

JACKY TO LILIAN.

Paris, Monday, April 17, 1899.

Little Lily,

Your nice letter, to hand this morning, only confirms what I have known for a long time, that you would be an exquisite woman, if you would only behave towards me with simplicity, truth, and straightforwardness, without your roguish manœuvres in such bad faith. Perhaps after all, it is better that you should be as you are for it is certain that if you added to your qualities of adorable prentice-whore, frankness and true faith in me, I should be madly, absolutely madly in love with you.

For the moment, I shall always feel this consolation, that if we were now separated, and it was nearly coming to that the other day—I should say to myself: "So much the worse, but after all, I'll not cry over my broken toys. Here lies Lily; she had an atrocious temper!"

What you say about the "other love," is exactly copied on what I have explained to you a thousand times, but—exquisite oddity!—you have done all that a woman could imagine, to destroy in me that very love you describe!

I'll not tell you of my orgies. If I "side-slip," I'll keep it to myself. But do you know that I should adore you to narrate to me your escapades. When you told me of the attempt of Gaston in the train, it produced an unimaginable effect upon me. When I saw you assailed by Lord Fontarcy, I was transported with lust; otherwise, why should I have done it?

And in other circumstances . . . in your house . . . how many times . . . I have seen . . . I have felt . . . it was lascivious . . . too nice . . . delicious!

You know what you have to do, if you wish to please me. Read between the lines, and for the love of God, and the love of Jacky, do not be a silly goose next Thursday.

Don't tell me that you are crazy at the thought of being alone with me for a few days, a few nights, for according to the loyal manner in which I have always treated you, and which I want to keep up, I feel that I should have a terrible desire to possess you properly. Oh! to stretch you wide, to rape you entirely, to feel myself inside you, burning, panting, bruised, wounded, crushed beneath me, and me buried in my Lily! . . .

No, I'll hurry to finish this letter. I'll only write a few lines in future.

Take all your precautions—beware of me—don't come if you are still a virgin; if you want to remain a virgin. Beware of a brutal embrace on my part.

Thanks for your plans for lunch with me. I hope you write in good faith; we'll talk it over.

I will come for certain on Thursday, if the weather is anything like fine. I must think of appearances. If the roads are not practicable—if it rains—what excuse could I make? I pray for fine weather.

I have no need to be disinfected.

I am curious to know what you will do to make me expiate all the harm I have done you for the last fortnight, in one single afternoon, and that in the rare intervals when I shall be alone with you! What saves me is that you know you are ugly when you sulk, or are in a bad temper.

I'll wind up this letter gaily with a little bit of English poetry. I'll no longer worry myself about you.

The first time I saw you in your Japanese costume, I began this little poem; at the table, openly, if you remember. I have been two months finishing it. That's a long time, but the result is extraordinary. 'Tis a masterpiece—sweet, charming and very dirty:

> Lily Arvel's a lewd little Jappy,
> Fond of Jacky—her poor silly chappie.
>> With her tongue she loves to lick,
>> His red sugar-stick;
> And when he comes in her mouth—she is happy!

(To be learnt by heart for Thursday.)
My sweet tongue in your dirty little pussy,

JACKY.

This day I have sent your Papa a big packet of English papers and magazines. There are three large fashion papers for you, with a band round them: *Pour Mdlle. Lili.* If you want them, look after them.

2

MARGARET. When to his lust I have given up my honour,
He must and will forsake me.

PHILIP MASSINGER.

I wonder why the chaster of your sex
Should think this pretty toy called maidenhead
So strange a loss, when, being lost, tis nothing,
And you are still the same.

JOHN FORD.

THURSDAY, APRIL 20, 1899.

I rode down on my bicycle, as arranged, arriving at 2:15, and
found the mother and stepfather in the garden. Mamma was neatly
dressed and tightly laced, not being in a dirty peignoir, and evidently expecting me. She wore a large pair of false pearl earrings,
which if real, would have been worth a thousand pounds. They
feigned surprise. Lily appeared at once, also neatly got-up. She wore
a bodice of black velvet, with large strass buttons; her black hair
nicely done, her face fully powdered, and her lips reddened. After
the usual compliments, inspection of my bicycle, which they had
never seen, etc., Lily took me away to show me a dress of which
she was superintending the making for her mother, who it will be
remembered, is a little, dark woman. It was a flaming red foulard

36

that they were having made at home, and Lily made game of it
and her mother. Being in the workshop with her girls, Lily talked
in English. It may be guessed that our conversation only ran on
one topic—the so-called incestuous trip—and Lily, who I watched
narrowly, flushed up deeply at each remark of mine.

Şhe stood up, leaning over her work-table, and I sat beside
her. I saw her only in profile and she did all she could not to let
her eyes meet mine. At each remark I made, I noticed a red spot
mount in her neck from the arteries, and spreading itself out from
the band of her collarette, gradually rise until it gained her cheek
and all her face. Then it would die away, and as surely come up
again at any fresh remark I made concerning her Papa.

She refused to make anything like a confession, but when I
plainly told her: "Whatever you do, I forbid you to 'put me away'
with him," she suddenly turned round and looked me full in the
face, her eyes dilated with a look of intense and horrified astonishment. She was quite dismayed and did not reply. "Do not force us
to quarrel, or make bad blood between us." And as she turned
her head away from me, without a word, I felt sure that she had
done all she could to prevent us two men ever being friendly together again, as we were in February. She wanted to "work" each
one separately, and I was now perfectly certain he knew all, or
what was worse for me, Lily's pet version.

Mr. Arvel had to go up to Paris on business in the afternoon,
as he did every Thursday, which accounted for me being invited
that day, and I was practically alone all the time with Lily. I tried
her all ways. My principal argument was: "I don't care what you
do if you are good to me. I love you, but why tell such useless lies
continually? Look at that letter I sent you in October. Why stick
to the lie that you never got it?"

"You never sent it!" she answered with a scowl.

And then she kept putting forth her great love for me. At last,
worn out, she said:

"To amuse you, I'll allow you to think that it is true, on the
condition that you never talk about it."

I agreed, exclaiming: "Hurrah! That is a confession!" and she immediately started off again herself on the same subject. I sum up here our principal remarks as far as I can remember them:

JACKY. "If your disgust was true, you could not remain under the same roof with him."

LILY. "But I go to London in September."

JACKY. "He will never let you."

LILY. "I hate him and discourage him all I can. For the last fortnight, he has left me alone."

I guessed from this statement that he could manage to ejaculate about twice a month, and the rest of the time his mouth and hands would be kept busy.

JACKY. "Then why did you caress him on the sly at dinner on April 5th?"

LILY. "I did not."

JACKY. "If you say that, I'll never speak to you again, for I saw you do it with my own eyes."

LILY. "Then I did! Why should I not caress him if I like?"

I told her of a woman I had known who could never sulk with me, but when she thought she was vexed and met me, resolved to scold and be angry, she would laugh, and put her hands in mine, give me a kiss, and say: "I cannot quarrel with you!"

I explained the folly of lying to me, who knew as much about female mendacity as a male fool could. I added: "A woman like you has no chance with a man like me."

JACKY. "If you tell me all, I can advise you. All conversation between us is impossible now. Imagine a drunkard consulting a doctor, who would say to him: 'Don't drink!' The slave to alcohol replies indignantly: 'I never touch spirits.' And he expects the medical man to cure him." Lily liked that little allegory.

She spoke of the novel Césarée.

"I think it is a lovely book, but when I read it, I see myself with you; not with Mr. Arvel. I should like to do all that with you. I am always thinking of you. When a young man, named François G., who is always running after me, and who lives down here, is speaking to me, I keep thinking what you would say in his place and how you would look."

"I like your smell. People smell differently. I don't like the smell of my brother, nor of François."

LILY. "Why don't you leave me alone on *that* subject? You have lost half the day, instead of spooning nicely with me. You might have had lots of kisses, instead of talking like this to me. I won't kiss you now. You made me very ill on April 5th."

JACKY. "Well, I'll have pity. You have been on the gridiron long enough. You are cooked now." At the word "pity," she fired up dreadfully, and said:

LILY. "If we quarrel, it is because you don't see me often enough. Why don't you come down more frequently?"

JACKY. "Oh, Lily, how can you say that? You know I can't come here unless it is arranged beforehand."

LILY. "Oh yes, that is true, perhaps!"

She meant that if I would give money, I might come there when I liked.

She spoke of her maidenhead: "I am still a virgin and you may do as you like with me. I don't care a bit about it, but I have always seen that when a man 'has' a virgin, he soon leaves her afterwards. That is what I fear with you."

I made no answer, but I supposed that this is what had happened to her, and will account for her returning me the novel *L'Anneau* without a word.

She wanted me to be a "woman." In this way: I was to have a meal with her. She was to order what she liked, as a man, and I was to be a "virgin," very docile and obedient, eating and drinking as she directed. She wanted to treat me as if I were of the weaker sex. She would perhaps remain dressed, and I was to be naked. She would undress me herself, as it pleased her.

"I would fasten your hands with that strap you left in my room last summer. I have kept it carefully."

This struck me as being strange, but conclusive. Evidently,

she had been keeping off me, not being a virgin, and this scheme would prevent me finding out her condition.

I told her how Papa had given me the story of her suitor, "who only wanted to poke her."

JACKY. "Why did he speak so coarsely about you to me, who never mentions your name to him?"

LILY. "He doubtless wants to lower me in your eyes. He is little-minded. That is the story of Teddy, who was bookkeeper at Myrio's. I did not know you then, so I can tell you without making you jealous, that Teddy made great love to me and I used to get awfully wet. I did not know what that meant then, and it used to frighten me."

She forgot she once told me that I was the first man who produced that effect upon her. I never spoke a word, as she dashed another of my illusions to pieces.

I explained that if he was little-minded, she had become imbued with Pa's doctrines, as she was like the daughter of a pettifogging lawyer.

I asked her too, ironically, how she managed to restrain her passions, having nothing but flirtations to feed upon.

"Oh, I am waiting for you, and I manage to get on by masturbating myself now and again."

Her cool impudence made me laugh, and I felt sufficiently indifferent not to contradict her in any way.

"If you do that, you'll be sure to have the 'whites' again. Masturbation brings them on."

"I never had the 'whites'!"

"Not last winter, in January?"

"That was not the 'whites.' "

"Let us say the 'reds,' if you like!"

She gave a little false laugh, making no reply which caused me to be certain of the *fausse couche* that ushered in the New Year.

Alone with the mother, after tea, I asked her whose daughter Lily was. She did not seem astonished at my query and gave me the following story of her life.

"Mr. Arvel was my suitor as a young girl. I did not like him. I got married to please my family to a man I did not love. I had two children, a boy and a girl, Raoul and Lilian. My name is Adèle-Lilian and that is why the house is called Villa Lilian. Then Mr. Arvel turned up again and used to meet me out with the babies. He would run after Lilian when she was but two years old. My husband died. I was penniless. Arvel helped me with money, and then was intimate with me, and I began to get over my dislike to him out of gratitude. We have lived together ever since. He never touches me now. I don't care. I never loved him. It was only habit with me. His temper was always bad, and he is very difficult to get on with. He is jealous, and envious, and full of curiosity."

Lily now appeared.

"How happy he ought to be between you two, both devoted to him. You, the mother, superintending the 'tit-bits' of the table he likes so much, and Mademoiselle waiting on him hand and foot."

Adèle got cross at this remark of mine, and flushing, her eyes sparkling with rage, declared he was not to be envied at all!

While concluding this conversation, Lily stood bolt upright behind her mother's chair, staring at me, but without speaking.

I afterwards told her that I had been pumping Mamma about her past life. Miss Arvel made no reply. She never even asked what her mother had said. Mamma knew all, and Lily's position in the house was secure, so she did not care.

When washing my hands before dinner, I was alone, and Mamma came and sought me out, a thing she had never done before, and said:

"Lily is not happy. Her business is too limited here, that is why she is going to London with her brother. What will the two poor children do in that great town? Suppose she does not succeed? She is too proud ever to confess a failure and come back home, and what would become of my little girl then? I want to let this place, which costs too much to keep up, and all of us would go to Paris and set up a millinery business. I would help her, but Mr. Arvel won't leave the country, where he is so comfortable."

"But he could stop here," I replied, "and she could work up

a business in Paris, you being with her as much as possible. It only wants a little money. Mr. Arvel could advance it."

"He won't give a penny. He says she is to stop here at home, and he will look after her, if she likes to be his secretary."

"Alas!" I answered, "I know what it is to want money. Look at my position now. I am 47 and I have got to begin life all over again, as I have no money."

My frank confession of poverty put an end to our conversation, but the mother, and Lily, and even the father, shutting his eyes, wanted me to offer money to set her up in business.

At dinner, Lily spoke in English of a woman near them, who had just died. It was rumoured that her husband had beaten her to death.

"Perhaps she liked being beaten," I said.

Lily affected surprise, and Papa and I agreed that it did women good to be beaten. Pa finished up as usual by telling Lily he would try it on her. No doubt he used to slap her dear posteriors a little. We were interrupted by Mamma, or I had intended pushing on the topic. That was why he liked me to be with him and Lily. But Lily was too jealous ever to let things go too far. She will always be between two people to put them at loggerheads. No doubt that was how she got her brother away from Lolotte.

Mr. Arvel, chattering privately to me, said that Lolotte's breasts hung down to her waist. I suppose he had reasons to know. He also told me that Charlotte's virginity being too heavy for her, some few years ago, she went to an oyster bar where she was known, and asked the young man who opened the bivalves to open her, and he did so. He also wanted to know if it was possible that Raoul could marry a girl, who earned no money and who wore silk chemises and drawers to match? He forgot Lily's beautiful batiste shifts and knickers, that covered her slight frame and limbs when she was "on the job." At home, she wore a thick flannel-like material for her drawers. I have had my hands there many a time. Her mother must know that now and then she would put on her soft pants of the spidery material you could blow away. They wash at home.

Now the day wears on, and the mother gets colics, and Lily

and I go to the chemist, who orders paregoric elixir, *i.e.* tincture of opium. We also drop in at the post-office and Lily registers a letter. The postal clerk is old and keeps us waiting. I tell my sweet companion that old men are always rather long.

We return home and Mamma takes a dose of the medecine. She dines on top of it, which is foolish, with neat Bordeaux wine, and a small glass of rum to top up with. Lily tells her boldly to go to bed. She evidently wished to be alone with Papa and me, perhaps not forgetting what I had hinted in my letter, as to her behaviour with her stepfather-lover, but Adèle gets quite jolly and will not stir. We—Lily, Papa and I—are to take the dogs out for a walk, before I go to the station, when suddenly Mamma spins round like a top and faints away. Lily never turns a hair. She does not love her mother; she is only disgusted at not being able to go out with us. Pa don't care either—he goes out with me, leaving Lily with her sick mother half undressed on the sofa.

There was no real love or tenderness in that house, nothing but appetites—sensual longing, gluttony and cupidity, with quarrels between whiles. That was how they lived. The master of the house cared for two things only in this world: cooking and copulation.

I had explained in the afternoon to Lily that life was impossible without genuine affection. We cannot be always spending.

"Oh! how truly you talk! I am very unhappy!" she exclaimed.

"You must not say that!" I quickly retorted. "It is not true. It is very wicked to pretend to be unfortunate, so as to make me miserable, thinking you are not happy. That is wrong of you, Miss Clever."

"Oh, Jacky! I'm not clever! I am foolish in many ways!"

"Not so foolish but what you try all you can to make me jealous, although you see how you fail. I wish you had a hundred men, so as to know what I am worth."

She was obliged to laugh at this fatuous outburst of mine, but would not explain what she meant by saying she was foolish. I was getting fatigued at Sonis now. This continual fencing was not to my taste, and only the thought of my book made me think of returning there. The idea that I was living a future volume and building up my novel kept me buoyant.

This new experience tickled my fancy and I had no sensual longings for Miss Arvel now.

Papa and I go out. I advise cutting off his wife's two daily glasses of rum. He does not appear to listen to what I say, but starts off again talking against Raoul and Lily.

Raoul had said that he would not come to see his mother at Whitsuntide. (Pa probably knew that Lily would not let him, and Lily had told me that day that she had made it all right with her brother for our journey to Belfort.)

"If he don't come and see his mother, I've got influence with the military and I'll look after him. He shall come out from England next year and do his twenty-eight days—the second service of reserve men in France—although I can get him off if I choose. My arm is long enough. Because he earns £5 a week in the wine business, he thinks the world is his own. They only keep him on because they know I could make it hot for them, as they robbed me with some shares in their concern, but as I held my tongue and did not prosecute, they gave the lad the berth. He is lazy, and speaks English with a Whitechapel accent. He wouldn't help me to clean the bicycles! (Again!) Lily wants to go to England. She shall have no money of me. Let him keep her. She is lazy, and vain, and fond of new clothes and jewellery. All her profits go on her own back. She wants us to live in Paris and set her up as a modiste. She would never be in until midnight and I should soon be known as her maquereau. Not for me! She was very ill in Brussels, but directly I popped in with a theatre ticket, she was off all right again. I tried to get her to learn writing for English fashion papers. I gave her a French article to translate (the one I arranged!), but she did it dreadfully badly. She would want a lot of practice."

"It was full of mistakes, I suppose?"

"Yes, indeed!"

He must have known I did it. I put in sentences purposely which it was not possible she could ever have written. Spangles, I called: "dainty, little, dazzling discs." A grey cloth became: "a fabric of a cloudy, pearl white, akin to the greyish tint of a fleeting morning mist." He must have known she could not knock off that stuff. A doll's tea service, I worked up as follows: "Those tiny cups, lilliputian saucers and wee plates, etc." He also feigned intense hatred for Lily's pet dog, Blackamoor. But winding up, he said:

"One thing in her favour is that she is very intelligent."

All this was said for me. He did not intend to let her go to Belfort.

We returned; Mamma was in bed. I told Lily some bits of his conversation. She was not astonished and showed no curiosity, which convinced me of their complicity.

"He hates your mother!"

Lily pretended to be surprised.

"You watch it. He hates everybody and everything, but you, and for you he shows false scorn to me, feigns to despise you perhaps—for me to share that feeling."

I did not say: "You hate your mother too." And in point of fact, all hated or despised each other. Papa despises Lily for being his plaything, and yet wants her ever between his thighs to feel and kiss him. He scorns his mistress for having sold him her daughter and prizes her as a servant and cook. Raoul hates his mother's lover for having debauched him and his sister, and Lily has no respect for any of them, nor for herself.

She then kissed me deliriously, and at the end of a long drawn-out, sucking, tongueing bout, she exclaimed with a loud sigh: "Oh, sweetheart!" as she had done to her brother in my presence on the eve of Shrove Tuesday.

She felt my sign of manhood outside my trousers to see if I stiffened by dint of her ghoulish mouth, as she had been doing on and off all day.

Then we went to the station, she kissing me behind Papa's back all the way in the dark. She "took sights" at him, continually, behind his back. But that was only to please me, as she is very fond of him, I fancy. But is she fond of anybody? She showed intense passion for me. Too much of it, I thought. She protested too much. I was getting very cool.

I showed her a photograph of my half-sister, with "yours

lovingly, March 1899," on the back. She said nothing at the moment, but later on pretended to be angry at my having connection with women! Then she was rude about my half-sister.

"How your thoughts run on incest, Lily!" I replied, and that silenced her.

Before wishing them a cordial good night, Lily told me that she would very likely try and get to Paris Sunday evening and dine with me. A visit to Lolotte was to be the pretext. She was almost sure to be able to manage it.

I smelt a rat about this visit on a Sunday night to Paris, so the next day I wrote her a few lines, saying: "That if Sunday was to be for her dinner with me, I should not be at liberty until 8 P.M. But if that evening she was passing through Paris, I should be pleased to see her, if only for an hour."

That was a trap, as I thought that if she had an appointment in Paris, I might meet her and learn something.

I also said: "I have had a conversation with Papa concerning your brother and his Whitsuntide holidays, which I had not time to tell you the other night." I may say at once that she never recurred to this important topic, showing that she would ask Papa when I left: "What did you tell Mr. S . . . ?" And he answered and narrated what I had said to him. The fact of her evincing no curiosity when I put forward conversations I had with him plainly showed that they were as one to deceive me.

LILIAN TO JACKY.

Undated (Received Sunday morning, April 23, 1899.,

My Jacky,

For to-morrow night—impossible, therefore we are obliged to put off our meeting until a fortnight, or three weeks hence perhaps. I am very vexed about this, as I confess that I have a mad desire—oh! but really an extraordinary wish to have you all alone mine own for several hours; therefore—

(Here we come to the bottom of the page, and turning over, the letter changes agreeably)—if thou art free the day after to-morrow, Monday, April 24, say so, and be at the Square Montholon at 11:45.

I will come and fetch thee and we will go and lunch together. Then we will see.

Wilt thou come?

I adore thee,

LILY.

I answered and acepted. She would have got my letter by the first post on Monday morning. I wrote as if she were a man, and I was the woman. I had also been calling her in my recent writings, "my wife," or "all my little wifie." And all this scribbling, and my apparent stupidity and calm on my last visit had thrown all of them off their guard. I was a fool, madly in love with their daughter.

I could not understand that Papa would let her dine out one evening and not lunch at home the next day. It was too good to be true.

Sunday evening, during dinner, I got this wire:

LILIAN TO JACKY. (Telegram.)

To-night at the American bar, near the Opéra. Nine o'clock.

LILY.

I went and found my charmer in a new flaming dress, made entirely of vivid red cloth. She had white kid gloves, with a nice hat, and looked very well, being very red in the face too. She had with her the Lesbian Lolotte, ex-mistress and ex-betrothed of her brother Raoul. They were both very jolly. I had never seen Lolotte before, but she knew me by name from Lily. I chaff them about their sexless kisses when alone together, and want to know who is the man of the two. It is the stereotyped stuff that is always poured out to a tribadic couple. Lolotte is a pretty, plump blonde. She was very free and charming; about Lily's age, 22 or thereabouts. We are soon very comfortable together in the back saloon of the bar, where, it seems to me, Lily is well-known. It was near the Café de la Guerre, and she went there with her brother on Shrove Tuesday.

Directly I saw Lilian, I exclaimed: "Hullo, all up for our luncheon to-morrow!"

"How do you mean?"

"Why, you fetching me out in Paris to-night proves it is all off."

"But that would not prevent us lunching tomorrow, although I can't come for the following reasons. How strange you should have guessed it! I had to take some hats to a customer in Paris on Monday, so I profited by that to get to you. This morning comes a postcard, which Mother sees, to say that the lady prefers to come down to the country. So I can't get out to Paris. My excuse is destroyed. If it had been a letter, I could have suppressed it, and seen the lady to-day, so as to stop her coming down. Thus our lunch is knocked on the head!"

"Lies!" I thought, but I said nothing. I should have liked to have seen that postcard.

"I have finished Césarée," said Lily. "It is beautiful. You have marked it well, and scored the best bits, but you are all wrong in one instance."

"About the bedrooms at the Swiss hotel, I suppose?"

"Yes. You know you are quite mistaken in your ideas about me!" She said this slowly and dreamily, not looking straight at me.

"I am absolutely convinced of the truth of my conjectures and stick to every word I have ever said or written on the subject!" I say this firmly, loudly, and impressively.

Charlotte was listening to the conversation, and Lily spoke quite openly, showing that her fair friend knew the secrets of Sonis. I told her that Lily was a liar, and had an awful temper. She knew it, and replied that all women were liars, out of necessity.

Lily's friend talked about London and declared that she would like to go there during the season. I offered, jokingly, to take her. She replied with emphasis, that it would be very nice, and people would take her for a daughter travelling with her Papa!

And she looked fixedly and archly at me. I had enough presence of mind to pay no apparent heed to her bold words, but I felt I had scored again. She knew.

I said I was impotent. Lily cried out: "No, he isn't!"

Lolotte said she was sentimental, and Lily was not. Nevertheless, the blonde confessed that she liked something stiff and rather long. I could see by the way she spoke that Lily was now like herself; a common, ordinary, middle-class, half-and-half kind of whore, always on the look-out for a man with money, and had I told her the story of her friend's virginity, she would have been quite surprised. It was a great pity that I knew Lily's stepfather-lover and all his connections and history so well. Under ordinary circumstances, they would never have thought of hatching these intricate and silly plots against me.

I spoke of Raoul, but both the girls begged me never to tell him of the meeting of the two beauties in Paris at night.

Lily told us the story of her day:

"I got up at nine, had a bath, lunched; then went on my bicycle, came home, dressed again; came to Paris, fetched Charlotte, and we both went to Narkola's to dine, us two girls alone (!!). We had lots of nice things—bisque soup and fine wine."

"In a cabinet particulier, both alone together?"

"Oh no, in the public room!"

All lies, but I say nothing.

"How dry you must both be now!"

They roar with laughter, and whisper together, and giggle; and again our conversation about the sexes becomes lewd and stupid. They have two American drinks each. I have a soda and Scotch whisky. Lily amuses herself dropping her saliva in my half-emptied glass, making me drink her spittle mixed with my beverage. She tells me that Gaston taught her that clean manner of showing affection. Lolotte gets on well with me and wants me to take her to London more than ever.

To lull Lily into security I thank her for having sent for me, and she alludes to how I said she sickened me, when she sent me a sudden summons by wire last September. She also spoke of my birthday, and remembered the date well. I merely quote these two facts to show that her brain was clear on technical points, and although she was artful enough to give no sign, all I had ever written to her, all I had ever said, had always gone right home to the mark, and remained in her memory. No doubt she read my letters over and over again. Poor, miserable Lily!

The girls kiss and say good night. We put Charlotte in a cab, and off she goes to her home, somewhere beyond the Bastile. Lily has a little, jealous scene about my freedom with her friend, as Lolotte had taken off her glove and held my hand and tickled it. We go for a ride to the Eastern station, to catch the 10:30 to Sonis. I am not to get out of the cab at the station, so as not to be seen by the neighbours who might be taking this train, or anybody, or somebody.

"When shall we meet again?" I ask.

"I don't know. You are aware how difficult it is for me to get to Paris."

"It used to be difficult. It ought not to be difficult now."

No answer.

I tell her I shall masturbate her in the cab. We get in. We exchange hot and luscious kisses, as we have been doing all the evening, more or less. After a lot of resistance, with cries of: "People will see us! Oh! They are looking, etc.," I get my hand up her clothes. I pull down the blinds. She pulls them up. At last, I overcome her feigned resistance and begin to excite her with my finger.

She has on her best drawers, and to my surprise, her cleft, generally smelling strong of the wonderful odour peculiar to the sex, is quite inodorous. It has evidently been freshly washed after dinner. My fingers afterwards were entirely without any feminine perfume. I knew also that a virgin's vulva is always more fragrant than that of a woman used to coition. I remembered that when her people were at Nice at January, she had a dinner at Narkola's, with Madame Rosenblatt and her male relations, who had purposely sent a false telegram to her Granny. Of course that was a cock and a bull story. Here is Narkola's again! Had I chosen, I could have gone there the next day, and inquired about an imaginary earring dropped by the young lady in the red dress, but I really was now quite indifferent, and would not have walked twenty yards to find out anything about her. I had spied upon her in Brussels—that was enough.

Suddenly, while gently caressing her clitoris, I turned half round, so as to get almost facing her, and placing my right forearm under her chin, on her throat, I drive her backwards into her corner of the cab, and while she is thus pressed there, unable to move, I thrust the middle finger of my left hand as far up her vagina as I can, until it is stopped by the knuckles.

I measure my finger next day finding 2½ inches, and my hand is small.

The 2½ inches of medius go up easily. I move my finger about inside, with a slight corkscrew motion. Within all is soft and damp, but not wet from randiness, only from the drink. She has not left me to void her urine since 9 P.M. She shrieks loudly and says:

"You hurt me! You hurt me!"

She struggles, but I have her tightly jammed in the corner. I find that her grotto is strangely altered. The outer lips were always very fleshy, but inside all was small, and the skin tightly drawn together, as on a thin hand. Now it is very fat, mellow, and as I said, not wet, as she was not feeling "naughty." My finger went in as in butter, and she has now evidently what I should call a large, fat gap, which has been properly stroked, doubtless by big, manly tools. But then, having been used that evening, it might be a little puffed up, as women's parts are after connection.

I cried out: "You are no longer a virgin! No longer a maid! Now I shall be able to have complete intercourse with you!"

I took my finger out and released her. She made a wry face, as she put down her clothes, saying:

"Oh, you did hurt me! But I'm still a virgin. Your finger went in because it was not in the right place. You were between the two!"

Possibly meaning just under the clitoris and above the hymen. I need not stop to point out the absurdity of this anatomical statement.

"You are a virgin? Bosh!"

"I swear I am! On my mother's life, I swear I am still intact!"

I was so delighted at having attained my object, that I did not realise the contemptible horror of the situation. It was only afterwards, when I was alone, that I gauged the depths of Lilian's baseness. At the moment, curiously enough, I thought of how I should describe the scene in my book. I saw it all in print, and it seemed comic and unreal, as if it was happening to someone else, and I was but the spectator of my own disgusted self. But there was a glorious warmth of triumph thrilling through my veins. I felt like a detective, who after many months has run his man down, and at last got the handcuffs on a criminal. I do believe that if I had found she really was a virgin, I should have been disappointed to find a maidenhead. It would have seemed like a monstrosity. Never did a surgeon operating on some special case of hidden cancer, feel more awful, intense joy than I did at that critical juncture.

"Come," said I, laughing, "and I'll finish you gently."

She was now quiet and subdued, and expected likely enough a storm of reproaches. She kissed me and let me put my hand up her clothes without any show of revolt. I began again to manipulate her rosebud, but naturally enough, she had no enjoyment. Then I got very stiff, but not too much, as I had been indulging that afternoon, and I got it out and put her hand on it.

She caressed and agitated it a little. Seeing we were getting near the station and having a sudden desire for her hot mouth, which I knew would make me ejaculate in a jiffey, better than her awkward pulling at me with her gloved hand, I said:

"Give me your mouth, Lily!"

She shook her head, and kept on with the movements of her fingers. I take her hand away and say:

"I must have your lips and tongue, Lily!"

She sulks and turns her back to me, looking out of the window.

"Well, I'll masturbate myself!"

"Oh no, don't do that!"

"I will! I'll spend alone! And you can go to the man with no finger-nails!"

At this rude remark, which called up the vision of the hands of her mother's lover, to my astonishment she turns round and kisses me. She was so pleased to find I showed jealousy of the wrong person. She was waiting for a scene about the people she had dined with. Out comes her hand again. I push it away, and rub my member a little, like a schoolboy. She turns her head away again, and to give her a chance, I say:

"I suppose your stays prevent you stooping down?"

She, the fool, cannot take my handsome hint, but has turned her back once more entirely towards me, and does not answer.

So I, in despair, cover myself up and button my pants. At this moment, we are just nearing the station.

Seeing this, she is evidently delighted that all is over for the evening, and turning, draws me towards her, gently patting my cheek with her hand, her arm resting on my shoulder, as I had often seen her with her Papa. At this Judas-like caress, I confess that I felt myself boiling over with rage.

She has disdainfully refused me her lips, without a word of excuse, although I have not spent with her since the 1st. of March, and have not had her mouth since the 1st. of October.

If she had said: "I am tired. How can I suck you in my tight stays, new dress, jacket and hat?" I would willingly have excused her, especially as I was not very lustful just then. But she had not even taken off a glove. Her stroke on my cheek meant: "Now that it is too late to suck him, I'll make it up with the idiot."

My blood boiled at this thought, and I repulsed her, pushing her from me by the shoulder. She was on my right hand. I felt like a brute and behaved like one. I dashed out my right arm and caught her a fearful backhander on the lower part of the left cheek and jaw.

She gasped for breath, and said slowly and quietly in a low tone:

"How brutal!"

"I am mad," I replied, "go and spend when you get home."

This was foolish, as she had freely emitted in Paris, and was not ready for me after her dinner, frolic, and two American champagne mixtures. She had had her enjoyment, and was not yet whore enough to play the proper part with another man at two hours' interval. Besides, her temper would not allow her to do so.

She was on the proper side to leave the cab, as it was now stopped, so she stepped out without a word, and I saw her go slowly and shakily along the station frontage, not boldly entering the first door in front of her, as she ought to have done, but sneaking along slowly, evidently thinking I was going to come after

her, or perhaps tipsy, or crying, or mad with rage at being out-
witted. Or going to the ladies' W.C. at the end of the building.

I slowly paid the cabman, watching her the while. I dared
not follow her, for I knew that if I did—God help me!—I should
have struck her again. So I turned away and walked home. How I
got along and what streets I took, I do not know. I am surprised
I was not run over. I found myself in front of my door, that is all
I can say. It was about 11:30 or 11:45. I got into bed and smoked
until 2 A.M. I could not settle to read. I could only smoke and
stare at nothing. I was very much upset, although I had known
the truth all along by intuition.

Then I found that the knuckles of the second and third fingers
of my right hand were torn and bleeding. I did not think I could
have burst the skin with the force of the blow on her face. I do
not suppose I hurt her much, as I had no room to swing my arm
in the cab, and she did not put her hand up to her face after the
blow. I hoped that I had torn my knuckles on her brooch, or
neckpins, or earrings, or garters, or something of the same kind,
while struggling with her, and these slight abrasions were only
coincidences.

Strange to say, but it is the truth, I had no regret for having
struck her and feel none now. When I wrote her that insulting
letter about the Belgian trip, and sent the analysis of her own
letters, I felt strangely delighted, and was surprised when she was
silly enough to answer.

It was the first time in my life that I had ever lifted my hand
to a woman in anger.

The next day I was quite calm again, and hugely pleased to
find how well I had succeeded.

I had quite deceived the infamous Trinity at Sonis and I had
proved to Lily that I knew she was no longer a virgin.

I had set myself a threefold task: to prove that Lily was Papa's
mistress, by exposing the lies from Lille; that her maidenhead was
gone, despite her assertions to the contrary; and that they were
all in league to conspire against me.

All I had to do now was to bide my time to taunt her with
her complicity, and then I could go away.

I wrote and sent the following letter, but it was not meant specially for her. It was for Papa,—and a little for my book which was rapidly taking a practical form in my brain,—and I composed the details of the famous ride, just as I have given it here, and leisurely prepared notes for the rest.

When I posted the letter I now give, I thought she would not answer me, and that I should never see her more. Anyhow, I made up my mind that she would never come to my arms again. I did not see how she could.

JACKY TO LILIAN.

Paris, April 27, 1899.

You arrive with Charlotte Sunday night, and tell me that the appointment arranged for the next day has fallen through. I say nothing, but I find the story suspicious. I should like to see the postcard of Sunday. But I pass that over. I don't care.

I hear that the two young ladies have dined alone. I venture to say they are "dry." They laugh, not understanding that I am mocking them. Lolotte must think me stupid. I say nothing. I don't care.

I make the following remark: in January, Lily also went to dine at Narkola's with Madame Rosenblatt. Put the two things together. Had I curiosity, nothing would have been easier for me than to have gone on Monday to Narkola's to find out about the lady dressed in red. I have not done so. Neither shall I. What better proof can I give that I don't care?

We get in a cab. I discover that she is no longer a virgin, in spite of all the stuff she has recently told me. I had already my suspicions when I did minette to her in January. Then I found her parts absolutely changed beneath my tongue. When a maid, she was rather thin down there, the skin tight over the bones, as with all virgins. Now all is fat. It is soft, as if swollen, but she is rather large, I find. Evidently she has met a strong sexual partner. It is true that she had just been enjoyed by a man, and at such a moment, directly after connection, the parts are always a little puffy. But she is too fat in the lips for such a young woman and I repeat—rather vast. But my examination was necessarily superficial. Her "pussy" was excessively clean, without any special smell. Therefore, there had been private, recent ablutions. Injection? After dinner, I think. The men were all married, as she was not perfumed.

I pushed my finger in freely as if in butter—six centimeters. The entrance was easy, all being open. She was not excited by me. There was only a little moisture through the drinks. The reason is simple; she had just spent a lot. Nevertheless, she swore on her mother's life that she was still a virgin, and that I had put my finger "between the two." Comedy! I said nothing. I did not care.

She did not try to caress me. She never even took off her glove. I did not care. (She used to say: "To you I would do anything.")

I ask for her mouth. She turns away without a word. I did not care. I give her a hint, telling her that perhaps her stays were too tight. I wanted her to excuse herself prettily. She did not understand. I did not care.

Then a wonderful thing took place, that I really did care about. Seeing that we were nearing the station, she left off sulking, and turned round to me, caressing my cheek. This is how I understand this Judas-like caress: "Fortunately, we are at the station. He can't ask me for anything now, the idiot! I have eluded the task. Now to coax him to get away."

In a twinkling, I understood the horror of this idea, and I made you feel severely the weight of my opinion. I struck you in the face—movement of brutal impulse. But whose fault was it?

She has dragged me down to the level of the brute—or would like to do so.

Do I regret what I did? I do not believe so. I don't care.

But what I do care about are the rude words I uttered concerning a poor man, victim of Lily, who I pity with all my heart. How he must suffer! How he will regret having let himself be seduced—if he does not regret it already. I understand the kick given to the dog. I understand everything, and from the bottom of my heart I ask his pardon for the insults I addressed to him by insulting the infamous Lily. If I could only make him understand the compassion and sympathy I feel for him, victim of Lily!

I, at least, possess common sense; I can reason, and I finish by regaining full mastery over myself. Then again, I do not live with her. Sincerely, I pity him. What a sad existence she will make for him—she does make for him! Poor man!

Why, Lily, this accumulation of lies, to enable you to play continually and solely for me, this part of the perpetual virgin, letting no one touch her but me, and yet always in somebody's arms? You are immaculate, of course. Jacky and you masturbate, or suck six times a year, and that is all.

Are you mad? Do you take me for a madman? Or are we all mad, and you alone sane?

It is laughable. But I don't care. When in a rage we say: "I don't care a damn; what does it matter to me?" Generally we feel quite the contrary. I believe that I prove, and I have sufficiently proved lately, the appearance of a slight commencement of indifference. And if you do not believe me, I do not care.

A few guesses:

Lily was certainly a virgin in October last. January she was so no longer, nor in December either. ("Don't be silly, darling!")

When sucking her in the dining-room in January, I felt the difference. I ask to be allowed to try with my finger. She consented, and cunningly put me off: "It is so tender now I've come!"

When did she lose her maidenhead?

In London in October? I think not. I saw her at the beginning of November, when she forged the hideous lie of the lost letter. At that moment, she wanted to be my wife. I still believe in her relative honesty, and she would not have wished to marry me if she had not been physically intact. You see, Lily, that I have still a little illusion. You are surprised? I do not care.

I think that the thing happened in November. With whom? After November, there is no talk of marriage.

I have two ideas: Mr. Arvel, or a stranger. I put aside the first-named, I don't know why, and from some signs that I have no time to set out here—especially as all this is very vague in my brain; I grope in darkness now—I lean towards a stranger, who, either because he feared the consequences, or else because he tired of her after once or twice, has not set eyes on her since. Or he is perhaps absent momentarily. And I believe he is an officer.

I suppose he abandoned her. Out of spite, she threw herself into the arms of those who she thought she loved a little: Mr. Arvel, who, on second thoughts, I think she loves a great deal, who she seduced; and Jacky, who she don't much care about, except to make him suffer, and excite Mr. Arvel. Nevertheless, she is always telling Jacky and writing to him how she loves him. I do not speak of the parties carrées with her Lesbian Charlotte.

A woman who truly loves cannot live without the man she has chosen. She only knows one thing; to see him as often as possible, although she may have to dig up the earth with her nails to get to him. In a word—'tis love. And when she sees her lover, she only knows one other thing: to get into bed, to open her thighs, to give herself up, and let herself be taken, virgin or not. Does a woman really in love think of her virginity? She loves. That is all.

Lily the liar does nothing of this with me. She loves not, neither Jacky nor anybody. Mr. Arvel a little, and the remembrance of her first real lover—that is all. She loves nothing. She fetched me out Sunday night through vanity, to show Lolotte that after having copulated in her society, she had yet another man waiting for her. I do not care.

Excuse all faults of French of your old foreign snob. I have a copy of this letter. Shall I make a few extracts for Lolotte, or do you prefer to read this to her when you see her?

This is a calm and sensible letter, without empty phrases; without tears, flowers, birds, or music. You like novels. This is better—here you have a living romance, of which you are the heroine.

You love voluptuous letters that you can show. Show this one, I'm not ashamed of it. I set forth my weakness, I allow, but I've no vanity. I boast of nothing. The part of victim does not displease me. And to prove that I should not blush if it be shown to who you like, I write it on paper stamped with my die, and I sign my name in full,

JOHN S . . .

But I have wagered with myself that you will not answer me. You are in a tight corner.

What lying bubbles I have burst since you became a neat little Césarée! I kiss you, and conclude—at last!

From a sensible point of view, it doubtless seems a silly thing to have sent the foregoing letter. The reason why I did it was because I was afraid that Lilian, perhaps half tipsy—she must have been so, or she would never have opened her thighs so wide—would not, or could not see my motives. Also, that I did not wish to spare her; I felt a savage pleasure in rubbing her nose in her filth. I wanted to drive her to give me up herself. I wanted to see how far she would go; whether she had any pride left; whether she was utterly debased and abandoned or not; and lastly, I was now certain that Papa knew all our story, and had eagerly devoured my letters, just as Lily and he had read all my obscene books together. I told her so; I told her I found his big, black thumbmarks in one of them. She never answered; she never did, when I guessed rightly. I thought he was putting her up to most of her tricks. In their narrow-mindedness, they cannot believe that I have always been truthful, and in spite of all I have said, think I am a miser and that there is still something to be got out of me; never mind how little—it is all profit. They were trying to "work" me. Pa, Ma, and Lily were all conspiring. They were accomplices, more or less, and I was to be the fool. Where they were all wrong, was that according to my mad letters and my still madder talk and ideas, they suppose and hope that I am absolutely gone crazy on Lily and that she can do whatever she likes with me. Habitual liars are the easiest people in the world to deceive. They believe everybody. But you must never lie to them. Tell them the truth or nothing, and they will be as children in your hands.

I had now to make a most dreadful sacrifice, with only the voice of my conscience to applaud me—the sacrifice of my passion; of my sensual enjoyment; of my thirst for lust with Lily, which I could have still assuaged had I chosen to be a weak coward towards myself. This holocaust, perhaps I am too vain in saying so, seemed to elevate me in my own sight, and I felt like a hero, in thus conquering my concupiscence in solitude, between four walls, all alone with my thoughts.

3

. . . . Go, call my daughter;
And if she comes not, tell her that I come.—
What sufferings? I will drag her, step by step,
Through infamies unheard of among men,

She shall become (for what she most abhors
Shall have a fascination to entrap
Her loathing will), to her own conscious self
All she appears to others.
. . . . I will make
Body and soul a monstrous lump of ruin.

SHELLEY.

ERIC ARVEL TO JACKY.

Sonis-sur-Marne, May 1st. 1899.

My dear Jacky,

If you have nothing better to do on Wednesday, will you bring
down your bike and come for a ride? We will breakfast at 11:30, *sans
façon*, and see you get home safely at night. Raoul has written, and desires to be kindly remembered to you. I was very much obliged to you
for the papers you sent.

Hoping you are all well at home, believe me to remain,

Yours very truly,
ERIC ARVEL.

P.S.—Look at the enclosed photo, and tell us what you think about "Mount Calvary"?

WEDNESDAY, MAY 3, 1899.

This postscript and the photograph, representing Lily between her brother and myself—taken by Papa in February—confirmed me in my opinion that Papa knew all, and so did Lolotte, for Lily never troubled about my threat of writing to her Sapphic friend. I sent a wire, accepting the invitation, and went down on my bicycle; my hands full, as usual.

I had made up my mind to be calm, cool, collected and merry, and not to say a word to Lily on the subject of our secret (?) relations, unless she spoke first. I half expected she would not be there. How could it be possible that any woman, even the lowest of the low, could sit unmoved in front of the man who, in the right or in the wrong, had sent her such a vile, horrible, loathsome letter, without counting his brutal assault on her? But knowing her petty thoughts, I guessed she would say: "How he must love me to write such things! How vexed he is!" And she would be proud to think she had got me in such a mad state. So Pa and Lily invited me to gloat over my supposed sufferings and make me suffer more. The best reason of all was, perhaps, that Papa did not want to quarrel openly with me, as I knew now too much about him.

I arrive. The servant tells me that Madame has gone to Paris early, and Mademoiselle will receive me. Not a soul to be seen, which was most impolite in a villa, when you are expected as the only guest. When the garden gate shuts to, somebody should run out to meet you, I think. At least, such was always the case with me, but not this time. I am ushered into the house and am left to wait five minutes alone. A cool reception. Papa comes downstairs at last and we go out for a walk to meet his wife at the station. We return, all three of us, and he talks of his "Calvary" joke, while I see Lily, peering at me from the summer-house workshop.

"That was your invention," I reply, "because she is between two thieves?"

"No. She mentioned it first. Where is she? Lilian! Lilian!"

And he bawls out her name. She will not answer. She does not appear until lunch, fully an hour and a half after my arrival, and greets me coldly. I am, I am pleased to say, perfectly indifferent and quite self-possessed. She does not excite me as she used to do. She has on an old dress, and no powder, or red on her lips. The beauty spot on her cheek is gone.

We lunch. During the meal, she has to get up and pass behind my chair. She puts one hand heavily on my shoulder, near my neck, boldly in front of her two parents. The lunch is a poor one, compared to what they used generally to put on the table for me. They are all dull. The duller they get, the gayer I am. I actually go so far as to imitate Sarah Bernhardt!!

"You do well in mentioning the name of the actress," says Lily.

"I always do when I give an imitation. It avoids all discussion." Then I add: "To-day is an anniversary! Four years ago, in May, I forget the day exactly, I brought the little fox-terrier, Lili, here. That was the first time I ever came into this house. How time flies, and what changes take place in four years!"

This with a little emotion, half real, half feigned, but I felt I had acted it well. I don't think they liked the little speech. There was no response, except from Lily, who saucily but angrily, sniffing, snorting, replies:

"I thought you meant her birthday, when you said anniversary!"

I notice that Papa treats Lily with mock gravity, and calls her Madame, all through the meal. Ever since the return from Brussels there has never been any romping between the pair as in olden days, but they treat each other with great seriousness. They have no need to play with each other in the daytime now. Perhaps too, Mamma's susceptibilities have to be reckoned with.

When the coffee comes on, the beautiful porcelain cups and saucers, which Papa brought from China, are no longer put on the table, as they used to be for me. Lily asks me how I will have my coffee—in a cup or in a glass. I see no cups on the table, so I reply that I will have it in the same way as Mr. Arvel. She says that

Papa takes it in a glass, and she pours it in his, on top of the dregs of his white wine, and serves me in the same way.

It is impossible that Pa and Ma did not notice these little shades indicating my disgrace in their house, and they must also see the way Lily treated me. Their collusion was glaring.

While we are drinking the coffee, Mamma goes and has an awful row in the kitchen, and kicks out one of her two female servants. The same thing occurred on April 5th.

Papa and Lily remain at table with me unmoved, and I feel dreadfully ill at ease to hear Adèle shrieking in the kitchen and the vulgar howling of the domestic replying to her. My interesting pair tell me that Madame Arvel is mad and can't keep a servant. They are like husband and wife, and Mamma is the housekeeper: Lily sneers at the muffled sounds of the dispute, and Papa swears and growls.

Mamma returns, very red in the face, and apologises to me for her outburst of passion. She must tell servants all she thinks of them, and give them a bit of her mind. This one had been talking against her in the village.

"Dear Madam," I say, "why get in a passion with hired menials, and expect devotion from them, when you see so often in families that even blood relations betray each other. You expect too much of servants."

Of course, Adèle never answered, and the guilty couple was silent too.

Lily stuck with Papa and me. I followed Papa about all day like a little dog and would not be left alone with Lily. She now began to look wistfully at me. She could not make me out, and was waiting for some advance on my part. I noticed her in the glass.

She talked about a new photographic lens and said to her Papa:

"Papa, you must photograph me as a Japanese girl and in all sorts of costumes."

And she looked at him with her sweetest smile, and her nostrils quivered nervously.

"Papa, I am going up to Paris at 2:37."

But she did not go. She never left us hardly a minute.

"Here's the postman," says Lily, and she rushes down to the gate. She returns with a letter for Pa, and cries out: "One from him!"

As she ran back into the house, Pa tapped her posteriors, where her pocket was, and said to me:

"She has got it in her pocket!"

I made no remark.

"Lily is not going to London, in September to live with her brother," he suddenly broke out. "She has found out that she would probably have to keep him."

"What is she going to do then?" I say. This is the first and last time that I ever asked him anything about her.

"She will stop here with me."

Afterwards, he speaks very affectionately to her in front of me, as he has never done before, and while he is talking, I wink facetiously at Lily. I am certain that he is trying to teaze me on behalf of his stepdaughter and secret wife, even as a mother might do, who would be the procuress of her own girl.

Finally, she manages to get me alone and chaffs me about being too thin. I retort that I look after myself, as the doctors advise me that if I get too fat, I shall be in bed again with rheumatism.

"I do not spare myself," I say quietly. "You find fault with my personal appearance, because you have no longer any feeling of desire for me. Qu'importe le flacon, pourvu qu'on ait l'ivresse!"

She throws up her head and snorts, but says: "No! No!" as I stroll away from her, back to the side of Papa.

She makes us two men take her out for a walk. She does not try to go out alone with me and never does again. Surely Pa and Ma can see the change?

She chatters about a certain fashionable actor, and turns very red; crimson are her cheeks, as I tell her tales of his amours. She says she does not like him any more, as although he looked beautiful on the stage, she would prefer him to be less of a rake. Lily declares that actors and actresses have strange ideas, but she adds

with a sigh that lots of other people have strange ideas too. Papa
smokes in silence. I play the clown, and they are both obliged to
laugh at my foolish antics.

I ask her if she is rich—if she has not a few hundred francs
saved up in a corner of her wardrobe, under her clean drawers.
She cannot help smiling as she wonders at my astuteness in feminine matters; that is exactly how her Mamma hides her money.
Lily's pocket money is limited. She got one hundred francs for a
pair of puppies, thanks to my advertisement. In spite of my advice,
they did not advertise again, but the other three pups were given
away—one to the officer; one to a friend of mine, the jeweller,
who made the ring; and the last to a brother-journalist, a friend
of Papa's.

Lily wore no rings that day. I never saw my poor ring on her
hand again.

We return to tea. Then Lily stands in a doorway, waiting
for me to speak to her. I repeat my movement of retreat, walking
away in the garden, after Papa, and she looks so wild; frowning and
black under the eyes, that I turn round, and thoroughly happy to
feel myself so free in front of her—for perhaps I feared I might
weaken—actually laugh outright at her. She goes in, but not at
once. Then later, she complains of a headache. Alone with me, for
I continually find her at my heels, I gravely advise castor-oil.

Papa and I go out for a ride on our bicycles. He is very slow,
careful and nervous. He does nothing but talk of Lily and how well
and fearlessly she rides. He confides to me that his member
shrivels up on a bike, and asks me if mine does! What does he
mean? Does he want me to ask to look at it? I answer that I have
never noticed this phenomenon in myself.

When we return, Lily's head is worse. She has got a face as
black as a negress. She comes to me and says:

"I have left all the books I have of you at the station. Here
is the ticket!"

After my laugh, while we were out on our bicycles, she had
evidently made up her parcel, and had gone to the cloakroom of
the little station of Sonis.

Unmoved, I take it.

"Thank you," I reply. "I have got a couple of novels ready for you. One is on the same subject as Césarée but much stronger."

"Where are they? Have you brought them with you?"

"No, but I will leave them at the cloakroom of the Eastern station and send you the ticket."

That was all. She got more sulky, and I gayer than ever. She calls her Papa.

"Pa, will you come down to the cellar with me?"

I used to do that. Papa puts on his gloomy look and is delighted to go with her, while I, all alone, recline on the famous divan, where we sat at Shrovetide.

I think they exchanged notes down below. Papa sent her up alone, and kept out of the way, to give her an opportunity to make me say something.

She rushes through the room, on her way to the kitchen, where her mother is, and says to me, in a voice choked with passion:

"Rest yourself; take things easy!"

"Thank you, Mademoiselle."

"Make yourself at home, quite at home!" She flounces out. In a few minutes, she returns and sits down. After a pause, while I watch her frowning, she again complains of her head, and in answer to my coldly polite sympathy, hints that she often suffers in this way—every month. She wants me to talk.

"Sexual causes, I suppose, and not the stomach?" Another pause. Then I add:

"When I got home that Sunday night, I found my fingers torn and bleeding. How was that? Do you know?"

"Of course I do. It is not surprising!"

"How did I manage to tear my skin?"

"Let us talk of whatever you like, but not of that evening. I will not talk about it at all."

Aghast at her impudence, I hold my tongue, and a few seconds afterwards:

"I don't think I shall come here again."

"I don't force you to come," she replies quickly, black with rage.

"There is no question of force."

Then another long pause, as neither of us speak, until Papa arrives, and I am asked to go and wash my hands in the best bedroom as I always do. I have stated that Lily used to accompany me, get me hot water, a clean towel, and kiss me. This time Pa takes me, apologises for a black residue in the cold rain-water of the ewer, tells me to pick out any dirty towel off the horse, and sits on a sofa, while I wash my hands. He never did this before. I take a long while purposely, as I like to see him seated, waiting for me. He is leaning forward, his joined hands passed between his thighs. I cannot prevent myself comparing him to an old bawd, and there is something womanish about him, as I think that he has espoused the quarrels of Lily with a lover. The day has been instructive for me, and I ask myself who has been the most ridiculous of us all? I vote for Papa, and fancy he would look well with a double-bordered cap, à la Sairey Gamp.

We dine and he starts the Calvary story again.

"Has Mademoiselle really suffered so much?" say I. "This is the first time I hear of a female Christ."

"She has a crown of thorns," replies Papa.

"The crown of thorns of a young lady can only be tight boots and tight stays."

He still calls her Madame all through the meal, as he did at lunch, and says, looking at her and me:

"Bitter! Bitter!"

She seems very worried, and I exult, as I am so self-possessed. I can see that Papa is resolved to draw words out of me, and create some scene for his diversion, and the more he tries to teaze me the more jolly I get. Nothing could have vexed me that day, or caused me to lose my temper that night, and as I watched Lily's bluish lips and Papa's snarling grin, I thought of my little growing manuscript at home and wondered if the great masters of the art of novel-writing had ever lived their stories in advance.

I was aroused from my reverie by Papa's loud voice, saying:

"Pass the sauce, Satan!"

I do not even start at this new jibe, but say very quietly, with a pleasant smile:

"I did not quite catch what you said. Did you call me 'Satan'?"

"Oh! I meant that for Lily. I ought to have said 'satin.' "

I am satisfied with his retreat and say no more.

Lily now wakes up, and she talks of a new red dress she has—meaning the one she wore when she dined at Narkola's—and says it is too conspicuous, she will never wear it again.

"Wear it as a dinner dress," I answer. Pa knows she dined in it on Sunday.

"It is cloth and tailor-made," she explains.

She wants to know what are masks to be worn at night for the skin. I explain that they are pieces of kid with holes cut in them, smeared with creams for the complexion. And I add that women not only wear masks at night, but very often in the daytime as well. All our talk is in English. Mamma does not speak English. She is a cypher. Now and then she joins in and wants to know what we are talking about. So we change to French.

"Women are fools," says Lily, "to bother so much about their skins."

"There is no such thing as a foolish woman," I answer, "I have asked several and they all told me they were very clever."

I get a laugh for this, but Papa for the sixth time murmurs his catchword of the evening: "Bitter! Bitter!"

Lily says she has been suffering from a swollen nose, big and red. It is only just better. Can it have been my blow? No, she is anæmic, and strumous. I remember a disabled hand from the bite of a mosquito; a stye in the eye; an abcess in the mouth. She caught cold in Paris, coming out of the hot restaurant or bar, insufficiently clad in the courtesan's cambric underwear, after the thick and comfortable everyday Cinderella combinations.

"Mademoiselle has had what we call in English—a nose . . . gay!"*

---

* A certain analogy exists between the nose and the genital organs, since both of them (and the nipple as well) contain an erectile tissue. Congestion of the nose is often regularly produced at the period of menstruation and excesses of ven°real enjoyment may provoke inflammation of its membrane.

The dinner is over. Mamma goes up to bed and leaves us three.

Arvel talks about the Dreyfus affair, being against the officers now, and I tell the story how an old Jew of 80 years of age, seeing the hetacomb of corrupt officers, had exclaimed:

"It is the justice of Jehovah! They tried to teaze Jehovah! Never teaze Jehovah!"

Lily asks what Jehovah means. Papa harshly interrupts her, telling her that she would not understand, and so I see how for years he has carefully diverted her understanding from all that was good and noble. Her life is wasted.

Her foot gently touches mine. I do not respond. Mr. Arvel asks me if I have ever been to Italy. I answer in the affirmative, and I tell how I took lessons, so as to acquire a little Italian before starting. To try my new knowledge, being in London, I went into a penny ice-shop, and said to a swarthy, moustachioed foreigner behind the counter:

"*Parlate Italiano, signor?*"

He lifted a cover off a zinc pail, and stirring up its contents with a wooden spoon, replied in a business-like way:

"Shtrawberry or cream-a?"

Lily laughed immoderately at this, until the tears came into her eyes.

"I am glad I have at last made you laugh, Mademoiselle, but I am sorry to inform you that this little story, which I am flattered to see has had the good fortune to so excite your mirth, is not true. I made it up myself. It is a lie, although as a rule, I do not tell lies. Do I, Mr. Arvel?"

And I turned to Papa. He smiled grimly, but did not answer, while Lily, perfectly black and sulky at hearing the word: "Lies!" seemingly very vexed, left the chair close to me on my right, on which she had been seated, and went off to recline on the divan with her dog, leaving Papa and me to cap each other's stories and smoke without her. She never took her eyes off me.

I make much of my bitch Lili, as I have been doing all day, and all my sentiment with the animal is met with icy coldness on their part.

Lily is in a complete fit of the sulks, seeing me so indifferent, and the time for my departure approaching, without my having said anything at all.

No doubt after my letter, which Lily never alluded to, from that day to this, they expected I should forget myself in some way, or show some wretched weakness. That is why they sent for me. The whole of the day, Papa never left me, and instead of doing photography, he walked round and round his garden, and took care to keep near the house. I followed him.

Lily, at one time, brought some work into the dining-room, so as to be near to us; but I made no sign, and they both circled round me as if watching an epileptic patient. I suppose they thought I might burst into tears, or faint away, or better than all, beg Lily's pardon and make a substantial peace-offering.

Do wicked women bleed foolish men's purses by excess of ill-treatment? Probably they do, or else Lily and her Pa would have behaved in a different manner.

I look at my watch. It is time to go.

"We'll take the dogs out, come back and fetch your bike, and take you to the station," said Papa.

Lily, who generally went with us, or alone with me, very dull and black, begs to be excused. She goes to Pa, says "good-night" to him, and putting up her face to be kissed, he salutes her on both cheeks. She never did this before. Papa looks surprised, and the light fades out of his eyes, as it always does when stirred by the power of his passion for Lily. It stirs me too, and I feel very lewd, as this is the first time I ever saw them kiss before me. I may say that I never saw Lily kiss her mother all the time I had known her, and it will be noted that Mamma was not present when Papa kissed Lily. She knew I liked to see her playing with Papa. Was she doing this to pander to my vile mania; or to excite my jealousy; or to please Mr. Arvel, by telling him that I was jealous of him?

I never knew. Had I been on good terms enough with Lilian to ask her, she would have only told me some lie, so when the pleasant quarter-of-an-erection sensation it created in me had worn off, I forgot all about it, and it is only as I strike the keys of my type-writer nearly a year afterwards that I see the girl and the old man kissing so chastely before me, both trying to get at the little brains and money I may have had. I bear no malice, as I led them on to believe I was malleable.

Lily says: "*Bonsoir, monsieur!*" to me very coldly. We go out. She goes with us into the hall, standing behind us, still hoping for a word, or a sly caress perhaps. I take off my hat and say very softly and nicely: "*Bonsoir, mademoiselle!*"

She answers, really hissing it through her teeth: "*Bonsoir!*" Quite curtly, and there is no "*monsieur!*" with it, which is very rude.

The sibilant sound of her last word betrayed the rage she felt, after a useless day of simulation in the face of my unfeigned indifference. And Papa would taunt her, and ask her what had become of the boasted power she had over me.

I go out with Papa, who must have noticed the change in his girl's manner to me.

He talks smut.

"Girls nowadays don't seem to care about real copulation—they like being 'messed about' better."

This was a bold thrust at me. I answer quite indifferently and insignificantly.

I let him keep up the conversation, and he gets on to sleep and sleeping draughts, in order to be able to say:

"Lilian sleeps well. When we were in Brussels, she would get to bed after the theatre at midnight, and never wake until eleven the next day. As she was away for her health, I never disturbed her, but let her have her sleep out. We had a fine, big, double-bedded room. There was a large screen and I rigged it up across the room, fixing it against the washstand."*

A month ago, he had told me that Lily was lazy and would

---

* "I think the washstand (one only), was against the outer wall, on the left of the fireplace and could not have been behind the screen. The room is about five or six yards square and the screen could not reach halfway across. It was the ordinary height of a large screen and one could only look over it by standing on a chair."—NOTE BY A. MALLANDYNE.

not get up. But that was nothing. He was a man who said just what came into his head, as it suited him. But what did he want me to reply that night? What was I to answer?

I felt inclined to be smutty, and chaff him about Lily, and her love for her Pa, and so on. But I would not take the trouble, and after all it might have been a trap. I simply said nothing. I expect he was pursuing his same old "bluffing" tactics. But there was an undercurrent of fear of me. He was too clever. It would have been much more simple to have said nothing, as I did in answer to him. There was now a very long silence between us, more significant than any reply I could have given. He broke it by talking of bawdy-houses. I explained that they were not much good. Some fellows, I said, liked to take a green girl there with them. But it is generally a bad move. He replied that possibly it was wrong to go with anybody you might care about. I put an end to this debate, by declaring that as a general rule it was not a wise thing to do.

He evidently had the idea of seeing Lily with him in a brothel, among its abandoned denizens, a favourite pastime among fast Parisians. Had she been with him; did he long to take her; or had she gone to one with a miché? This was the second time he had spoken to me of lupanars. He had got them prominently in his mind.

There is nothing new under the sun of sexuality, and nearly all old debauchees, when they get hold of a young woman, new to depravity, or who they fancy is not quite corrupt, feel a great delight in going to a brothel with her. Each one thinks he has been the first to be so diabolically lecherous. What fools we old voluptuaries are!

I thought he would have liked me to speak out and go about Paris with him and Lily. I hardly knew what to think. Lily had stopped all friendship between Arvel and Jacky, by her lies. It was a very difficult position for me to be in, especially as I got no help from the wretched young woman. Suppose I had begun to talk lightly about her to the father and he had turned round on me? So I said nothing. By this time, we had returned to the house.

A light was burning in Lily's room. Immediately, Arvel's head goes up, looking at the bright window like a boy of twenty. He puts up the dogs for the night, and conducts me to the station. He is very cordial and says he will soon have me down again. He wants me to go and visit some ground he has bought on the Western line. I promise him some special photographic printing paper—which I send him a day or two after—and we part.

I get my parcel of books at the station. There is Césarée; the first volume of "Gynecocracy," and volumes 2 to 6, inclusively, of "Justine."

In volume 6, I had marked the paragraph about the pleasure of seeing one's mistress in another man's arms. I had asked Lily if she had noticed and read it. She swore she had seen no marks. I attached no importance to this, thinking that perhaps after all I had pencilled some later volume that she had not seen yet.

That idea did not suit Lily's plans at this juncture, as she wanted me to become jealous, so she told this lie; as when she pretended to ignore the Mademoiselle Bismarck missive. How I discovered her prevarication again, was by looking through the books in the train, when I found, not only my underscoring and marginal lines, but the place in the sixth volume was marked with a long strip of orange photographic paper such as I had seen plenty of at Sonis, but I possessed none of that kind. This made me more sure than ever that Papa had read the book, and that he would have been more free and geniune with me, shutting his eyes to my connection, had she not worked him against me, as he was, to a certain extent, a puppet in the hands of Lily and her Mamma. The two women can kill him by inches, if they choose. The mother has but to tempt him with her choice cooking, which he cannot resist, and Lily will follow suit with her cunning caresses. To regain fresh strength daily, he will eat heavily, and drink rich wines, followed by fiery, cheap whiskies. No man, especially at his age, can burn the candle at both ends with impunity.

I give here, out of curiosity, the odd notes I jotted down the day after my visit, just to show the state of my mind, with all my doubts and contradictions.

It is all over now. I cannot visit there again, unless Lily was to come forward and go down on her knees to me. This she will never do. She is too hard. I know her. What will the next move be? An invitation from Papa? If so, I shall probably decline it. I must do so. Besides, I am tired. If I go, it will only be to tell her of the fact which is now perfectly clear to my eyes: that every hand at Sonis is against me.

Papa behaved all day like an old procuress, trying to put two lovers together. I remember how silly he looked at her side, the day the officer arrived to see the puppies. Papa has spoken since about the two that were sold; and of that presented to his colleague; while Lilian has oft recurred to the fate of the one my jeweller had, but there has not been the slightest reference ever made to the animal that was given to the soft-eyed soldier, whose appearance and bearing pleased me so much. He was a man any woman would have been pleased to be seen with.

She cannot come near me now. Even her Whitsuntide journey must now be knocked on the head, if ever it was sincere, as Papa will not hear speak of the brother spending his holidays away from home, and she is going to live always at the villa now.

She depends on Papa for everything, even to her food, and I know he is very kind to her. She too, evidently likes him very much. He is not married to her mother, but he will have to do so now, so as to reward her for the sacrifice. The trio are firmly bound together by their material wants and pecuniary interests. Mamma's "courses" are leaving her, and she has no more feeling. She hinted as much to me. So what chance have I in such a household? With Lilian's obstinate lies and her desire for money against me too. She has spoilt everything, and I must retire.

I now know all I want. She is the mistress of her mother's old lover and her maidenhead has been gone some months.

She only cares for me for what she thinks she can tear out of me. If I was wrong in this surmise, she would simply try to see more of me, or work for me with her Papa, as she seemed to do so nicely before she left for Brussels with him.

MAY 3, 1899.

I took to the Eastern railway station, two novels, as I had promised, and left them in a parcel at the cloak-room, sending the ticket to Lily in an envelope, without a word. I wrote on the fly-leaf of one of them that I did not want them back, as they were of no value, except for reading.

One was Suzanne, by Léon A. Daudet (Paris, Charpentier, 1897), and the subject was the incest of a bad girl, a liar and a hypocrite, who glories in her wrongful lust for her own father. He takes her away on a trip to Spain; her health being the pretext, and both alone together, they put up at a hotel, when he gives her a ring, just as Papa did in Brussels. It is one of the most powerful works of the kind. I underscored all the erotic passages, with any remark which seemed to touch on Lily's case, and there were many.

The second novel was La Femme et le Pantin, by Pierre Louÿs (Paris, Société du Mercure de France, 1898), which is a pretty little story of a wicked woman and a weak man, who continually returns to his torturing mistress, in spite of her vile treatment of him.

I think that Lily was egged on me for marriage from the very first, and flirting was allowed, but perhaps her visits to me in Paris were added by herself? Or they knew she came to me, but she would tell them at home that I walked her about the parks and squares and sighed over her.

Another proof that Papa knows all, and had read my last disgusting letter, where I spoke of the kick to Blackamoor: this time, in front of me, he feigned to get in an awful rage with Lily's dog, and took a big stick, pretending to hit him. Lily seemed (?) distressed. Then he brought the cudgel softly down on the crouching body of the trembling pet and burst out laughing, caressing the animal. That was clearly an answer to my allusion to his cruelty to Blackamoor.

———

Papa had asked me if I knew the price of nickel saucepans in Paris, intending to replace all his kitchen utensils by that new metal. I got him some tariffs and catalogues of these goods, with the offer of a very large discount, on account of my efforts. But I soon suspected that he would have liked me to make him a present of these utensils, and when he spoke of a new photographic stand camera, as he only had a fine detective apparatus, or of chemicals and requisites, of which I got him some catalogues, it was only mendicity in disguise, and I was required as a dupe to feed them all.

———

Lily was contemptible. She was capable of everything that was bad, and why? For nothing, through that invincible force which drove her alternatively from good to evil, from evil to good, in the same irresponsible way.

Her absence of all moral sense was unimaginable. She had no idea of rectitude or honesty, nor of what was allowed or forbidden. She had no conscience of her acts. She felt she was despised, even by those she pleased, and those who were the most indulgent towards her, would judge her as eccentric and lacking brain equilibrium. She realised the impression she created, but did not try to overcome it. Subtle, loving, caressing, kind; full of curiosity; crafty, and above all perfidious; adoring intrigue; stopping at nothing; obstinate, bad-tempered, and sly. She was full of coquetry and false pride, with the low tastes and bad language of a prostitute, although not vulgar. Yet without animosity, I should be insane to take any interest in her, despite her evident perversity.

Lily belonged to the category of hysterical unfortunates. I am certain that she had a certain instinct of sincerity. She would have liked to have been loyal, but she could not. She lied, in spite of herself, without knowing it, and always for the sole reason that the one simple characteristic of hysteria is the madness of mendacity.

Like the tongue of the fable of Aesop, Lily was, or could be good or bad. Doing evil, as suggested by the stronger will of Papa, she loved good actions, and passed long hours teaching one of her illiterate workgirls to read and write. To another, she advanced money when in trouble and was never repaid, and I felt certain that if she obtained gold by her prostitution or her millinery, she would freely give her earnings for her family. Strange mixture of qualities leading to vices; of vices conducting to virtue; all these contradictions were united in her.

Perfidious, she was clumsy; cunning, she was credulous; courageous, she was cowardly; a young lady, she liked the company of paid hirelings; indefatigable, she was lazy; perverted, she was devoted; vain, she was humble; witty, she was silly; and ugly, she was very pretty at times.

She inspired disgust and excited desire; in a word she troubled the brain of whosoever took an interest in her.

4

Un amant qui perd tout n'a plus de complaisance
Dans un tel entretien il suit sa passion,
Et ne pousse qu'injure et qu'imprécation.

. . . .

Son devoir m'a trahi, mon malheur et son père.

CORNEILLE.

Thou think'st I am mad for a maidenhead; thou art
cozened. . . .

BEAUMONT AND FLETCHER.

ERIC ARVEL TO JACKY.

Sonis-sur-Marne, May 28, 1899.

My dear Jacky,

I have been so busy of late that I have had no time to call my own.
I had intended asking you down last Monday, as Raoul had got forty-
eight hours leave, but I am under the impression that you were in the
midst of a family fête, so I was afraid to disturb you.

I just had time to take a photograph of Lilian and Raoul, copy of
which I send you.

We still are as badly off as ever, as far as servants are concerned,
but if you will come down and take pot-luck, bicycle and all, with us
on Tuesday, we shall be very pleased indeed to see you, and do our best
to entertain you.

With kindest regards from all, believe me to remain,

Yours very truly,
ERIC ARVEL.

MAY 28, 1899.

I sent a polite wire in answer and some of my perfumery for the mother and daughter, and went on my bicycle, arriving in the morning.

The photograph represented Lilian in her Japanese costume, standing up, her head reclining on the left breast of her handsome brother, who is swathed in the Japanese robe I had once put on. His arm is round her waist; he holds one of her hands in his, and presses it on his shoulder, while his cheek touches her hair, and she looks out of the picture with a wicked smile on her naughty face. Raoul seems sly, sardonic, and serious, as was his wont.

This group had been shown to my brother at the Bourse a a few days before I got mine, much to his surprise. He asked Mr. Arvel what it meant.

"It is a brother and sister," was the answer. My brother found this very funny, as he thought it was slightly lewd.

When I got in, Papa was in his little, photographic dark-room near the garden gate, and he was evidently quite gone with admiration on this Japanese group. I extolled it, and said it was very voluptuous, giving an impression of indecency, by reason of the flowing drapery of the girl, as one could see she had no stays on.

"You mean the backside!" he replied, coarsely.

I said it was very beautiful, and continued:

"Why don't you get photographed with her? I should like to see you two together."

He did not answer, but I saw the usual change in his face, and he began arranging some bottles.

He told me he would photograph me that afternoon with my bicycle, and I could take him, as I expressed the wish to have his likeness. I said I wanted him, as I had already got Lilian and Raoul, and he gave me some more copies of the Japanese couple on other papers, as there were several hanging up to dry.

I had brought a fancy little trick photograph, representing Lily as a ballet girl. They sell in Paris cards without heads to print photographs upon, and if you have a negative you can get your friends' faces on comic bodies. Arvel liked the joke.

After some conversation, Lilian appeared to invite us in to breakfast, and greeted me with marked and studied coolness, still playing a part for her Papa. She looked old, worn, and seemed to get uglier every time I saw her. Her skin was dark and sallow, and a moustache was coming. She was black under the eyes. She was dressed without any care, and had no powder, or lip colouring. There were no rings on her hands.

I was very gay and quite self-possessed. I chaffed her about the Japanese photograph. I told her that her brother looked sly and devilish: as satanic as myself.

"My brother says it is indecent. He has seen it. Your Papa showed it to him at the Bourse. He is now quite gone on the little Japanese girl."

"Pa," said she, "you are mad to have shown that at the Bourse. I suppose everybody has seen it?"

And I persuaded him to have it enlarged and coloured. We now went in to breakfast, and I told her quite loudly before her Papa, not to be sulky that day.

"Don't put on your black face, and show those ugly, violet, distorted lips. Last time I saw you, you looked like a Christy minstrel."

She walked rapidly away in front of me, turning her back to both of us, quite surprised, and he, of course, said nothing.

I had on for the first time at Sonis, bicycle breeches and Scotch stockings, and I began to make fun of my own calves, as we sat down to table. I said that all the ladies were in love with me, since my relations and my half-sister had forced me to put on cycling costume.

"Oh, your love! That must be very precious!" exclaimed Lilian, sneeringly and loudly, so that both her mother and father could not fail to hear her.

"Precious or not, once tasted, women always return for it," was my quick rejoinder.

She made no reply to this vain boast. The rest of the talk at déjeuner, although I made as many jokes as I could, and caused them all to laugh, does not concern our narrative.

I said that I had been to London just before Whitsuntide.

"I wish I had known," said Papa, "you could have brought me over a camera. There is no duty on it."

"I should have been very pleased to do so. I went to see some friends, had some clothes made, and I purchased this bicycle rig-out."

I said, which was perfectly true, that every Sunday, I had been coming to Sonis, to lunch in the pretty village, with a party of cycling friends, but that the weather had been too cold. They were astonished. I said I should come down next Sunday. They told me they were all going to the races in Paris. I expect Lily got me invited, after nearly a month's silence, to tell me she was going to the races. They evidently thought I should go too, and walk them about, give her and her Mamma drinks, and gamble a little for them. Instead of which, I said I was coming to Sonis with some ladies. I, of course, did not tell the principal lady of the party—no other than my Lilian at home—that the Arvels would all be absent on Sunday. So that was all smoothed over. And my artful puss of a "missus," who thought I dared not go to Sonis with her, was now thoroughly mystified. At the end of the lunch, Lily broke out with her old lie:

"I must go to Paris this afternoon to get some cottons, etc."

"You can't go now that Mr. S . . . is here!" said Papa.

This was her usual comedy. I said nothing, but it will be seen later in the afternoon, that it was only a fib to teaze me and hide the fact that my invitation had been deliberately planned by the pair.

Now comes a big parcel from the Louvre, with household goods, brooms, etc. Papa will not pay and flies into a passion. He does not pull out handfuls of gold, as he did in February.

Ma runs out in a huff. Lily chides Papa for getting in a rage, just as if he were a little boy: "Temper, Pa, temper!" she says.

"Let her go mad if she likes and tear her hair and grit her teeth, as she did the other day," snarls Arvel.

They must quarrel horribly at times.

"She has no money left," says Lily quietly, "and she will only send the things back. It is silly of you."

Papa reflects, and then relents, with a heavy sigh.

"Well, go and pay it out of your money."

Lily goes and gets the money upstairs and he is alone with me. He groans about the two women's extravagance.

The meal is finished and I am to go out on my bike with Papa. Lily refuses to accompany us. I do not ask her. She has customers coming. She also takes piano lessons now. She says she has a new bicycling costume.

Papa starts his parrot-cry again: "Bitter! Bitter!" And then he says, apropos of nothing:

"Raoul spells 'bitter' with one 't'." He chuckles at this.

"Ah, that makes 'biter,'" I reply. "The biter bit!"

His laugh stops suddenly and there is a pause, enabling me to add:

"Sometimes people try to trick you, but you see through them and they lose the game."

"In that case,"—and Papa spoke with some warmth—"the loser retires, and don't go into mourning for so little."

"How can people try to trick you, when there is not any interested motive to be seen?" broke in Lily, as she rolled up the napkins and put them in the drawer of the buffet.

"But if the motive is hidden?" quoth I.

No answer came, and Papa and I go and work at photography. He takes me in two positions. I take him in two others. He is a handsome man, or was. Lily comes now and again to see us at work, and once in a fit of rage, she tears up her photograph as the ballet-dancer, which has been shown to Mamma and all the work-girls. I could see that they had still some lingering idea that I was a jealous lover, full of agony at Lily's coldness, and she hated to see me so natural and undramatic.

I tell her in front of Papa that I am cleverer than he is.

"He does you, Mademoiselle, as a Japanese girl, because he has got you in front of him, but I transformed you into a ballet-girl without seeing you!"

I inform her that I have got her negative and shall make a dozen more dancing girls, and send her one every week. With her black face, she goes off in a huff to see her customers, who now arrive.

Papa remarks that Lilian has a devil's temper and he coolly adds that she is wicked, and a liar.

My photograph is now finished, and I say that I shall go and show it to Lily and dare her to tear it up. Arvel tells me to be careful, as she very likely will. She appears again, and I tell her that I will not show her my picture unless she kisses me. This is all before Papa. I never spoke so freely to her before in the presence of her parents. She is really quite surprised and is obliged to say:

"What is the matter with you to-day? I have never seen you like this!"

I now feel I am master of the situation, and I become more of a wag than ever. I chaff her about having a husband soon, and tell her that Papa will get her a nice little man and she shall have twins. They glance at each other. I continue to play the clown.

The negatives are now finished and dry, and I go and find Mamma in the kitchen to get a petroleum lamp for printing purposes.

I joke with her too, and tell her that my calves are such a success, that a lady in Paris makes me put on a pair of her black silk stockings every time I go to see her. Mamma says I am very gay. I ask her if her daughter always tries on hats and bonnets on her customers' heads down in the country, or sometimes goes to Paris to do so.

"I suppose now and again they countermand her by postcard, or so on?"

"I never saw a postcard countermanding anything," she answers, and then adds sadly:

"My daughter don't tell me everything!"

All mothers who know their daughters are foolish virgins pretend never to know what is going on under their noses. Adèle, I think, shuts her eyes to everything, puts up with anything, waiting for her old man to marry her. He told me again he would at the end of the year, Raoul having only one year's soldiering to do as the only son of a widow. If his mother was married, he would have to serve three years.

Back with my lamp. Lily says Papa is too fat. She makes me pinch his ribs. We talk of women's bellies. Lily says she has none and what little she has, she keeps down by wearing suspenders instead of garters. I say that a woman with a belly does not exist for me.

"Hush!" exclaims Lily, "Ma may hear you!"

Adèle was quite near, having come into the garden unobserved by us. Papa hears all this loose talk, but is dumb.

"You should be very nice to Mamma," says Lily to me, after she has left us. "You ought to try and make love to her."

What does she mean? I dare not guess. Papa is right beside us, but he is mute.

I now go after Lily alone in the garden, as the customers are gone and she has had her piano lesson besides. How about the visit to Paris now?

I ask her how she liked the novel of Suzanne I sent her. Not as much as Césaréc it appears.

"That is because Césarée is a good little virgin and Suzanne is vile. How did you like La Femme et le Pantin?"

"Not at all!"

"No, because it shows up women like you. Come here, I want to talk to you for the sake of old times."

And we go away behind some trees, she looking very happy, thinking I am going to be very nice, from my opening words. As we walk together, I say to myself: is it really to be believed that by sheer strength of false letters and lies, the truth, the whole truth can be entombed? It cannot, shall not be. She has lied enough. It is impossible to lie more. The strength of lying is doubtless enormous, but it finishes by being exhausted. She has tried to build a very wall of falsehood round her house and fabricate with forged sentiment, supported by lies, a monstrous idol of seeming truth, before which I am, forsooth, to stupidly kneel.

Now I have been all round the circle of lies. I know, I understand, I judge, and that gave me the tone of authority which ought to have impressed her greatly, had she loved me.

I felt myself soaring above all humane consideration. I forgot my book. I was no longer myself. I was the impersonal mouth of truth, and the grandeur of the part I played gave me simple, strong, and luminous facility with which to speak; and ample demonstration gushed forth abundantly.

I told the facts and classified them, unrolling the chain link by link before my victim. I explained all, and showed all. Each hypothesis became a reality, accompanied by a procession of proofs, without any jesuitical insinuations, or sneaking blows in the back.

"I very much enjoyed my last visit here, when after that Sunday night in Paris, you thought I was going to come round again and humble myself. You waited all day for me to speak. I said nothing and have held my tongue for a month, until it pleased you to send for me. And I am not asking for anything now—not even a kiss—as you are the vilest creature that ever breathed. I am not the weak hero of "The Woman and the Puppet."

I pass over her denials, and her false laugh of scorn, which she puts on, trying to show me that she did not care what I said to her, but will continue with as much as I can remember of all I forced her to listen to. I was quite calm. She did not excite my lust as she once did, and I found a peculiar pleasure in insulting her and dragging her through the ordure she kept on shovelling up herself, until she should get tired of trying to drive me silly by her stupid wickedness. I think that is all she wanted to do. Did she really know what she was about?

"I gave you a turquoise ring. Strange, I have just found that 'turquoise' means November. I 'had' you first November 26th., 1897, and in November 1898, you got deflowered."

"It's a lie! I'm still a virgin! Oh, that month of November!" she added, with the half-groan, half-sob, that I had already heard when I taunted her with the remembrance of Shrovetide.

"A virgin of three inches of finger! I don't care if you are a virgin or not. What made me angry was your imposture, extending over three months, when you kept me from touching you between the thighs, as much as you could, and told me"—here I could not help sneering—"how you were keeping your maidenhead for Jacky, and how you would like me alone to have it."

She was silent. Her jerky, imitation laugh stopped, and she bent her head.

"You were free to do as you liked, but not to try and trick me who never did you any harm. You invented that lie about the unregistered letter; how you suffered at Lille and Brussels; and how you were always a poor, persecuted virgin, adoring me. You are worse than any woman I ever met. How much do you get, when you dine out with Lolotte? A hundred francs between you?"

"You talk to me as if I were a common prostitute. I want no money. I have plenty."

"You are lucky. I have none. I want to tell you that you have been trying to trick me, and I never was your marionette. You invented a cheating dodge that I never heard of before. You give a rendez-vous by letter, knowing you cannot keep it, and then you countermand it, and if reproached, say: 'But I meant to see you and could not. It is not my fault. Did I not make the appointment?' The last one made by you and stopped by a customer's postcard that your mother saw, was a fine cheating joke. You Ma has just told me that she never knows what you do. Your letter with the appointment for Mi-Carême was a lie. Your Papa, as a man of business, knew in advance the date of his departure. It was a slack time with him in Paris and the Carnival was on in Brussels. And your 'monthlies' were just over, for you went out cycling with me on the first of March."

I paused for a reply. None came, and even her spasmodic laugh was hushed.

"And I hear no more about your trip with me to Belfort. You knew it was impossible."

She turned her head from me. I could not see her face.

"I never went to Brussels. I sent there, and I have got a long report all about you and your Papa in the double-bedded room, in writing. That is better than if I had gone myself. All my letters since were got up to lead you on in your cheating lies. You have shown them all to your father, and both of you have been trying to work me, and exploit me, and trick me for some base and mercenary motive. You have both fallen into my traps. Your mother even knows all about the books I lent you, 'Justine.'"

She had been silent, but this last blow went home, and she

was mad with rage, as with flashing eyes and curling lips, showing her gleaming teeth, she exclaimed:

"How can you be so wicked? How can you imagine such horrors? Ma knows nothing. You think and think until you do not know where you are. You know nothing. You guess all wrong. I am a virgin. Pa has never touched me. Now let me tell you once for all that he knows nothing about all you and I have done together and he must never know. That I ask of your loyalty."

Not all, certainly, but as much as she had cooked up for him.

"Then why does he always talk dirt about you to me?"

"Perhaps he is jealous of you." She said this very slowly, and with averted gaze.

"I never answer him about you."

"That is good of you and quite right."

"No, no! you are accomplices here in this house to cheat and harm me!"

"Say that again, and I will never invite you here any more!"

"I don't want to come. You have always run after me. I still say you are all in league to play with me and against me, but you have not got the best of me yet. I am too clever for you. And you yourself are not cunning enough to beat me. That article I translated and the 'passionate' letter of lust, written by your order, were all for his amusement."

"You are awfully bad. You must be very wicked yourself, or else you could not imagine that such horrors could exist in others. I will go to Papa with you now and tell him all."

"Come on," I answered, and I stepped towards the studio. She did not move, but remained still, trying to laugh sarcastically at what she called my "stupid imagination."

"I don't care what you say," I continued, "I now know all I want to know about you. I could have gone to Narkola's and found out more. I could, if I chose, go and sleep with Charlotte."

"Why don't you?"

"Because I won't take the trouble. I know enough. You are a common whore, dining, and letting all men enjoy your body in cabinets particuliers for a few louis, and without the excuse of a poor prostitute who does it for bread. You have got all you want and your Papa as a lover. You dined at Narkola's regularly last winter with your subscribers."

She was not offended. She did not feel my insults. Never had I so insulted a woman. The hot blood comes in my face as I copy it out now, months afterwards, and she was able to find the following lie to clear herself. It is true that she had had three weeks to concoct it.

"I will explain about that," she now replied. "Lolotte was going to marry Raoul. We broke that off. Pa won't let her come here and I won't go to her place. She has a big brother, and I want to keep him from doing harm to mine. To talk with her we dined alone together at Narkola's. Papa must never know I went there, or that I was out with Charlotte. You must not betray me."

"You put on cambric drawers to dine alone with Lolotte?"

"I had no cambric drawers!"

"You had no drawers on at all perhaps? And where do you wash them? What does Ma say to you putting them on, when you go up to Paris alone at night? You are a nice, amusing, incestuous little viper!"

"Now let me be! Go away! I want to work! I won't listen to any more of your ravings."

"You must. You shall. I enjoy telling you all this. I have lots more to tell you."

She ran from me, but I followed her into the workshop, continuing my vile talk in English.

"I'll slap your face, if you say more!" cried Lily, through her clenched teeth.

"Do so!"

She slapped one side, half-angry, half-laughing. I offered the other cheek and she slapped it too. She did not hurt. This was in front of her workgirls, and she told them in French that I was teazing her and would not let her work.

"You can work." I speak now in English, as she takes up her needle and a hat. "See, your hand does not tremble; you don't make a stitch wrong. You don't care."

"I do. You hurt my feelings terribly. I never knew you were such a bad man. But now I will go and sleep with my Papa, although I have never done so yet, just to spite you."

"That lie I expected. I know that old trick—one lie to cover another! You will say: 'When I wrote to you from Lille, I resisted him. It was true what I wrote then, but now I am his mistress!' And as for being a virgin, you will declare: 'When I swore on my mother's life in the cab that I was a maid, the night you slapped my face, I told the truth, but I was so disgusted with you, for whom I was keeping my maidenhead, that I immediately went and gave myself up to somebody else!' You will have to invent some new lie.—Now tell me, Lily, who had it? Was it not in November, just when I wrote to you after your lie of the lost letter, in which I enclosed the fifty-franc note, that Lily was dead?"

"You never sent that letter."

"Then why, when I told you I had done so in November last, did you at once write back wanting to marry such a scoundrel?"

"Because I was very fond of you then, and would have done anything for you."

"Yes, because you thought I was rich. That night in the cab, you must have been tipsy, else you would never have opened your thighs as far as you did. In January and February, you always gripped them close together."

No reply came, so I tried the following little artifice upon her:

"Look here; I'll tell you something that will astonish you. If you will come with me to a doctor, not chosen by you, but somebody I'll take you to, and let him examine you; if he says you are a virgin, I declare, without swearing on mothers' lives that I'll marry you."

"I am a virgin and I'll go to any doctor you like, but I'll not marry you now!"

"Because you think I've got no money."

"I know you haven't. Pa always told me so."

Then, after a pause, as I take breath, turning her face from me; not daring to look at me, she says slowly, in a low and tremulous voice:

"I think you would marry me without caring if I was a virgin or not."

"No, I would not. After all, the least I could ask for as a huband, when I think over what passed between us last year, would be your virginity."

"Last year I had somebody else as well as you."

"What do I care?—Your Pa tells me you prefer feeling and sucking to proper coition."

She was too surprised to answer, and she waited for more. I had gathered this from his statement that modern girls preferred superficial caresses.

"How about the Mount Calvary? That proves he knows all."

"He only meant that I was between two thieves."

"Then why did he add a remark about your crown of thorns?"

She was strangely mute.

"He meant that you had suffered, going up the mountain. And why does he call me Satan? He will tell me all in time, if I like. I ought not to say so much to you, as you will now stop his mouth. I can imagine you talking to him, in your bedroom, just after I went away last time:

" 'Well, Pa, what did he say to you?'

" 'Nothing! But what did he say to you, Lilian?'

" 'Nothing, Pa!' What fun for me you both are! It is grand to be able to read you all here, wanting for nothing, caring for nothing, and telling you all I think of you. I am going to put our adventure into a novel. I have already written a lot of it. I shall call it 'Suburban Souls.' I shall alter the names and places."

"That is the least you can do!—Now, will you go away! Leave off, I say. You do not know what nonsense you are talking and how you are mistaken in every way."

"If I am wrong, I am an utter rogue. You have never yet called me a liar, because you know I am not one. But say so now; spit in my face, and tell me to go!"

She turned away without a word, and her mother appeared.

"Don't say any more, as Ma can catch up a few English words she may know," whispered Lily, hurriedly.

So I saluted the workgirls and retired.

It was always the same. She could not tell the truth. Driven in a corner, she covered up the first lie with a second one; then if wanted, placed a third one over them, and so on as long as necessary. It is true that she deceives no one, as she must always be detected sooner or later; but she gives herself the satisfaction of believing that she has blinded her victim for the nonce.

I went back to the dark-room. Papa was hard at work, finishing my second photograph, and his own. I help him a little, as it is too late to go out cycling.

I now make up my mind to do what I have never done before: to "work" him a little, and talk to him, as he has tried to talk to me. If he knows all, as I think, it will not matter, and if he does not—I shall see what comes of it. So I begin to talk smut. That soon draws him out, and I boldly tell him about virgins, and how girls swear you out that they have never been penetrated by a man.

"You can't tell," he says, looking at me with a puzzled expression.

"Can't you? You've only got to put your finger up."

"That is not a test, but still if you thrust in four inches or so, they can't be virgins. My fingers are no use. They are too short."

And he stared at me with increasing uneasiness.

"Then I am right. You agree with me. My experience has proved this."

"But then, there is no certainty. The hymen gives!"

What a splendid, strange remark for him to make! An elastic maidenhead! Surely he knew all, and was trying to make me believe that Lilian's membrane still closed up the vaginal passage, and was like a bit of india-rubber!

"You can't tell," he continues. "They can make a virgin cleft with alum water."

"That is no use against the medical exploration with the finger."

"Ah, you've never tried to get into an alum girl!"

I cannot help shrugging my shoulders disdainfully, and keep on:

"What is really difficult is not to have children. To get them is easy, but to enjoy a woman and not impregnate, is hard work."

"To get children," he answers, evading my proposition, "the best way is to have connection dog-fashion, and not let the woman empty her bladder for twenty-four hours afterwards."

I can hardly keep from laughing at this new cure for female sterility, and we prepare for a walk before dinner, when Lilian appears from the kitchen. She looks so ill—so black, dull, and rancorous—that even Papa notices it, and asks her what is the matter.

It is the effect of my talk, and she has been having a little explanation with her mother about what I had said. She chaffs me and I retaliate gaily, all before Papa. I tell her how rude she was, never to thank me for some English fashion papers I put in Papa's parcels. She curtsies down to the ground with ironical politeness, saying:

"I thank you, sir!—Are you satisfied now?"

"Hardly. You are not overpolite as a rule."

"I shan't take lessons from you."

"You might do worse."

She tells her Papa that she is going to Paris the next day, and she says:

"I must have a little cheque: fifty francs will do!"

And she pirouettes in front of us, lifting up her skirts slightly, but turning her head away. When in a fix, she hides her face. Papa does not answer, but looks at her with his most gloomy air, showing how strongly she stirred him then. This is also to vex me, and show me what money she can have of him! With this she runs in doors, still with averted face. Shortly afterwards, I am alone for a few moments, while Papa has gone up to his room, and I hand her the preface (see Appendix B), and the first eighty pages of "The Double Life," a rough proof; with all the incestuous passages marked, and some newspaper cuttings: "An Infamous Father" (see Appendix F) and "The Tête-à-tête" (see Appendix G). I give her to understand that I have arranged this preface. She seems very pleased and is evidently delighted that I do not sulk after the blowing-up. Her lips twitch, her eyes laugh, and her nostrils quiver, exactly as when she used to get "wet." Can she make her nostrils palpitate at will? Yes—women can do it.

"Don't spend!" I say, and she runs away laughing.

Papa and I go out with the dogs. We talk more smut and I tell him:

THE TALE OF TRIXIE.

A few years ago, I was carrying on an intrigue, to use a polite term, with a married lady, and she used to give me a *rendez-vous* somewhere in Paris, during the afternoon. Her lord and master was rather jealous and she was obliged to take great precautions, frequently changing the place of appointment. One quiet spot I had found out was the Terrasse de l'Orangerie, in the garden of the Tuileries, where one might have thought oneself to be in a dull provincial town, had it not been for the roar of the distant traffic. My sweet adulteress very often never appeared at all, as a whim of her master might stop her many a time from going out.

At least, so she told me. One fine day in June, I was at my post, under the trees, and I knew by the time I had been there that she would not come that day. I felt rather glad than otherwise, and was debating with myself whether it would not be better to give up such an unsatisfactory *liaison* altogether, as I lazily smoked a cigar, and fell to idly watching the movements of a trim-built little lady who was impatiently trotting up and down, all alone, with a bunch of roses stuck in her waistband. She was simply, but neatly dressed, and it was easy for a man used to the ways of a big city, to see that she was not a common wench, seeking the acquaintance of the first man who would accost her.

She passed in front of me, and went to the stone parapet that borders the terrace, and like Sister Ann, looked out afar, but nothing was to be seen. With a gesture of impatience, she tore the roses from her girdle and flung them away. Then she looked at a tiny watch and made as if to leave the garden. I got up and followed her, and although repulsed at first, I managed to make her conquest, and finally, after a deal of trouble, she told me that she was seeking an adventure, and had answered an advertisement in the *Ruy Blas* newspaper, where, under the cloak of matrimony, kindred souls poured out their desire to find fitting mates, and restless spirits sought for their affinities. Trixie, for thus I shall call my new friend, was fresh to Paris and its ways, and she had answered one of these announcements, when she had been directed to come to the Tuileries, with the bunch of roses as a signal, so as to make herself known. The correspondent had not kept his appointment and so she made my acquaintance.

I may say at once that, after two or three appointments, she let me do what I chose with her and I found her to be a most charming little woman, and possessing all the qualities that I always sought for in a mistress: strong sensuality and no squeamishness or false prudery.

Before giving way to me, she told me that she had already been seduced and abandoned by her lover. Her parents had got to know all about this intrigue, and although they let her live at home with them, they made her life very unhappy, reminding her daily of her fall, and she was naturally never allowed out after dinner. She was exceedingly well educated, and spoke English, French, German and Spanish, writing all the four languages without faults. She could play the piano and seemed domesticated. Trixie spoke vaguely about giving lessons to earn a little, albeit she confessed to not being in want of money.

She was not of a mercenary disposition and soon got to be very fond of me. Being of a passionate nature, she was delighted to fall across a man who was not jealous, and who taught her, or thought he taught her, a few new tricks and turns of vice. She dubbed me her "professor," and in truth she was an apt pupil in my hands.

Trixie was fond of her own sex, and frequently asked me to introduce her to some nice girl, promising me that I should join in the fun. We made up our minds we would try all sorts of strange games together, and taste of all the fruit that the orchard of passion could possibly contain.

I had not known her a month, and none of our projects of lust had as yet been put into practice, when one morning, the *Ruy Blas* contained an advertisement, stating that a young couple desired to meet with a lady and gentleman with a view to friendly intercourse.

I showed this to Trixie and asked if I should answer it. She demurred at first, but finally consented, and I entered into correspondence with a person who turned out to be a tall, handsome gentleman of about thirty years of age.

He came to a meeting that I gave him on the terrace of the Tuileries, and I saw he was perfectly sincere and acting as I was, without any base motive. He told me that he was married, and had taught his wife that the heart and the senses were two distinct things. He was far from being jealous and left her entire liberty, although he preferred that when she took a lover, she should do all with him and without concealment.

The idea of a partie carrée pleased him greatly, as I told him we were both perfectly free to keep our names to ourselves. I had no curiosity, and wanted nothing but pleasure.

I let him know at once that I was not married, but that I had a little mistress, named Trixie, whose story I told him, and it was agreed between us that the two ladies should meet. If they liked each other, as we two men did, we would arrange to dine or lunch together and change partners, besides letting our companions enjoy themselves in Lesbian fashion, as he confessed that his wife was not averse to playing the part generally ascribed to the poetess Sappho. This, I knew, would suit Trixie.

We arranged to tell our ladies of the result of our interview and I said it would be best for us all to meet on the terrace, and as soon as I could see Trixie, who could only come out in the afternoon, I would let him know.

The next time I enjoyed my new sweetheart, I told the story to her and drew a highly-coloured sketch of the cultured young married man I had met, but she did not seem enthusiastic. I was myself very hot on the scent of this honest rake's wife, as he had offered her to me in exchange for my Trixie, and no doubt he felt the same towards me.

At last, my lustful little woman promised to come to the Tuileries at three o'clock on a certain day, and after the exchange of a few notes and telegrams with the young husband, an appointment was made by me and accepted by Trixie, who was to meet her "Professor" in the public garden, where she and I would await the coming of the advertising couple, when the two men would introduce their brace of beauties to each other.

I was punctual, but Trixie did not turn up, which annoyed me not a little, as I thought that if the young fellow appeared with his spouse and found me alone, he might reasonably suppose that no Trixie existed and that I had invented my story with the sole object of getting to see his wife.

While fretting and fuming up and down the terrace, my new friend made his appearance and he too was alone.

I told him at once that Trixie had not come, in spite of her

promise, and that I was very vexed. He replied that his wife had
been taken ill just before getting dressed to go out with him, and
had gone to bed, refusing to accompany him that afternoon to
meet Trixie and myself, although he had told her everything,
described me to her, and had extorted from his wife a promise to
go on with the adventure.

I begged him to excuse me, and I could only say it was not
my fault. Trixie had promised too and Trixie had not come to me.

We adjourned to a café, and he once more expounded his free
love doctrines. It suited me admirably to agree with him. I promised to let him know directly I heard from Trixie, as I did not
possess her real address, but only wrote to her at a post-office, as
I was doing with him, and he with me.

A few days later, I was called to London, and wrote to the disappointed gentleman that he should hear from me on my return.
I dropped a line to Trixie too, giving an address where a friend
would receive the answer for me, informing her that I had not met
the young wife I ought to have seen, and I scolded her slightly for
not having kept the important appointment.

I had not been a week in the British capital before I received
a long letter from Trixie in reply, covering about eight sides of
notepaper. She seemed to be in dire trouble lest I forgot her, or
would be eventually disgusted with her, after what she considered
it was her duty to write to me.

My Trixie and the free-love gentleman's wife were one and
the same person!

He had drawn up the advertisement and put it in the paper,
without consulting her, as she was in the habit of obeying his
strangest behests.

When my letter arrived, she knew the writing, but kept her
own counsel and let everything go on until the day came for the
meeting of the two men and the two (!) women, and then she
got out of it at the last minute, exactly as her husband had told me.

She concluded with a piteous appeal to her "Professor," not to
abandon her, and added that if now, knowing all, I cared to see her
naked in the arms of her husband, she would try and do it for me.

I had nothing to be offended about, and had I felt sore at her
little trick, her frank avowal would have disarmed me entirely.

On my return to Paris, we met again and I tranquilised her. I informed her that I had no curiosity, nor any wish to see, or know her husband, and I was perfectly content to enjoy her, in any way she liked.

She was delighted at what she called my generous magnanimity and we became fast friends, as well as eager lovers.

Anything I wanted, she said she would always try to do for me, and would even consent to introduce me to her husband officially, but she plainly showed that she would not care for him to enjoy her in my presence. She would go with delight from my arms to those of any man I chose, but not her husband, unless I desired it, and would be resigned to any sacrifice of her body or her affections, sooner than lose me.

The idea of witnessing her conjugal copulation was not a tempting one for me, and I put her completely at her ease, by petting the poor little woman and informing her that she could do precisely as she chose.

Trixie had married very young, and had two children, a boy and a girl, although no one would have guessed it to look at her, with her clothes on or without.

She was petite, very slightly built, with no breasts to speak of. Pretty features; fine grey eyes; beautiful mouth and good teeth; long black hair, and every other charm in proportion.

Trixie was a woman among a thousand, as she was a perfect female rake, and at the same time perfectly honest, truthful, and sincere, ready to do anything and join me in any extraordinary caprice and freak of lasciviousness, whether men or women, or both were concerned.

Her husband had debauched her, soon after the birth of her second child. He had often propounded his theories of love and liberty on both sides, and that husband and wife should be partners in passion with mutual confidence, and no jealousy; but she had repulsed him with horror, having been brought up strictly, and married to him when in her teens, very soon after leaving school. Her parents were in trade, and her mother and father of different nationalities had lived in various countries, not being those they were born in, which accounts for her polyglot talents. Her husband was, like myself, an Englishman, who had passed his life on the continent.

He had made the acquaintance of a young cavalry officer, who I will call Achille. He was married too, and with his wife visited Trixie and her husband, and a slight cordial friendship sprung up between the two couples, with mutual pleasant intercourse; dinners out and at home; visits and return visits; theatre parties and so forth.

Achille and Trixie's lord and master seemed to be, strangely enough, of the same opinion as regards sexual liberty, and Madame Achille had given herself freely to the latter gentleman, with full permission of her husband, and the two men had been together in the same bed with her.

Trixie was quite unconscious of this trifling intrigue, and busy with her two pretty dolls of children, refused to listen to the theories of her spouse, which seemed loathsome to her.

But he was resolved to drag her down to his level and corrupt her entirely, for such was his mania, and a conspiracy was formed and carried out in the following cold-blooded way.

Achille and his wife came to dine with Trixie and her lord and master at the latter's house, and champagne was freely drank. After dinner, the conversation turned on the subject of female sexual inversion, or the love of women for women, and in front of the two men, Madame Achille made love to Trixie, as a man would have done. The young mother was horrified, and at last, out of patience at the bold advances of the half-tipsy officer's wife, who dared to approach her with audacious fumbling fingers and mannish kisses; disgusted with the applauding leer of her wine-flushed husband, and the brazen words that Achille, excited at the scene, let fall without restraint, she rose to leave the table, pretexting a headache, which she ascribed to the champagne.

Seeing the quarry about to escape, her husband rushed towards her, and seizing her hands, called to Achille to help him. In an instant, the military voluptuary full of lust, was upon her, and despite her struggles, shrieks of shame, and appeals for mercy, the two men bore her slight frame, as light as a feather, more like a pretty boy than a mother, to an armchair, and threw her backwards in it. Her husband held her hands and kept her seated against her will, while Achille on his knees, threw up her skirts, and roughly separated her well-built little legs.

She kicked about as well as she could, struggling and calling out, until she was quite exhausted, and Achille, with the consent of her husband, exhibited a magnificent weapon, which Trixie could not look at and closed her eyes not to see. Madame Achille now came forward, threw herself madly on the panting victim, and began to undress her, or rather undo her clothes as well as she could, considering the position she was in, held down in the chair. Achille, with coarse jokes and worse than rude remarks, clumsily assisted his wife, and between the two, they tore her garments off, and left her nothing but a few shreds of torn linen.

Achille's wife, telling her husband to pull the outraged mother's legs well apart, then applied her mouth to Trixie's secret spot, and despite her shame, notwithstanding the horror of her position, the tongue of the Lesbian was so cleverly worked, that finally she succumbed and emitted into the mouth of the sly, sucking woman. At first, the feeling that a strange woman's mouth was kissing that part of her body, which no one save her husband and a doctor had hitherto seen, filled her with disgust, and she so violently upbraided her treacherous female friend that Madame Achille seemed inclined to relinquish her purpose, had not Trixie's husband forced her to continue.

It was only by dint of sticking to her task that the continued lingual onanism of Madame Achille produced its effect, and when that was evident by the change that came over poor bruised and outraged Trixie, a roar of triumph was started by the two men, who relaxed their hold and left the young novice to be finished off by a last few rapid touches of the tricky tongue of the officer's wife.

She rolled to the ground exhausted, and Achille boldly plunged his perforator into the palpitating body of Trixie, and emitted freely in the vagina, all moist with his wife's saliva, while the father of her children gloated over what was for him a delightful spectacle—to see his wife ravished by his friend, after being outraged by a woman in his presence.

Directly he saw that Achille had finished and was forcing his tongue between Trixie's lips; he turned to Madame Achille, and she responded to his mute and significant appeal by boldly unbuttoning his trousers, and searching for the staff of life, which was as familiar to her as that of her husband.

She was soon riding over him, while Achille tried to pacify Trixie, who had begun to cry, and to the sound of Trixie's tears and sobs her husband ejaculated close to the neck of the greedy womb of his friend's wife.

Trixie recovered from the shock, and for the sake of peace, yielded now to her husband, and soon finding the forbidden, but juicy fruit, sufficiently palatable, she threw all scruples to the winds, with the idea that if she did not help her husband in his salacious pastimes, he would get other women to help him. Her passions being now thoroughly roused by the efforts of her husband, she plunged into the vortex of depravity, and fell into my hands, just as she was ripe for any devilment.

Puritans will shake their heads sadly as they read this story, and say that such a life could not last; that the laws of divorce would be called into play; and that such a lustful couple would soon separate, with talk of the mutual respect necessary between husband and wife. They are entirely wrong, as Trixie and her spouse lived perfectly happy together, devoted to each other, and bringing up their children with the utmost care.

Trixie visited all the secret haunts of Paris in my company, and the history of what this darling little woman did with her "Professor," would fill a stout volume.

Suffice it to say, that although she loved her husband more than anything in the world, she had a great deal of affection for me, and she proved it, because she never told me a lie. I mean that no doubt she may now and then have uttered a fib or two, but she did not invent mean or wicked falsehoods to teaze and worry me. On the contrary, she told me all about her lovers, always kept her appointments, and never quarrelled with me.

I was very fond of seeing her in the arms of another woman, and I gave her orders to entrap and entice young girls whenever she could, and we used to enjoy them together.

She was always ready to obey my bidding, and, my dear Mr. Arvel, if I had asked you to dine with her and me, and after the meal, had told her to go away with you, she would have done so cheerfully, if I had desired it. We had many parties carrées together, although I must confess I did not care about them. I liked to possess her with another woman.

The foregoing rapid sketch was an enormous success with Mr. Arvel. He constantly kept recurring to it. I told him I had lots more to tell him. I also consulted him about a married woman I was just then trying to get hold of, and I asked him if it was honest to try and debauch a friend's wife? My conscience pricked me. He advised me to get her if I could.

"If you don't, someone else will!"

"Alas!" I say, "there's no honesty when our desires are aroused!"

He concurs, and tells me some of his experiences. They are silly, schoolboy yarns. I continue to astonish him with some of my adventures. I want him to retail all this to Lily.

Then he talks of the books he likes. Miss Braddon is his favourite author. He does not like French novels, as a rule, but he wants to read that celebrated book on the vice of masturbation, *Charlot s'amuse.* I promise to get him a copy. He does not like "Fanny Hill." I tell him it is good, and written in good English too. He hates reading philosophy. He prefers "Tit-Bits" and "Answers." He has read the book I lent him—"The Romance of Lust"—twice since February! He is going to send it back to me. I shall then go through it and see why he liked it so much. He gossips anent flagellation, and tells me how much he likes books on that subject, especially "The Mysteries of Verbena House," which he had from me, and which I passed on to Lily.

I narrate to him some recollections of Trixie's birching experiences with me. I have never been like this before with him. He listens with open mouth, and his pipe goes out. I cannot now remember all I told him. A huge budget of stories of the same kind I unpacked for him after dinner.

I begged him never to sneer at novels, except very farfetched stories of travel and murder, because authors simply hear of strange doings in private life and write them up, when by practice we can, as we read, pick the truth even out of a mass of lies in a three-volume love-story.

I confide to him that a gentleman friend of mine had written a vile book, and having gone away travelling, had left me to correct the proofs. I promise him a copy when done, in a few months.

"What is it about?" he asks.

"I dare not tell you. It is so awful. You shall see it when finished."

"I should like a copy, but I must not keep it. I will return it when read, as I am frightened of the girl getting hold of it!"

Of course, I am alluding to "The Double Life," the proofs of which he got from Lily soon after I left his house, I expect.

We return to dinner; he still saying, as he opens the door:

"That story of Trixie is wonderful!"

I must remark that they had cut off the afternoon tea, and I have not washed my hands since the morning. It will be remembered that they used to take me into the best bedroom, which communicates with Lily's. Have they altered their sleeping arrangements? I walked behind my man, chuckling as we go in to the evening meal. Trixie has kept us out late. It is eight o'clock. Mamma and Lily are awaiting us impatiently. We sit down talking "dog," and I say:

"Mr. Arvel and myself disagree on one point. I will not allow that in-breeding is good. All your dogs will have faults, unless you get some outside cross."

He has just had another brother and sister put together. They are also by a brother and sister.

I notice that Lily and her Papa have not yet been able to meet that day. I have never left one or the other, so I know I can continue to try and talk to Papa again after dinner, before she has time to tell him that I have declared they are accomplices in every way against me. He is charming to me all through dinner and until I leave; quite different from last time, when he was probably under the influence of Lily's story to him of the little drama of the cab, told in her own way, of course, as she has a certain set of lies for him, no doubt. Perhaps he is glad I am no longer friends with her?

I am certain he is quite bewitched by her and she likes him very much. But still I fancy she has not yet found the man who can influence her. Will she ever? I think not.

How a young woman of 23 can allow a man to talk and write to her as I have done, surpasses my comprehension. And still she sends for me. The lowest street whore, or brothel wench, would have shown some little pride of some sort ere this; or would have fled from my awful talk; or shed one or two tears, if only of vexation. She must be hysterically mad. She is lustful, but cold-hearted, in spite of her heated centre of love, which is like a fire on an iceberg.

I am forced to come to the conclusion that she no longer cares for me—if she ever did—and I make up my mind that this shall be my last visit. I have a scheme for closing the doors of this House of Lies against myself, so as to guard against any future weakness on my own part.

We sit down to dinner. Lily gets up occasionally, and once she stands over her Papa, and plunges her eyes in his as if she was fascinating a dumb animal. He looks at her for a few seconds, and then, quite confused, unable to bear her glance any longer, drops his head sheepishly into his plate, like a boy sick with passion.

We talk of legs and calves again. Lily says she has no calves. Mine are false, I say. She determines to see if what I declare is true, and feels them under the table, finishing up with a sly pinch.

She passes me the salt, with the remark that she is helping me to sorrow.

"Dost hate me then so greatly?" I exclaim, in the exaggerated, gruff tone of the stage villain. She does not like that remark and says so.

There are asparagus which Mamma tells me Lily went and got specially for me. I ask her to mix me some sauce of oil and vinegar, as she is doing for herself. She consents, and when finished, puts her finger in it to taste it. Mamma chides her. I say I will be re-venged, and when she is beginning to eat her asparagus, I put my finger in her plate and taste her sauce. She offers me more asparagus. I take some from her hand and say:

"Thank you, Madam,—Mademoiselle, I mean!"

At this, which I say loudly and boldly, her face shows true temper; the black cloud comes over her features, and her lips are blue and distorted.

"I hate being called madam!" she cries angrily. Both Mamma and Papa are curiously silent during my encounter with Lily.

We talk of types of character. I tell them that if the negatives of the photographs of the illustrious personage, who died in February in a woman's arms, of Papa, and of myself, were all superposed and drawn off together, the features would mix and melt into one face, as we were of the same race, tastes and temperament. No one replies to me. I do not think they understand, or else they have read my thoughts. I add that I really think my host is a Jew, and appeal to my hostess. She answers coolly: "I know he is not!"

"No one knows better than you, madam!"

She does not turn a hair, nor does Lilian. They make as if they did not know what I am talking about. Of course, Papa is silent.

Dinner is over. Papa leaves me alone with Mamma and Lily.

Mamma tells me about Raoul as a soldier. I had told him that if ever he got into trouble privately, and there was anything he did not want his mother or sister to know, he was to write to me. This I now told to his mother and she thanked me. An officer has taken a dislike to him and he is being persecuted. He is unhappy. I say that there is perhaps a petticoat in the case. They agree with me. Raoul has never been punished. Both the women say that it is thanks to the good advice I have given him. I do not quite understand. Lilian tells me that he never forgot how I instructed him to behave at the regiment last November, and if he has got on so well, it is all on account of my counsel. And that was eight months ago. She never told me this before. Ma informs me that Lilian is not going to London with her brother in September, but is going to give up bonnet-building, as her health will not permit her to remain the long necessary hours in the workroom, and that it is a fearful trade unless you have a very good connection. She requires plenty of exercise in the open air, and to live in a pure atmosphere, not inhaling the rebreathed air of the stifling workshop, with a stove in it.

Here Lily grips her lips with her hand and hides her mouth; her elbows resting on the table.

Mamma continues: "She is not going to take any fresh customers, but gradually drop the old ones. I want her to shut up at once, but she wishes to wait until September, when the season here is over. She will become her Papa's secretary (*I kick Lily under the table*), he will give her a salary (*a kick*), and teach her the business (*a kick*); so that she will become a lady journalist (*a kick*); and remain comfortably at home with her Papa!" (Kick, kick, kick!)

I agree heartily with Mamma. "Certainly, she cannot do better than always remain with her Papa!"

Lily holds her lips tight and does not move. Papa returns and says that she does not help him. She retorts that the other day she prepared a lot of newspaper cuttings. Papa says:

"You were to have worked a day with me, but you never turned up."

She takes some medecine, which I opine is for cramps of the stomach, a well-known symptom of poor-blooded hysteria, and the dogs come in.

One bitch licks my ears. Lilian pretends to be disgusted. Mamma not being present, I say that ear-licking is nice and that lovers lick each other's ears.

"When you are married, you will be glad to lick your husband's ears!"

"Horrible!" she exclaims. Papa smokes in silence.

Mamma returns and the talk turns on theatres. Lily tells Mamma to go to bed. Lily has a pleasant, cool way of saying curtly:

"Go to bed, Mamma!"

Her respectable parent refuses. Lily talks of the plays she saw in Brussels.

"You went to a theatre every night?"

"Not every night," answers Papa, "as she was ill part of the time. She caught cold during a drive in the Bois de la Cambre, and went to bed early.* I wanted to go out and leave her. She would not allow me to do so."

"No, certainly not!" protests Lily. "Pa wanted to see the Carnival. I wasn't going to let him gad about alone."

Mamma laughs and looks at me with sparkling, aggressive eyes.

"She only let me go from her side once the whole time we were there, and that was for ten minutes," said Papa.

And he then held down his head and looked quite silly and delighted. And so did Lily. They were really, without exaggeration, like a newly-married couple talking of their honeymoon. Mamma beamed on the guilty pair, and glared defiance at me, with glitter-

---

* More irregular menstruation!

ing glance, as if to show me that she was on guard, to defend the happiness of Papa and Lily against a wicked stranger. Poor foolish mother! She too, was trying to torture Jacky.

"How about taking the dogs out?" asks Papa.

"Lilian! Why don't you go out with Mr. Arvel and Mr. S...?" says Mamma.

"I don't like three people walking together," retorts her daughter.

This was a hint for me, but I refused to take it.

Lilian thanks me for some of my own make of Eau de Cologne that I have brought her. She is going to be rubbed with it, as I have advised her. She says that Mamma does not know how to "friction" her. Ma declares that she is a bad nurse. Lilian replies freely before her mother that Pa alone knows how to rub her properly. Papa says he will come and wake her up early as usual, and rub her with Eau de Cologne. Lily answers that she will not be woke by him any more, and forbids him to come into her room in the morning. So Mamma goes to bed, looking at me with a triumphant air, and Papa and I go out together, leaving Lily alone. There is no more strolling for me alone with her. They are punishing me.

We walk and I talk. Again Papa recurs to Trixie. He asks what has become of her. I reply that she had a slight illness. That I lost sight of her, and during the Easter holidays I saw her husband in deep mourning with the children.

If a husband walks out in black at Easter with his little family and no mother, it is a sure sign that their Mamma is dead. I often caught sight of him since, but always in mourning, and never with Trixie. He cannot get over the fact of her having procured women for me. I explain to him that a woman who really adores a man will do almost anything, and suffer a martyrdom; or go through the most disgusting vicissitudes, enduring what seems sometimes beyond human strength. (He ought not to be surprised, for has not Adèle given him her daughter?) I quote wife-beaters, and how they refuse to charge their husbands. It is all love.

"Lust, you mean!" he adds, with a snarl of deep scorn. He is a man who despises women, and hates them because he cannot do without them in the kitchen and in bed.

We speak of jealousy. I tell him that Trixie was always ready to go with any man or woman I told her. Jealousy is a ridiculous feeling. He declares that he is jealous and that he could not care for a woman if he thought she had anybody else. He could not enjoy a *partie carrée*. This interesting talk takes up so much time that when we return, I have missed a train. There is none now until 12:20. He will sit with me another hour.

Lily is alone, reading one of my magazines. Papa leaves us.

"Well, what do you think of me?" I say. "You did not imagine I was so clever with women? I should like to have your frank opinion of Jacky."

"I think you are not clever. You are very bad. I could never have supposed you would have had such horrible thoughts of me."

I laugh disdainfully.

She then says, slowly and sadly, with a sigh:

"*I am very wicked sometimes.*"

This is the nearest approach to remorse or regret that I have ever heard from her.

I do not reply, and a moment later, Papa returns, and she shortly afterwards touches his cheek with her lips, chastely, and he salutes her on both cheeks as on the occasion of my last visit, and she bids us both "good night." After this kissing comedy, she says "Good night," softly and kindly to me specially, and gives me her hand. She is sad. Still she does not go at once, but hovers round Papa and strokes him gently on the head with her book. At last, she goes, gliding away gravely, bidding me good night for the third time, gently and warmly, as if regretfully. I rise respectfully from my chair, touched in spite of myself by the misery of her tone, and return her good night as she goes by, and she begs me to be seated and not derange myself.

Thus she passes out of my life. I have heard her speak to me for the last time and her last words were: "I am very wicked sometimes!"

Could a novel-writer find a better exit for his heroine than that?

Papa and I are once more alone together. Still more bawdy chat. I say that I had a *demi-vierge* all the year before and that I respected her virginity. Did I do wrong or not? Am I not a fool?

"No," says Pa, "you acted properly."

"But she went afterwards and gave herself up to somebody else."

"You can't help that. You did your duty."

He would like to meet a woman with an elongated clitoris. I talk to him of hermaphroditism. I am getting tired and sleepy. I remember that in January, Lily was greatly struck by that character in "Justine," called Dorothée, who possessed a penis-like clitoris. Miss Arvel frequently mentioned it. The idea tickled her fancy. And now Papa talks of the same anomaly! How they must have enjoyed my bawdy books together!

Again he says that girls now-a-days prefer being "messed about" to honest coition.

"Ah! they tell you that to please you," I reply, "when you don't have connection with them nicely; or when they don't like you; or when you can't."

He pauses and reflects, and I think that masturbation and prolonged and unnatural caresses, when practised before the age of puberty, or shortly afterwards, at the dawn of woman's sexual career, lead to an aversion for normal coition in later life. In such cases, some abnormal stimulus trains the sensual desires to respond to an appeal which has nothing to do with the fascination normally excited by the opposite sex. Anything will therefore serve to produce the orgasm: man, woman, or child; an obscene book, or their own finger, without counting purely mechanical means. There is no warmth or tenderness: one man being as good as another to them. Indeed, once their venereal sluices opened and shut, the presence of the male, or the active agent, becomes more wearisome than otherwise, and they evince no desire to return in kind. The organs are quickly excited and as quickly dormant again. The private parts, thus so early brought into use, and subjected to such sudden strain, revolt against the repeated unnatural shocks, and becoming flaccid, lose their tone. All is soft, stretched, and open, and lovers are bewildered to find a young face on the body of a woman, whose soft flesh seems to be dropping from the bone, while they go away wondering how such a darling little chit should carry between her thighs the yawning gulf of an older mother of a family.

Love, in its essence, becomes distasteful, and the feeling of natural lust, engendered by real affection, being entirely foreign to their nature, all sentiment forms the object of their mockery; they fall back on the pleasures of the table, or think of nothing but money, jewellery, and dress.

But I do not take the trouble to tell him all this, so I explain succinctly how girls learn to practice onanism with the hand or the mouth, alone or with their lovers, in countries like France or North America, where conjugal frauds are practised. They learn such tricks from their mothers, who teach them early how to satisfy men without getting enceinte. All this, he pretends is new to him. I can see he is surprised to find me speaking so freely.

I tell him of some of my amours in tropical lands, for I have been round the world. I can see he is quite astonished. He tells me that all girls having Spanish blood in their veins are largely made; their private parts seem to spread out early in life. Here is another part of my last letter answered by Papa. But why does he systematically try to always lower Lily in my eyes?

It is time to go. I promise him more bawdy experiences for later on, and he sees me to the gate. He excuses himself for not accompanying me to the station. He does not talk of any future visit. He is evidently displeased at my free and easy attitude and is in a hurry to go and ask questions of Lily, and tell her my stories, and my hints and innuendoes. This is the first time I have been left to go to the railway alone. I know too, that I have kept them apart all day.

I cannot find my gloves. He promises them to me with the negatives of my photographs, so that I can print them off myself, and to return me "The Romance of Lust" shortly, and so I go away.

I should like to hear what Papa said to Lily as he went up to her room, after my departure, and how much of my scathing diatribes she retailed to Pa and Ma.

I am now heartily sick of the whole lot of them, and I resolve never to put my foot in Lily's house again. And there is my own smouldering weakness for Lilian Arvel to be guarded against. I have been patient, but can be so no longer, and have carried out

my scheme to the bitter end. I now resolve to do what I think few
men would be capable of. I am going to "put myself away" with
the family, and at the same time calm my mistress's growing
jealousy, and make a neat finish for my romance.

I really think that Papa and Mamma have been pushing Lily
on to me for "the good of the house." In order to get anything out
of me, it was necessary to forge these elaborate lies with Papa's
help. If Lily confessed that she was merely the easy, satisfied mistress of her mother's lover, she could have no hold on me. If she
tells the truth, she would be saying: "I want for nothing. Papa
keeps me in idleness. I am no longer a virgin. You can possess me
now without fear or remorse." There is no money hanging to the
truth in her case.

SUNDAY, JUNE 4, 1899.

My mistress is tolerably well. I dress her up in her best, with
all her diamonds and jewellery, and a friend and I go on our
bicycles to Sonis, meeting my lady, who takes the train, at the
restaurant I told Papa, Mamma and Lily I should choose, and we
sit in the open air at a table on a low terrace giving on the road to
Paris.

MENU.
Hors-d'œuvre.
Truite saumonnée, sauce verte.
Entrecôtes grillées, pommes sautées.
Poulet rôti.
Salade.
Fromage.
Fruits.
Café.
Liqueurs.

At 12:45, a hired victoria appears in sight. On the box, next
to the coachman, is Pa, in a large Tyrolean straw hat. He frowns
and looks straight before him. Ma, in the red foulard, turns her
head away. I touch my cap. Lily looks up defiantly, tosses her head,
and snorting, laughs scornfully. They roll by. They are silly. They

should all have returned my salute, as the lady who is with me, for aught they knew to the contrary, might have been with my friend. They have never seen and do not know my mistress. I have never spoken about her to anybody except Lily. And if they had pulled up a moment and let me run and speak to them, it would have been cleverer still, and would have quite damped my rocket. It must also be noted that Lily's mother is not married either.

Ten minutes afterwards, one of the workgirls appears on the road, and inspects us carefully. Then she goes back again, having turned up her nose at us and sniffed, as if we were a parcel of bloaters. She had evidently been left a roving commission to go and see whether I was at the restaurant, and who I was with, as I might not have had a table giving on the road, and Lily might have gone to the races without seeing me. She must have given her orders before leaving.

After lunch, we stroll past the house. The workgirl is at the window. She sees us three. She glares.

At the window of a neighbouring villa is the sister of François. She visits at Mr. Arvel's and knows me well.

JUNE 6, 1899.

No doubt my offence is great. But my great desire for bringing about my own downfall is not yet satisfied. I want it to go home to the hilt. I want to show Lily that I have really done it purposely and that I do not want her any more. I write the following letter, so that it is impossible for any of them to fathom my conduct, and know whether I am a fool, a madman, or a cold-blooded joker.

The worst they can say is: "How he must be gone on Lily to take all this trouble!" Even that I do not mind. But I think the Queen of Liars cannot like it. And my poor mistress looked really very nice, being in one of her best days. Woman-like, she brightened up at the idea that she was playing a trick on two females she was jealous of. She is pleased, poor thing, at what I did. So I have killed two birds with one stone. My poor ailing girl! So devoted to me, really fond of me, rich or poor. If she could only have her health again! But that is impossible.

What I did, flaunting my mistress in front of the Arvels, was silly and bombastic, but it pleased her, and teazed Lily, for whom I have no more consideration.

Papa writes an article in a London magazine for June, and alludes to men touting English visitors on the boulevards for bawdy houses. It is very unusual and in very bad taste. (See Appendix H.) It shows what his mind was running on.

I post this letter to Lily, addressing the envelope boldly in my own handwriting, and underlining the word: "Mademoiselle."

JACKY TO LILIAN.

Paris, Tuesday, June 6, 1899.

I think, perhaps wrongly, that I owe you a slight explanation of my lunch at Sonis on Sunday. This hasty letter is useless, but I write it principally for my own self, for conscience sake.

The poor woman, formerly divinely handsome, who is my faithful, devoted, and disinterested mistress since 1880, has become very jealous and sour-tempered, knowing that she is suffering from a mortal malady which declared itself about four years ago. Her rare beauty is gone, and she feels that she no longer possesses any influence over me. She had long since asked to visit Sonis, where she had never been. That was out of jealousy. And then she has been "worked up." Of course, she believes herself to be in a position of inferiority, despised by my friends of Sonis, who she knows are legitimately married. She is only the mistress of a common Englishman, formerly a "runner" at the Bourse.

Envy, vanity, jealousy, curiosity—you know what I mean.

Is not life sad, with these terrible ironies? Is not all this petty and vile? Such is the punishment of social irregularity.

I constantly refused to take her to Sonis. But a month ago, in the face of the welcome of my last visit but one,—after the scene in the cab—I gave way, and granted the trip. I was happy to know you were all going to Paris. That is all the story. Must I excuse myself? I hardly know. Put yourself in my place. Should I show any delicacy or have any regard for you?

I have nothing more to say. It would be too easy to overwhelm the Japanese girl. I have had enough of rummaging in your heaped-up mass of disgusting lies. All this is adulteration, fabrication, sophistication. Anyhow, I have left the game easy for you to finish—Suzanne-Césarée, false virgin; falsely incestuous; falsely cunning. Your "Papa-lover" told me you were a liar and wicked. Strange woman! Must then all your lovers scorn and despise you? What will become of you in a few years? Soon you will tire of the unnatural life you lead. Will you become a Miss Pawle* or worse?

Here is your pretext for closing the doors of your house against me. A few words thrown out about the audacity of S . . . coming to your town with his whore, and you are all well rid of me. Am I not a good fellow? I take all the wrong-doing over to myself. Such is my last act of delicacy. Final coquetry of your ex-lover, the son of Satan. That devil Jacky!—one never knows if he is mocking or no.

So, adieu! Keep a good recollection of me. That should be easy for you, as I am the man to whom you gave the least. Do not hate me too much. You will never more help me to salt. Only say this to yourself:

"Of all my lovers, both beneath my roof and out of doors, this one never did me any harm."

With the remembrance of the last lingering kiss of your lying lips,

JACKY.

P.S.—I shall always send the papers to your "Papa," as I have done for years.

I enclosed two newspaper cuttings. They were, "Divorce Among the People," (See Appendix I.) and, "The Alleged Offence under the Criminal Law Amendment Act." (See Appendix J.)

JUNE 14, 1899.

Lily sends me back the two novels: Suzanne, and La Femme et le Pantin, together with the proofs of "The Double Life," and the newspaper cutting: "Tête-à-Tête," but she did not return the two paragraphs I had enclosed in my letter of rupture.

---

* Miss Pawle was an American girl, once very pretty. She wrote for the New York fashion papers, and was a well-known Lesbian and discreet whore. She had been "gay" about fifteen years in Paris. She was supposed to have supported her family by her prostitution.

I had expressly told her I did not want the books to be returned, and I had so written on the flyleaf of one of them. Nevertheless, she sent the whole lot by post. This was for me to write, I think, but I did not reply.

JUNE 20, 1899.

No acknowledgement being received by Lily, she consults Papa, I suppose; because I receive, six days after the novels, a parcel containing my gloves, the negatives of my likeness as a cyclist, in two positions, and all the books he had of mine, including "The Romance of Lust," which had been in his possession since February.

I examine this obscene work and find that the corners of several pages have been turned down, and one which has been so treated with very dirty fingers—page 72, vol. II. On that page is the description of a young woman named Lizzie, with a little clitoris sticking out like a boy's penis.

In January, Lily talks incessantly of the character in "Justine" with the elongated clitoris. In April and May, Papa mentions this deformity twice to me. He returns me "The Romance of Lust," marked at the page where such a thing is described. Comment is needless.

I do not acknowledge the parcel.

In my letter of adieu, as in all my others since the return from Brussels, I had not put everything that I exactly thought. I always tried to "keep a little bit up my sleeve," for a future time, or until I could find more evidence on certain points. It will be seen that I never alluded to her frolics with Raoul, nor did I ever write, or even speak about the visit of the officer.

I also pretended that I thought an officer had been the first to possess her entirely. It was prettier and more romantic. Whoever it might have been: Papa, or a man who paid, it is not of the slightest consequence, but the work was done before the 11th. of November 1899.

After the lunch with Lord Fontarcy, at the end of September,

I did not see her until that latter date, and then she was full of grief; denied receiving my letter, with the money in it; was behindhand with her "courses," and had a fit of hysterical weeping. She then asked me to marry her for the last time, believing me to have more money than I actually possessed.

No doubt she was already hymenless at that juncture, and this was her last desperate move to regain her lost position. Had I accepted, she would have kept me from getting into a bed with her until after the ceremony, with the aid of Papa and Mamma, who would have taught her how to bring me an alum-made virginity on the wedding night. To fully cheat me, she wanted a night in a bedroom. It could not be done otherwise, and this accounts for her strange behaviour ever since, and her continual plans for travelling with me to London and Belfort. She feared the free play of the Rue de Leipzig, when she would fling herself unrestrainedly about, stark naked, outside a bed in the open light of day.

That is why she dared not confess the slightest thing to me, as the comparison of dates with what she had written, and which she hardly remembered herself, would have damned her in my eyes. At least, so she thought in her petty way, little knowing that a frank avowal at any period would have disarmed me at once. And so she had gone on from falsehood to falsehood, until she had piled up such a scaffolding of lies about her, that if she had made the slightest move towards the truth, the tottering fabric would have fallen down and crushed her.

When I lifted my mask of stupidity in her pretty garden, she had to choose between my love and her lies. She elected to remain rotting in her silly infamy, especially as I had plainly made her understand that my pockets were empty. That last thought would be her supreme consolation.

Finding that her daughter's young life was spoilt, her mother—poor, tactless, ignorant, avaricious creature—preferred her to become a prostitute at home, sooner than drive her out into the gutter. It was also to her advantage for Lilian to lend her body for her keeper's lusts.

There are many other strange little secrets in this peculiar and patriarchal family, but it would be useless to say all here, and I do

not wish to drag on the tiny stage of my theatre of living mario
nettes a variety of characters who were more sinned against than
sinning. The figures passing like frightened shadows through the
crude confessions of my worst passions and vices, are vile enough in
all conscience, including the wretched writer, but he has had
moments of remorse, and has not made many of his actors half as
bad as they really were. He has done penance publicly and without
stint, but he has handled his old friend Eric Arvel with comparative
discretion and tenderness, and has let him off easily, suppressing
much that he knows about him, because he sleeps with step
daughter Lilian, who formerly played at being Jacky's incestuous
half-virginal offspring.

5

I had no news of the Arvels, and carefully avoided Sonis-sur-Marne, devoting myself to my invalid mistress, whose health seemed to get worse and worse.

I still sent Papa his bundles of newspapers and magazines, and suddenly I got the following extraordinary note:

ERIC ARVEL TO JACKY.

Sonis-sur-Marne, July 13, 1899.

My dear Jacky,

I have been going to write to you over and over again to thank you for all the papers which you have sent me, but I have been upon the shelf for nearly a month from the effects of some violent poisoning with bichloride of mercury.

You know what you gave me was put away in my *cartonnier*. It

117

got all over my papers, and when sorting them I got a full dose, and only just managed to scrape out with violent salivation.

I am going over to London to-morrow for a few days and then to Ireland for a change.

Can I do anything for you when in the little village?

With best wishes, in which all join, believe me to remain,

Yours very truly,
ERIC ARVEL.

I answered as follows:

JACKY TO ERIC ARVEL.

Paris, July 14, 1899.

Dear Mr. Arvel,

I am very sorry to hear you have been so ill. I hope you will soon pull round and will profit by your trip.

I ought to be away myself, for fear of fresh rheumatics next winter, but all my people have been ill. And so I stick in Paris.

I got the negatives quite safely, and the prints thereof have been a great success wherever shown. For which many thanks.

I am grateful for your offer to be of use to me in London, but I have nothing I can worry you with this journey.

Renewed health, pleasant journey and a happy return home,—that is all the harm I wish you.

Yours faithfully,
JACKY.

I was, rightly or wrongly, so disgusted at his letter, that I hesitated a few hours about answering it, and at last sent him the foregoing, out of common politeness, but I took good care not to mention Adèle or her daughter: his two concubines.

The story of the "violent salivation" seemed diabolically fantastic, if true.

Salivation by inhalation is possible, but rare. I feared to think that the shadow of syphilis was hovering over the villa of Sonis, and that my quandom host had simply been taking mercurial frictions, thus accounting for the malady of years ago.

Anyhow the lips of Lily, that I once thirsted for, were at the disposal of a salivated man. She was the mistress of her mother's old lover, with rotting gums and fetid breath; sore lips, and ulcerated mouth and tongue.

I prefer not to write more on this subject, and hope that his letter was strictly true.

Although he had only spoken of the British Isles in his letter, I heard afterwards that he was seen in Brussels. I did not verify the statement. I could have written to Mallandyne again, but I resolved to try and forget. I cared very little. I was a subscriber to a newspaper, where Arvel contributed articles regularly, and he would date them from different places he used to visit, so that would have been a slight indication of his movements, and the whereabouts of Lilian. My subscription was up, and I did not renew it.

This peculiar mania for writing half the truth to me suddenly and without cause or reason, betrayed a strange hysterical frame of mind in a man of his age, and made me think that most of Lilian's later letters, including the famous one from Lille, were suggested and dictated by him. It was not nice to say: "the bichloride you gave me." I got it at his request.

This poison story made me very angry and as I still continued to send Mr. Arvel his bundles of newspapers, I resolved to teaze him a little, as he was trying to do with me, and at the same time to offend him thoroughly.

I amused myself by marking with a red pencil all paragraphs that seemed to have a bearing on illicit connections between fathers and daughters, or brothers and sisters; and cuttings from periodicals, together with any matter that seemed to allude to my amours with Lilian.

I found a number of stories, scandals, policecases and gossip in society papers, which had a special meaning for him and me, but I will only mention a few of the most remarkable ones.

There was a small article in a number of "Answers," called: "That Wonderful Number Four," and I did not fail to frame it with crimson dashes.

In "Society," during this month, I marked a few lines about Napoleon the First. (See Appendix K.) I took the paper regularly and Papa had it as soon as I had read it.

JULY 28, 1899.

Here are a few specimens of what I sent him:

A prospectus of a new work on sexual anomalies, entitled: "The Ethnology of the Sixth Sense."

I wrote on the first page in pencil:

"I have a copy of this book, which I can lend you, if you like to say the word."

The second page gave a table of contents, and following the mention: "Monstrous clitores," I added:

"Compare with Dorothée. ('Justine.') Conversations in January.
"Compare conversations on the same topic in May.
"Compare 'Romance of Lust,' vol. II, p. 72: Lizzie."

What could he think of the month of January being mentioned by me? At that time he was away in the South, and the allusion was plain to the fact of Lilian and him being in complicity, by the mention of the two books, one lent to him, and one to her.

I also added two cuttings, one relating to the crime of Bordes, an incestuous murderer, and the other headed: "A Horrible Crime." (See Appendix L. and M.)

ERIC ARVEL TO JACKY.

Sonis-sur-Marne, August 2, 1899.

Dear Jacky,

If you have not anything better to do, will you come down tomorrow Thursday, and have lunch with us? We shall all be delighted to have you. Raoul is here just now, but is going back on Friday.

Hoping to see you and have a good chat with you,
I remain,

Yours very truly,
ERIC ARVEL.

I was greatly surprised at getting the above invitation, after the mercury missive and my selection of insulting paragraphs. What made me smile bitterly was that the invitation arrived Wednesday evening, August 2nd., and I was to go the next day.

Most of the letters from Sonis were type-written, and I could nearly always tell whether the father or the girl had used the machine to write to me, as there were slight differences in the writings.

It would be too long to describe how I arrived at the knowledge by comparison, but I was certain that the above had been composed and typed by Lily and signed by her Papa.

Besides, it was the beginning of the month and she would be under the influence of her "menses." Immediately before and immediately after the flow, there would be a heightening of actual desire and she would think of me, for such is the effect of menstruation on unbalanced individuals.

The time I saw her, after I searched for her maidenhead in the cab, was May 3rd., and she is complaining that she is about to be unwell.

She gets me invited again for May 28th. I am not sent for again until August 3rd.

I felt a little pity for her, as I thought of her monthly martyrdom, and I asked myself if she were not perhaps only a miserable victim of the workings of her womb.

When we think of the debased, mercenary whore, who counts upon the weakness of men to feather her nest, we must keep her image distinct from that of the normally healthy woman, with true equilibrium of the reasoning faculties, who has nothing in common with poor-blooded neuropaths hardly responsible for their actions every twenty-eight days, and who pass half their lives seated on a cold custard.

A woman to keep her secrets should never let her male victim know her diaper days.

During the menstrual period of these hysterical women, we find falsehood united to wickedness and craft; cowardly slander; calumnious denunciations; the setting of perfidious snares, and the invention of satanic fables and even robberies, while they cleverly arrange things, so that suspicions shall fall on innocent parties.

My reader has only to run through the dates set down in this book and he will see that all the principal events take place between the 20th. of one month and the 8th. of the next; except when there is an irregularity, as when Miss Arvel denied receiving the money I had sent her, and during the fausse couche of January.

No doubt all her life was controlled by her "flowers," being a hereditarily neurotic subject, and on such a morbid soil, early masturbation and the tantalizing practices peculiar to half-virgins, and women who refuse to have children, would produce neurasthenia with its manifest symptoms.

I made up my mind that if Lily wanted me, she would have to come forward herself, and I sent off the following telegram at once, so as to stop Mamma going to market and providing for me:

JACKY TO ARVEL. (*Telegram.*)

August 2, 1899.

Thanks for amiable invitation, but regret, impossible to leave Paris at present. Very busy.

So they had to pass the day without me. I suppose they thought I should appear at once at Lily's beck and call, with presents for the Mamma and girl, and cigars for the boy; papers, books, gossip, news and smut for Papa, and he and Lily could teaze me at their ease and so get him an erection for when I was gone.

And I should have had to play clown all day to make them laugh, when I was full of worry, and trouble and grief in Paris! Not that I mind acting a part in society; I am very good at it, and would go splendidly through it, if the girl had been sweet and tender and I knew a rendez-vous would follow the visit.

It must be remembered too that it was my birthday on the 19th. of July, and Lily knew it well. She had also made me send a wire to her Papa on his anniversary. I got nothing from them, and I wanted nothing, expected nothing; but why invite me suddenly?

Lilian Arvel would never forgive me this refusal to see her, as both Papa and Raoul would sneer at her, and her vanity would be wounded to find her power was gone.

AUGUST 16th., 1899.

In that lively London weekly, "Society," since the month of April a serial story had been running, entitled: "The Confessions of Nemesis Hunt," giving the history of a clergyman's daughter, who becomes an actress, going through the most extraordinary experiences and cynically talking of her various loves and lovers.

She becomes the mistress of an actor, who is a member of the same travelling troupe, and in the number of August 12, 1899, this tale took such a strange turn that I am certain Papa would think I had a hand in it to annoy him and Lilian. (*See Appendix N.*)

It was simply a strange coincidence. I also sent him a cutting relating to another incestuous father, condemned at Troyes. (*See Appendix O.*)

The prospectus of "The Double Life," which was now announced as soon ready, went to him as well, and I pencilled the following note on it.

JACKY TO ERIC ARVEL.

(*Note.*)

Dear Mr. Arvel,

This is the prospectus of the book of which you saw a few rough proofs in the early days of June.

I shall send you my own copy, as I have been foolish enough to subscribe, as soon as I get it, probably in September.

You will read it, enjoy it, just the same as the others I lent to the Villa Lilian, and return to

Yours faithfully,
JACKY.

I was now finishing the revision of "The Double Life," and I had inserted the two following paragraphs,—Vanderpunk did not know English,—and I do not think my additions spoilt that otherwise extraordinary work:

Page 237.—"Her nostrils quivered with fresh rising lust; her lips were moist. She clung to me, murmuring:

" 'Papa! Papa! Don't be silly, darling! F . . . me last. Just one little tiny spend of your poupée. Tiny! Tiny!' "

Page 419.—"I have a vision, papa! I dream that we are living in a pretty cottage in the country amid trees and flowers! We are happy there with poor dead mamma come to life again. All three we play together. Our bedrooms communicate. Sometimes you take me travelling alone with thee to foreign climes. I shall have a beautiful, tall brother. He shall have a sweetheart, and we will all enjoy her. He shall frig and suck with me, and thou shalt be jealous. Thou wilt make me cheat and deceive all men, and I will rob them for thee and mamma. And I will hoodwink them, telling that I am a virgin, and how papa teazes me with his infamous love, and they will take pity and give me gold for my dress and the house. And I will try and never get the pox, so as not to give it to my darling old papa sweetheart!"

It was sweet after having been something like a puppet to turn round and make a marionette of the showman.

It was rather bold to mention that "you saw a few rough proofs," especially as they had only been lent in secret to the girl, his daughter-mistress, and he always told me what wonderful precautions he took so that "the girl should not get hold of any book you may lend me."

I had picked up an original edition of *Charlot s'amuse*, which I sent him in a packet of magazines on the last day of August; and on September 5, a number of "The Illustrated Police Budget," containing the "Awful Story of a Daughter's Shame," heavily marked by me. (See *Appendix P*.)

On the 16th. of September, I forwarded to him by registered bookpost, a clean, fresh, and uncut copy of "The Double Life," which had arrived the same day from Rotterdam, and I received the following letter:

ERIC ARVEL TO JACKY.

Sonis-sur-Marne, September 18th., 1899.

My dear Jacky,

I am half ashamed to write to you. It is so long since I was "going to" do so. When I went away to Coblenz a month ago, I made up my mind I would write to you during my travels, but I have such a lot of work to do manipulating the promotions of these new Anglo-German companies for the English market when I am in Germany that I have hardly time to eat.

We went down the Rhine to Cologne, and then from Cologne by

train to Brussels, to Blankenberghe and Ostend, returning to Paris in time to spend Sunday, the 10th., quietly at home.

I cannot tell you how much I am obliged for all the papers I found waiting for me at the Rue Vissot, and also for the loan of *Charlot*, and of "The Double Life," both of which I am returning to you to-morrow with many thanks.

I think the last is very erotic reading, but there is nothing real about it, as there was about the four little volumes,—"The Romance of Lust,"—which you lent me previously.

They were really good as such things go, but what I should like to find would be a book written really by a woman, giving us the contre-partie, and probably convincing us that the act of copulation which plays such a large part among human pleasures is simply based on the vanity of men who "kid" to themselves, while the women are simply relieving themselves of a more or less troublesome itching, and simply regard the male as a *parfait jobard*.

This idea no doubt came to you when you were out in Samoa?

Can we ever think we hold a woman by her senses? I do not think so, and I have an idea that the mere act of copulation without a love which has been mutually ripened by long acquaintance is not worth "twopennorth of gin."

I have not had time to work at my photography, but I hope to get into full blast when some relations, who are going to stop with us, have concluded their visit.

I saw your brother at the Bourse yesterday. You never come there now.

I hope all your people are well.

I am very, very much obliged to you for all the papers, although I do not think much of "Nemesis Hunt," who is rather too much of a whale for my swallow.

Yours very truly,
ERIC ARVEL.

JACKY TO ERIC ARVEL.

Paris, September 22, 1899.

My dear Mr. Arvel,

I am very pleased you like the papers I send you. All the magazines that come into the house are always put on my desk after perusal by the different members of our family, as they all know they go to you. And when the pile gets troublesome, I send it off. Therefore I deserve no thanks.

I am afraid you do not approach erotic tales in a proper spirit. Of course "Nemesis Hunt," and "The Double Life" are unreal, but still here and there are incidents relating to passions, natural and unnatural, which are such as take place every day. I prove my words by enclosed cutting. (See Appendix Q.)

Work up the amusements of Mademoiselle Vial into a little story, and everybody will say it is all lies, the outcome of the writer's diseased imagination.

Your idea about a woman writing her own double life is a very good one. But as there exist no really truthful autobiographies or confessions written by men, how can you expect women to have less vanity and more veracity than we have? Nevertheless, women are always confessing, if you only take the trouble to listen to them. They are so cunning and clever—not intelligent, for malice and craftiness do not betoken intelligence—that they continually overreach themselves, and if you coolly think over all a woman has said and written to you, you ought to get very near the truth. A man who can't do that, is of no use with women. But all are not daughters of Judas. There do exist loving, tender, truthful women. Sensible people know how rare they are. Their lives would be uninteresting, so we could only get revelations from wicked creatures.

A man need not take much trouble to "hold a woman by her senses," or otherwise. Be natural, straightforward, and patient, and if she loves you, she will hold you herself. But she must feel something with you which she feels with no other. She must prefer you.

I have a pet theory, although in these matters there are no hard and fast rules to be laid down. It is this: a man may love many times in his life; a woman loves but once. If you could get at a woman's heart, you would only find one name deeply engraved upon it, even though she may have had countless lovers. Some women meet that one man at the outset of their career, others later, and many never.

Some have come across the one man they could have loved and have kept their secret. They have never been "had" by him and he never knows how he was loved. If you have fallen across that genuine, disinterested tenderness during your life, you are all right. If not, you have never known the real love of a woman.

I am most happy to hear you have been enjoying good health and been taking pleasant journeys.

Since June we have left off subscribing to "The Stock Exchange

Review," so I do not see your articles, which I suppose you still contribute and send from the different continental towns you visit?

All my family, you will be pleased to hear, are very well indeed, "as it leaves me at present."

Yours faithfully,
JACKY.

P.S.—I didn't have "Nemesis Hunt" last week.

There was a slight retard. Not surprising when we think of what she gets up to,—and down to, as well.

It's a far cry indeed from "Mord Emly" to my sweetheart "Nimmy Hunt."

"The Double Life" got into Mr. Arvel's hands on the 17th. of September. On the 18th., he wrote the letter saying he would send me back the books "to-morrow."

It is a stout volume of 446 pages! He and Lilian were reading it together, no doubt, and he wanted to lead me to believe that he could get through it in two days! In point of fact, he sent it to me back a week afterwards, on the 24th., after he had received my answer to his letter. When he wrote on the 18th., prompted by Lily, they had not got to page 417, where I talked about the daughter hoodwinking men by pretending to be a virgin, whose Papa teazes her with his infamous love, while she gets money out of her lovers for her dress and the house and is masturbated by her own brother, etc.

All this, however, is only to lead up to this concluding and amusing result:

The book came back entirely cut open for reading, with but one exception: one page of the preface,—the one containing the lament over the daughter's death,—of which I had lent the proof to the girl only, in May, was not cut. This was a damning oversight.

OCTOBER 8, 1899.

During the whole of the month of August and the best part of September, my faithful mistress had been in the country and had not been well at all.

She returned about the 22nd. of September, and went to bed.

It was her last struggle. The doctors gave me no hope, and this morning she is gone from me, after suffering such agony that to stand by the bedside of a loved one, and see her hellishly racked, fighting for life, as each essential organ gave way, would make an atheist of the most fervent believer and he would ask himself as I did: Is this the work of the Almighty? Is God a cruel Chinese mandarin or a torturing Torquemada?

In repose at last, on a bright Sunday morning. How beautiful she looked! During her illness I could not recognize her as the handsome, strong lass who had footed it merrily with me over peak, crag, and glacier but a few short years before in Switzerland.

Many a time she would fatigue our guide and he would drag himself slowly from the valley, while I, in despair, would lie down panting by the side of the steep path and looking up, admire my devoted companion's perfect frame, profiled against the clear sky, as alpenstock in hand, she stood triumphantly perched on some projecting rock.

And now she is gone. After death, the pristine beauty came back to the loving face, as if the mocking devils who had torn at her poor heart for years with the red-hot pincers of disease, had relented, and pleased to have finished their horrible task at last, satiated with her sufferings, had allowed her to look her best to show us poor mortals what fragile, feeble shadows we are.

And so she sleeps. Her big, blue eyes will never more brighten at my footfall. I shall never see their laughing light again.

I kissed her still warm cheek passionately and lengthily. I could have kept my lips to her face for an hour, but my tears fell upon her and that I did not like.

I am sorry I did not send for a photographer. I thought of that too late.

And so she sleeps. For the first time in my life I have seen a cherished being die and gazed at my love after death.

Up to now, I think I must have feared the end of all things. At present, the skeleton may come with his scythe, because I saw on the peaceful features of the white figure on the bed, who had been my girlish sweetheart, my wife without the priests, my devoted woman who lived for me alone, that she was at rest, and I really grasp the fact that death is the only true release.

And so she sleeps.

OCTOBER 15, 1899.

My fair Lilian is dead. She knew of naught but her love for me. The black Lilian lives, and she hates me by now. She will never forgive me for having seen through her tricks and wiles, aided in her natural cunning by the artificial villany of her salacious stepfather, and her selfish mother.

The fathers are generally responsible in these cases, but when the mothers are weak, and sacrifice their daughters to keep the man at home and get all his money for the house, we must pity the young lass whose flower of virginity is torn from her by those who should be its most vigilant sentinels.

Corruptio optimi pessima, the corruption of the best is the worst,—is not only true for the victim, but also for the seducer. Women who have been debauched in their teens, or earlier, under ordinary circumstances, often rise again. But those who have been led astray by their fathers, who have known a villanous priest, as it sometimes happens, never succeed in getting out of the mire. As criminals of olden days were marked with a branding iron, it would seem as if the defiling culprit seared his youthful living plaything with an indelible mark of shame.

At the same time, the unnatural parent, who may have shown an honest face up till then, acquires in his features an expression of savage hatred. He becomes quarrelsome and morose, and like Mr. Arvel, his soul torn by his unholy passions, knowing that the slightest whisper may render him a thing to be scorned by friends and neighbours, he hurries to snarl at everybody, as if preparing an everlasting defence of his conduct; as if he found an excuse for himself in vilifying his wife and speaking with scorn of the daughter-prostitute, whose caresses he would go and humbly beg for a moment after he had traduced her.

Women of infamy, like Lilian Arvel, are seldom perfect types of beauty. Our passions are printed on our features, and wicked thoughts make wicked faces.

Sensual women are sad, until aroused. Their development of breast is rudimentary, as was the case with Lily, who in male attire might have been easily taken for a young lad. Her maternal grandmother, I have already said was more than eccentric, and her mother flew into tremendous passions when put out, and was unreasonably jealous. Lily had always a very bad temper; she was a liar, vicious, and thought of nothing but men, jewellery and dresses. I fancy that she suffered from chronic inflammation of the intestines and that would account for the peculiar bluish tint that overspread her features whenever put out. But I am no doctor. Her menstruation was tolerably regular. There were nervous troubles, spasms, cramps of the stomach, stifling, but never a complete hysterical fit with me. Her nerves troubled her during her monthly derangements. She had been some time at a convent-school, and in answer to my inquiries told me that she had never witnessed, or been invited to take part in any acts of saphism. I remember on one occasion, before I was unduly intimate with her, that some young women from Myrio's dined at the villa while I was there. One of them was called "Mahogany," in allusion to the colour of her hair, and she was supposed to be married, but she had all the freedom of manner of the kept mistress. After the meal, Lily went and sat on a garden bench with her, and by the way in which she sprawled on her friend's shoulders, I felt sure they were all disciples of Sappho.

Lilian's conduct was lax and provoking with all the young men she met, and some elderly financiers, from the London Stock Exchange, who had been invited to dinner by Arvel, came away with the conviction that the daughter of their host was a dangerous flirt, if nothing worse. Four years ago, she ran away from home and took refuge with her grandmother.

Lilian Arvel is a neuropath, who has unfortunately not found in her dwelling, between her mother and her mother's lover, the advice and examples that might have had a happy influence, so as to modify any bad instincts she may have had within her. She has much false pride; extraordinary ambition; her tastes lead her towards dress and debauchery; she hates her mother, and she surely despises her Papa, although she accepts his caresses. He serves as a machine to calm her lust. But she can reason perfectly well on all subjects which have nothing to do with the satisfaction of her passions. The manner in which her mother lived, combined with the conversations of her customers, all professional harlots, adulteresses or kept women, showed plainly that there was little chance of her moral sentiments being nurtured, or of her receiving the good advice and education which might have changed in some slight measure the disposition and tendencies of a young woman of uncontrollable imagination. She is endowed with very lively intelligence; her repartees are pointed and prompt; her memory is surprisingly precise. But I perceive a great change when I proceed to analyse her feelings and nature. Here I find enormous gaps, and I note the excessive development of egotistical feelings, vanity, and a yearning to be talked about and always play the principal part. If I call to mind her childhood, when she served as an aphrodisiacal plaything, in the bed of her mother; afterwards toying with her brother; then eagerly drinking in the bawdy chatter and risky songs of the milliner's workshop; her dangerous flirtations with Gaston, Ted, François, and all the others I know not of; her connection with Madame Rosenblatt and Charlotte; without counting officers, actors and myself, I can only reconstitute a type of character much more often to be met with than many people think. The principal characteristic of this style of person is the complete absence of all idea of morality. Such individuals are quite capable of saying what they ought or ought not to do, but all moral notions are abstract for them, and have no bearing on their determinations. Lusts, appetites and instincts predominate and their perverted impulses carry an intellectual activity, which is often intact, towards the goal of selfish satisfaction only. Acts entirely at variance with all moral and social laws do not excite their horror, but are quietly accepted by these curious unmoral people, who are as those suffering from colour-blindness.

They are afflicted with moral cecity, and do evil deeds with complete indifference. And as their intelligence, seemingly without a flaw, is only superficial; as the versatility of their feelings is as great as that of their ideas, they have no remorse. They may suffer slightly from an annoying obsession, when they cannot have their own way, but never from the remembrance of a bad action.

My poor dead Lilian had a great liking and esteem for the Arvels. She was proud to find that they invited me so often and delighted to know that her Jacky should be so sought after.

It proved her own good taste. She would see that I was well-dressed to go to Sonis and would wake me early so that I might not miss my train, after having chosen my cravat herself.

She had respect for them too and never thought of herself on the same footing, for were they not married, whereas she was but my concubine? I never deceived her. During the last year of her life, she began to get jealous of them all at Sonis and suspected me of being in love with one or the other of the women of the villa.

When I had been preparing a new chemical product in 1897, Lilian Arvel had done some type-writing for me. My poor girl knew of this and was always grateful to the young lady who was so kind to Jacky. She was sure the good wishes of a pure maiden would bring luck to my new invention.

On her deathbed, although her approaching end had been carefully concealed from her, she had forebodings and said to me:

"Jacky, I am dying. I know I am. You will marry Miss Arvel. You know,—the young lady who typed your prospectus two years ago. I am not jealous of her now. I can't be jealous if she loves you. Don't sleep with her in this bed. We two have passed every night in it for well-nigh fifteen years . . . You made fools of us both this summer."

NOVEMBER 8th., 1899.

In my packets of newspapers for Mr. Arvel towards the end of October I enclosed a curious cutting from the "Figaro" (see Appendix R) and an extract from Zola's latest novel that was just out (see Appendix S) copied on the type-writer, as, to change the current of my sad thoughts, I had bought a machine and was beginning to practise with it.

Then Papa wrote to me and the following correspondence took place. I was evasive and elusive. He was incomprehensible and bitter.

I only note a sort of rage and hate to think I had got to know his secrets, had read him and his daughter-whore through and through, and had walked away when I was tired of their intrigues.

If the girl was still at home, living quietly with him and Ma, and "getting her own living"—this was Arvel's pet phrase as applied to women—by carefully moulding the weak brains of moneyed lechers; there was no excuse for him to write as he did, and drag his own concubine in the mud, to "bluff" an ex-lover, trying to convince him that he had never played at the game of incest with her. Surely I should never believe that he would so vilify his own mistress?

If she had left him, disappointment might be a motive.

Be that as it may, his long and prosy letters did not trouble me much, as will be seen by my vague answers, and my mind was perfectly at rest as regarded the triumvirate of Sonis-sur-Marne. I never asked anybody about them. I knew nothing of their movements.

ERIC ARVEL TO JACKY.

Sonis-sur-Marne, November 7th., 1899.

My dear Jacky,

I ought to have written to you some time ago to thank you for your long and philosophical letter. I do not want to argue, or I could show you that you are sanguine on points, which picked to pieces, would show but a bare canvas, to be covered by the daydreams and fancies of the man who has forgotten the grand truth that all is vanity.

Women keep their secrets well, and they know how much they are pandering to the vanity of men, a knowledge which prevents them from disclosing the secrets of the charnel house. Men may write such tales as "Nemesis Hunt," and give spice to the commonplace adventures of a gay woman, by introducing the incestuous intercourse between her and the lover of her mother, supposed to be her father, for the amusement of those who are fond of gutter literature.

I must confess that the idea of any save platonic intercourse with the wife, or relation of any friend has always been very distasteful to me, and I have often thought, when running my eye over the legends in the Old Testament referring to the chronicles of the Jews, that the low system of enlightenment remarkable among whole colonies of Jews in Southern Russia, is fostered by those intermarriages, which to my mind, are as incestuous as the coupling up of Nemesis Hunt and Jean Messal.

Among the early Jews, and no doubt among many of the present day, incestuous connection is no crime and quite a matter of course.

I can understand that every one has his opinions on the subject, and I know that I had to pay very dearly once for expressing mine, when the son of a twin sister married the daughter of his mother's twin. I am told this was according to the Jewish rite. Naturally the object was to keep the money in the family.

I do not want to inflict any long sermon on you as to the virtues and vices of "Nemesis Hunt." The book will take, but it will not come up to my standard of "blue" books, according to the samples you have so kindly placed at my disposition from time to time, and while there may be some excuse for the lover, who was not sure the woman who offered him such rapturous embraces was in any way related to him, there was none for the woman who suspected the truth, from the time she met her father on the steamer.

I owe you so many thanks for the papers you send me with such charming regularity that I am ashamed to say I look forward to them as a right.

By the way, I was very much entertained with the volume: "The Scarlet City," which I will return to you next week, as I want to read it over again for the references it contains to men I have known.

I see you have taken to type-writing. I am sending off this by twilight, as I can only just see the letters on my machine. I am sure you will never feel inclined to take your pen up again, once you get into the swing of type-writing, and though you may often strike a wrong letter, the thing is so easy that you would never be persuaded to mess about with pen and ink for any consideration.

My dear Jacky, will you let me offer my most heartfelt sympathy for the loss you have so recently sustained. I only heard of it recently, and if you were thinking of the person whom it has pleased a higher power to remove from this earth when you last wrote to me, and so ably championed the affection of woman, then your loss must have been severe indeed, and I might say irreparable.

Yours very truly,
ERIC ARVEL.

JACKY TO ERIC ARVEL.

Paris, November 9, 1899.

My dear Mr. Arvel,

I am always flattered and honoured to hear from you, but more so to-day, as I am deeply touched by your kindly expression of sympathy.

There were lettres de faire part. I did not send you one. I did not want anyone to see me that day, nor did I wish to see anybody.

I begin to think you are right in all you say. You have evidently had a greater and more varied experience with women than I. I see that I have been spoilt. I never had to make love . . . at least, not much.

Now, I suppose, I must swell the ranks of the michés (Le Miché malgré lui, Molière . . . slightly altered), or else go and "listen to the band," instead of joining the merry maze of mercenary, menstruating Messalinas!

Glad you like the papers and books. When you send back "The Scarlet City," I will lend you another of the same sort: "A Pelican and a Pink 'Un." Also, an "indigo" novelty: "Dolly Morton," the true (?) confessions of a lady fair. And lots more.

I have only taken to typing since the 26th. ult., plus two lessons with a fairy-fingered maiden. I had some work to do which necessitated it. I thought I would try myself and have hired a "Nonpareil" for a month. I am a rare cuckoo at it! (Sounds like a fable: "The Cuckoo and the Type-writer.") Thought I should save money with it, but am spending a small fortune in erasers. There the love of gold, from my Bourse education and frequenting the Jews, peeps out again!

And yet a lady-authoress told me the other evening that she "had never met such a sensitive Christian."

I should like to know how long it takes to get to real speed on this clattering monster? I must stop at home with it a night or two, and have a real tussle with it.

Faithfully yours,
JACKY.

ERIC ARVEL TO JACKY.

Sonis-sur-Marne, November 10th, 1899.

My dear Jacky,

Many thanks for your letter, but I am afraid you are a sad flatterer. I am finishing "The Scarlet City," for the second time, and I will send it to you on Monday. I shall be very pleased to read the "Pelican and the Pink 'Un," as also the "blue" volume, purporting to be the confessions of a lady fair, although I am afraid the mother of most of the ladies fair and frail was "Moll Flanders," and that the supposed petticoated authoress wore bluchers and smoked a short pipe. By the way, talking of what is "blue," you said you would lend me a "blue" book, the prospectus of which you sent me, relating to various mal-conformations of certain organs.

(*The rest of the letter was all about the art of type-writing.*)

About the 20th., I shall be going to England, where I shall remain possibly three weeks, trying to get something to do, as times have not been over brilliant with me of late, and the expenses of my Bourse telegrams have increased so much, that working for the financial press has become bare bread and cheese.

Whenever you have any idea of taking a lesson on your type-writer, think of me, and remember that I shall always be glad to have your news, which I hope will always be good and couched in your usual happy strain of mind.

Very faithfully yours,
ERIC ARVEL.

I wrote a very short note in answer to the above, thanking him for his kind offer of tuition on the type-writer, and announcing that I was sending him the books he asked for.

I noted that Papa did not bear malice, as he coolly demanded the volume of which I had annotated the prospectus in such a vile manner a few months before. This is the first time he alludes to any of what may be called, my obscene innuendoes. So he got "Dolly Morton," "The Pelican," and "The Ethnology of the Sixth Sense." This last work I took the liberty of marking here and there in the following manner:

"The first shape of the hymen, almost invariable in infancy, and which is sometimes prolonged beyond puberty, consists in a labial arrangement of the membrane, the edges of which, separated by a vertical opening and facing one another, make a projection at the entrance of the vagina, which it closes, if I may say so, like a fowl's anus." (P. 275.)

". . . we often see tall and strong women showing a small vulva, and a mount of Venus without hairs, while little dwarfs display a largely developed vulva, followed by a vagina capable of satisfying an enormous penis." (P. 291.)

". . . an abundance of hair under the armpits, and . . . a slight moustache on the lips. Most frequently brunettes alone have this advantage." (P. 292.).

"EXAGGERATED AMPLITUDE OF THE VAGINA."

"In certain women, the vagina may acquire a considerable amplitude. If it is congenital, and the woman is salacious, and indulges beyond measure in the pleasure of love with men who have a large member, her vagina may become a veritable gulf, in which a penis of ordinary dimensions finds itself quite lost. There is no remedy for this deformity, except to endeavour to palliate it with tonics and astringents within the limits of possibility." (P. 311.)

". . . If a woman has a small one, she makes no difficulty in showing it, and displaying the neatness of her receptacle. But if she has a large one, she never permits it to be seen, for fear of revealing her disgrace." (P. 313.)

It will be noticed that mention is made in this last letter of Mr. Arvel to the well-known romance of Daniel Defoe, "Moll Flanders."

Papa was always alluding to this book, which had evidently made a deep impression on him. It will be remembered that the heroine unwittingly marries her brother. So whichever way we turn with the master of the Villa Lilian, the incubus of incest must always seemingly oppress us.

There was now a desire to see me again at Sonis. The lessons of type-writing were a pretext, and there was the hint of his departure to London, showing that the coast was clear for me in his absence.

ERIC ARVEL TO JACKY.

Sonis-sur-Marne, November 21st., 1899.

My dear Jacky,

I am returning your three volumes, which I have read with much interest and I tender you my very best thanks for the loan of them.

The "indigo" one reads like a true story, as it might fall from the lips of a woman who had given herself up to circumstances, and set perhaps the correct value of a "jewel," which is simply a marketable commodity, appraised by the vanity of man, held up to him as a temptation to commit all kinds of follies, in the hopes of obtaining a *primeur* from a source, which has, in ninety-nine cases out of a hundred, been tapped in a moment of curiosity by the *demi-vierge*, who wanted to go one better, having learnt from friends of her own sex, that there is still a resource in the *sonde* of the angel purveyor.

The interesting young lady who relates her adventures, bears out my theory that the "Sixth Sense" does exist, not as the outcome of Love or Affection, but as that of lust, played on and developed by the art and wiles of woman, the past mistress in converting vain man to the worship of Priapus, whose altar reposes on a solid foundation of *rosserie*.

When some ten or fifteen years have passed over your head, and your shoulders get bowed with age, and your whitened hair cries out: "Ichabod!" to show that some of the glory of your house has departed, you will find that Youth looks on you with smiling eyes, and that the tempting morsels are offered you, with the hope that they will be as the Dead Sea fruit to you, and with the determination to give you nothing better than the husks which have fallen from the trough of the swine.

Go on the boulevards and see the *vieux marcheur*, who can but limp, and watch the play around him, as he stops at the shop of the *modiste* or the jeweller, and then exclaim with Hamlet: "To what base uses may we return!"

There are a few exceptions to the general rule, and the endeavour of the woman seems to be to compromise actually or morally the weak, vain mind of man.

The husband of "Mademoiselle Giraud" *would* marry, and the comedy she played to disarm the man who thought he was on the point of possessing the woman he had yearned for, has been copied over and over again. The woman often throws herself into the arms of a man, decided that he shall, even with a show of a complete abandonment of herself, enjoy no more than the *petites privautés*, into which she has been initiated by her comrades.

You see I am drifting into the zone of platonic friendships, and getting by experience to know how to discount that mendacious exclamation: *Je t'aime*, which seems to warm the cockles of our hearts. All is vanity. It is given to some of us to learn that woman is capable of pure devotion, and that at times she can abandon herself to a kindred soul, but as a rule, woman is the author of such a book of follies in a man, that as Bulwer said: "all the tears of angels could not blot them out."

Some of these days I must try and write my life, with all the follies I have committed "writ large," but perhaps before the idea is carried out, I may have gone over to the other side, and buried a long record in the silent grave, where the wicked cease from troubling and the weary are at rest.

Yours very truly,
ERIC ARVEL.

P.S.—Many thanks for the budget of papers, which have just been brought down to me and will accompany me to London to read on the way.

My address will be Potteton's Family Hotel, Trafalgar Square, W.C., for the next three weeks, so that if you want anything from London, you will know where a letter will find me.

At last, Papa began to show a little temper. He preached me a sermon to let me see what a silly man I was, and how badly the "half-virgin" had treated me.

I suppose the couple was annoyed at my indifference to their timid overtures, and the marked passages in the "Ethnology," to which book Papa took care not to allude, must have shown them sufficiently that I did not wish to renew with Lilian.

His position was a strange one between Lilian and me, her old lover, with whom he corresponded, never mentioning her name, and I never asked after her. And now he suddenly breaks out in the foregoing letter, to my great delight.

A few days afterwards I replied evasively. I was resolved not to say anything that would compromise me in any way, or enable him or her to have the least idea what my real feelings were.

As I read this over, correcting the proofs, I cannot help thinking from the outburst in the foregoing letter and the allusions to female vice and treachery in the following ones that Lily had gone away. The month of November was always a fatal one for her. It is not possible that a man could so write if the wretched girl was at his elbow, as in former days.

Not that the quarrels of such people mean anything. They may hurl the vilest insults at each other, and even come to blows, but like dogs, it does not prevent them licking each other afterwards.

Even had Lily departed, whenever she met Papa again she would be at his disposal, if he so willed it, until death should part them.

But in the meanwhile she had exhausted his two purses and was no longer at Sonis.

The unbreakable chain that united Lily and Eric was no heartfelt attachment. It was a double heavy yoke of dissimulated interests. Their *liaison* was a commercial partnership.

JACKY TO ERIC ARVEL.

Paris, November 29, 1899.

My dear Mr. Arvel,

I received the books and was glad to see you liked them. I too fancied that "Dolly Morton" sounded as if half true, perhaps in part told to a man who knew how to listen. I did not like to say so, for fear of being wrong.

I sent you to London, three newspapers that ought to have gone in the last bundle, and would have been too stale if kept three weeks longer. I shall collect your papers and not send any until three weeks, counting from the 21st.

I did not flatter you when I said that you had greater experience than I with the fair sex. Your letter of the 21st. proves it beyond a doubt, and what is more strange, you seem to have the power of reading my thoughts to a certain extent. I have not your knowledge. I am all theories, and that is not much good, I know. It would take me a long time to explain all I mean and to answer your clever and deep-thinking letter properly. In September and before, I could write; now I cannot.

So you must forgive me if I do not reply to you as you deserve. I will try later on if I can, but I shall never be able to discriminate and reckon things up as wonderfully as you do.

I have read your letter over and over again, each time with more absorbing interest.

I would be ungracious not to thank you for your offer to try and render me any little service in London, but I have absolutely nothing that I can ask you to do for me.

Before writing any of your erotic recollections, you must read the "Memoirs of Casanova."

If you have never done so, I will lend you the work in French or English.

Faithfully yours,
JACKY.

DECEMBER 8th., 1899.

I liked the above letter, because it was a masterpiece of emptiness. I sent it to his hotel in London, but I knew he would not answer until he had seen Lilian. I fancied too, that Lilian had told him how I spoke about publishing the story of my intrigue with her, and that is why he wrote concerning his own autobiography. But I was not to be drawn.

I was musing on these things, on a dark evening about half-past five, as I was slowly going home, passing the St. Lazare railway station, when suddenly I thought I saw a ghost.

It was Trixie tripping gently along, her eyes bent on the ground.

She might not have been alone. Her husband, or a lover, might have been just behind her. I cared not; nothing could have stopped me from speaking to her just then.

I rushed towards her, and I refuse to write the sweet joy of our meeting.

Trixie cried a little, but I soon petted and soothed her, and we had a cup of tea together in a fashionable resort behind the Opéra.

And how she did talk and tell me all that had happened to her since I had last seen her!

Her husband and children had been in mourning for a near relation, and she herself had been in bed with pleurisy all through March and April; and afterwards, she had been away from Paris, during a long convalescence.

Achille was dying. His brain had given way under the strain he had put upon it, by his unnatural cravings and curious practices for years, and I began to think that we have to pay dearly for all our excesses in life; be it the bed, the bottle; or even common gluttony.

Over-indulgence with women and the searching after extraordinary pleasures and uncommon delights in the higher grades of sensuality, will lead us eventually to the padded room, while the masturbating Lesbian,—a menstruating fiend,—who makes such inordinate use of her tender organs; sucking, injecting, checking conception, washing with all kinds of lotions, teazing and tickling, without counting natural coition, must in due course fall beneath the surgeon's knife. The medical Jack the Ripper removes ovaries and the womb itself, and leaves a female eunuch, and thereby partly demented. Lucky will she be, if only the operation is needed and succeeds, and she does not have to sojourn for a short or long period in a private asylum; her plump arms hidden in a straight waistcoat and her luxuriant tresses ruthlessly cut off.

ERIC ARVEL TO JACKY.

Sonis-sur-Marne, December 22, 1899.

My dear Jacky,

When I was over in London, they sent me such a dreadful machine that I had no inclination to sit down and write. Otherwise it would have been my duty to thank you for the papers which followed me to London and your interesting letter of the 29th. ult. which afforded me pleasant reading. I have never read the "Memoirs of Casanova," in fact as you may hardly credit, the first obscene book in print ever read by me were the poems ascribed to the Earl of Rochester, among the State Papers in the British Museum, and then after perusing the *Ecole des Biches*, and "Fanny Hill," I have been permitted to fall back on your well-stocked library. Would the "Memoirs of Casanova" aid me in jotting down from the tablets of memory the old, old story of how man is caught in the snare, like the bird in the net of the fowler, and how neither experience nor age can prevent him imperilling all that he otherwise held most dear and sacred, for what? For what the veriest courtesan in the street can sell him for a mere song, as part of her daily business. Analyse the whole thing and the absolute sameness sickens one from a rational point of view. When the heart beats, and the innermost soul is moved, who can say that the feeling we conjure up under the name of love is reciprocated or exists in either the passionate woman, seeking relief from the heat of animal passion, or in the man who is offering a tribute to his amour-propre by taking possession of a woman, who draws her calculations from the vanity of the man to whom she offers herself, not with the unreserved franchise of the courtesan, but with the mock-modesty of the demi-vierge of the XIXth century, decided to take advantage of his weakness. What more can I say than others have said before me in writing their memoirs? I can plead that *plus ça change, plus c'est la même chose*, and the only difference is to be defined by the student of the sense of lust. That calculating philosophy and logic which makes a man in close contact with a woman recoil from actual sexual intercourse might be described by those who argue in favour of platonic love. The world taxes all such hesitation with a less polite term and Brown Sequard is advised. This may be correct when we are judged by the standard of youthful desire, but there are few of those over-ardent temperaments, who have not often wished afterwards that they had possessed the same dose of philosophy as the older man, who seeks out the courtesan, and opines that Love has very little to do with the mere connection of two bodies. I might write for a whole year without changing anything or without being able to fathom the depth of the feminine deceit. In woman there lies no truth at the bottom of the well. There are however, close friendships, and women have surrendered themselves to men to whom they have shown the deepest devotion, and for whom they are ready to give up their lives; and when you find such a one, tie her to you with every link a reciprocated affection can forge. Were I to write my "erotic" recollections, the cry of "Chestnuts" and "Rats" would be raised, as I wandered through the list of clergymen's daughters, and offspring of officers who have ministered to me carnally, and gradually come to more recent experiences, proving perhaps that "There's no fool like an old fool," and that however philosophically a man may be inclined, there is the old leaven of vanity which bright eyes, a smile, and youth know how to turn to advantage. Eve was the tempter, and her daughters have been armed to give battle successfully to man.

My dissertation is long and wearying, no doubt, so I will end it and turn to another theme more interesting, by wishing you and all yours a very merry Christmas, and renewed health and prosperity for the coming year, with plenty of health to enjoy everything Providence may send you.

Truly and sincerely yours,
ERIC ARVEL.

This letter contained a *lettre de faire part*, printed in silver, setting forth that Eric Arvel had married his mistress, Adèle, and he had written the word, "Private" upon it.

JACKY TO ERIC ARVEL.

Paris, December 26th., 1899.

My dear Mr. Arvel,

That you should enclose in your last letter the announcement of your union, causes a variety of conflicting emotions in me; the principal being the thought that you consider me worthy of being apprised of such a delicate piece of news. I am vain enough to suppose therefore, that you count me among a privileged set of *intimes*, and if so, I fully appreciate the honour you do me. May I say you *both* do me? I have learnt by my own experience that a mere ceremony, or writing down of signatures, does not constitute a real marriage, and some of the unconsecrated associations are several degrees more perfect than the legitimate ones, because the man, if he is a man at all, tries by untiring devotion and continual solicitude, to make the woman he has chosen to share his joys and troubles, forget the loss of worldly consideration, which she sees vouchsafed to others, who are often wicked shrews or worse, but they are called "respectable" because they have gone through a legal process.

I should not dare to speak so freely and boldly on this matter, were it not that I look back ever so sadly, and see nineteen years—nearly half my life—of the same companionship. But I was not fated to find the rest and peace that you will now enjoy, combined with the sweet sense of gratitude, of which you will reap the benefit.

I always envied you, I confess that fault, every time I saw you in your pretty villa, and now I envy you still more, as I think of what might have been, and how I lived for years, trembling lest the secret confided to me by the doctors should reach the ears of my Lilian, and powerless to arrest the sure progress of a relentless malady.

Nobody ever knew. But I purposely cease writing on this subject, as I do not possess the necessary talent to describe my sad existence, and even if I did, I do not think I could summon up courage to put my thoughts on paper. And besides, why should I come and throw a shadow of gloom over your happy household just at this festive period of the year?

I thank you for your good wishes expressed for Xmas, and am deputed by all my family to wish you the same, continued far into the next century. To make us quits, I personally return your Xmas greetings with my best hopes for your felicity, good health and prosperity during the new year: "OO," which I hope will not turn out a "naughty" one for you. You terminated your beautiful letter by saying that you feared to weary me, but I wished it had been much longer, as I can learn from you. I have met no man knowing the wiles of women as you do, and you have also the power to set forth your ideas in polished style, which I try in vain to imitate.

You must not be offended if I now take the liberty to put a question to you; and I tell you frankly that I shall not mind if you do not answer it. Do as you think best; whatever you do will be well done.

You write that "your more recent experiences prove that there is no fool like an old fool," and I fully agree with you, taking the lesson for myself, and accepting it as I have accepted other deserved strictures, with the pleasant thought that you take a kindly, friendly interest in me and are writing to me for my good. But it seems to me, and perhaps I am wrong, that you reproach yourself, and one or two sentences are ambiguous and might apply to the writer as well as to the receiver.

To sum up: what are those recent experiences? That is my audacious question.

I now give you my humble opinion of erotic recollections in print, but I fear this letter is far too long. I must ask you, if you take in "Le

Journal," to cast your eye over the feuilleton: Le Partage du Cœur,* where you will find a good model of psychological writing, where the author seeks to penetrate into the innermost souls of his sensual characters and show the motives, desires, jealousies, etc., that sway them. The adventures should be presented so as to demonstrate the peculiarities of passion, and the downright filthy part only becomes readable when it falls naturally into its place as the outcome of circumstances previously sketched, and which should be out of the common, as rapid sordid encounters and swiftly-ended passades with prostitutes are not of the slightest value. Mere meetings of men and women and descriptions of what they do, even if true, are of no use. Those who can throw a light upon the workings of the female mind, when under the influence of lust, real or feigned; or show us what a man feels, thinks, and does when "in the net of the fowler"; or becomes crafty, fights, escapes; or mayhap enjoys the humiliation of his captivity; will be rendering a service to all students of sexuality, surfeited with impossible tales of artificial amours, written to order.

I have just left at your bureau, Rue Vissot, a litre of my best Eau de Cologne, as a most trifling wedding present for Madame, and also to prove that whatever my faults, I possess, at least, the reconnaissance de l'estomac.

Faithfully yours,
JACKY.

ERIC ARVEL TO JACKY.

Sonis-sur-Marne, December 27, 1899.

My dear Jacky,

Many thanks for your nice long letter and for all the good wishes which I most heartily reciprocate. I hope that the year about to commence will be a happy and prosperous one for you and yours, and that the healing hand of time will efface from your memory all those pains and sorrows which weigh at the moment so heavily upon you.

Mrs. Grundy still holds a certain sway in society, and compelled us both to legitimise those ties which have bound us so close for many years past. Each act is weighed in a certain social balance, and though bell, candle and book were not required to cast any halo about a union

---

* Since issued in one volume: Paris, Fasquelle, 1900, 12mo.

based on mutual inclination, we thought it best to place things on their proper social footing, so that when I have passed over the river on to the other shore, what I may leave will rightly be claimed by the woman who gave herself to me. What I have done was due to the woman who gave up her fair name for me. I am deputed by Mrs. Arvel to offer you her sincere thanks for your present, and to tell you that she has no faults to bring to your door, save the one that you are more happy in the giving than in the getting.

Now to your "audacious query." I do not read any feuilleton. I lack the necessary patience to await the suite à demain. I told you that any attempt to write the biography of any man as you would have it with the heart laid bare, and the "Sixth Sense" analysed, would raise the cry of "Rats" and "Chestnuts." Every line written would come home to you, and the words inscribed upon the wall at the feast of Belshazzar would haunt your eye for ever more. The recent experiences I allude to are those of later years, the outcome of observation, and of the sayings and doings of those we find on every side, in a world where women discount the vanity and self-assurance of the man, who is about to double the cape of platonic affection. Surely you have analysed the furtive glances of the trottin, and the frôlements of the woman by your side as you gazed in the shop of jeweller and bonnet-maker? You have not been without knowing how with looks and implied promises the "Sixth Sense" has been cultivated to the highest degree of tension, and then how bitter has seemed the deception which has followed. You may have found the "Sixth Sense" so overstrung by doubts and apprehensions that even when the promised fruit falls ripe to your lips, you close them, not to give admission to the foul thing which will be more sorrowful to the heart and more bitter to the taste than the apple which drove Adam from Paradise. Is there anything new under the sun? Is it not always the old, old story, and what divine hands will ever weave the crown of golden myrtle, which shall adorn the head of the man who can conquer himself, who in the burst of youth can control his passions, and remember how Solomon warned us against the lips of the strange woman and that end which was bitter as wormwood and sharp as a two-edged sword? Have you never studied the philosophy in the old German ballad "Die Handschuh," where the knight courts death to please his lady-love, and then indignant at the peril he has been exposed to at the mere whim of a woman, refuses the reward the proud Cunegonde had in store for him.

"Have you been at the cockles?" Why do you see any stricture in what I write of past and present experience? You do not know what each year will bring forth, and how the human mind becomes more and more as an open book, as age creeps on and desire is fanned to sleep. The time will come for you when each day will bring its lesson, and then you will say with me, not from the experience of the hour, that there is "no fool like the old fool," but from the experience brought about by that spirit of comparison which never deserts us? Who has not been fooled has never sought. The seeking is mere lust; a simple satisfaction of the amour-propre, aroused by the wiles of woman, who is in her heart of hearts a much better judge of humanity than you or I are inclined to believe. How she delights in bringing out the weaknesses of the "idiot" who calls her "the weaker vessel," as though her capacity for giving pleasure did not long outlast that of the man for imparting it. The older the man the more susceptible he becomes to the charms of a sex, which has given him so many pleasant souvenirs in the store-room of his mind. He is easier beguiled; he thinks that Spring and Autumn can be linked together, and when the "Sixth Sense" has been roused, prudence and most of the other virtues are cast to the winds so that the passion of the hour may be indulged in.

"Have you been at the cockles?" Why try to fit the cap of generalities? Experience bitter as wormwood and sharper than a two-edged sword has taught me, not to-day but long since, how readily we embark on the journey to Cythera "as the bird hasteth to the snare knowing not that it is for his life." Will my experience benefit you? If so, you should have it, but the only experience of value is that bought with tears and lamentations, when in the solitude of our chamber we open our hearts and say: "I have sinned."

Recent experiences have I none. I have sunk to anchor in my haven of rest, with plenty of time for reflection, for examining the past, and making the general confession a man makes to himself, when he feels that the time is approaching for him to turn his face to the wall. I have not offered myself as a candidate for the crown of gold and myrtle, and I am as full of those faults and imperfections as any man who is human, and God alone knows if I can affect the same indifference as the good Saint Anthony, when the temptress comes across my path. Perhaps age will by that time have conquered the *folie érotique* which warps our best intentions, and I shall have *sang-froid* enough left to ask myself the why and the wherefore of the wiles of her who seeks to ensnare me. Possibly prudence and caution may cause me to ask myself why the *appât* has been so tempting, and Passion tempered with

Age will enable me to see through the plot made against happiness or honour. Many have succumbed, and if I follow their example I shall only be one of the few who have sacrificed so much to gain so little. Human resolves are as the words which are written on the sand of the sea-shore, and yet there are men cowardly enough to say with their first parent: "The woman who thou gavest to be with me she gave me of the tree and I did eat." When the cup comes to your lips, will you dash it aside and say that there was the warning in the words that "there's no fool like the old fool"? Believe me, it is hard even to aspire to friend-ships with the young, when a certain period of life is attained, and women have the instinctive desire, the unhealthy curiosity, to see how far they can arouse the old Adam. What are the peculiarities of Passion? Sordid motives on the one part, and vanity on the other. Passion is not devotion, and in my opinion Love only comes when the man has learnt to appreciate the sterling qualities of a woman, apart from the carnal pleasure she can afford him.

I hope my sermon has been long enough, and that you are con-vinced that when I wrote to you, there was no secret sorrow gnawing at my heart, and no desire to throw stones in the glass house inhabited by my neighbour. Age enables me to philosophise, and when I have time to sit quiet in my own room and review the past, analysing my own feel-ings, wondering whether I could withstand the smiling promises of the temptress, I am impressed with the wisdom of the man who said there was "no fool like the old fool."

Here on let me again thank you for all your kindness, and good wishes, and hope that the new year may bring you and yours the re-alisation of every wish.

Yours very truly,
ERIC ARVEL.

I wrote no more to Mr. Arvel, and ceased sending any papers. I gave no sign of life.

JANUARY 1, 1900.

As I awoke on the first morning of the New Year, I received the following from Trixie, and I cannot refrain from giving it here, as it is such a triumph for my theory of true love and affection, which Papa affects to sneer at.

TRIXIE TO JACKY.

Paris, December 31st., 1899.

My dearest friend,

For the last few days I have not had a moment to myself. I wish that all these holidays were passed; they do not amuse me.

Thank you for the pretty paper, it is quite in good taste, like everything that comes from you, and when I use it I shall often think of you, and that will prevent me from gathering my ideas together.

For the year 1900, I send you, with all my heart, my most sincere and best wishes. May it be luckier for you than the one that is gone. For myself, I ask you to keep me a little corner in your heart, for you know that I love you very much.

I want also to tell you once for all, that I will no longer let you put on your little sardonical look, when I say that I love you for yourself,—or, if you like, for myself,—without any desire for money.

I will not let you compare me to other women. I am almost happy that you are hard-up just now, as that gives me the opportunity to show you that I wish to abandon myself to you, entirely, for love, without any other thought than that of making you happy and so becoming myself at the same time the happiest of women.

I have been deprived of your caresses too long; you must never leave me again,—do you hear me, darling? Be good to me, dearest, and let me love you. I will overwhelm you with so many caresses; I will be for you such a perfect sweetheart, that you will be forced to succumb beneath the weight of evidence, and you, who are so straightforward, possessing such perfect common sense; knowing so well how to judge men and women, I want to force you to say to yourself and to me also, that if I have faults, as is only natural, I have no idea of lucre with you.

So see how I am dragged hither and thither: I would that you remain poor, so that you should have the proof that I love you for yourself alone, and at the same time I wish that you were rich and independent. I hope that you may become immensely rich, and yet if that was to happen, I should live under the eternal apprehension of seeing later on that you have the idea that I have only loved you in the hope of being enriched by you. After all, you are only a man. . . . Pardon me if I foresee that you may become like all other men.

To-morrow, on returning from your walk, come and wish me "Good morning," at the post-office, Place Victor Hugo, about 11 o'clock, if you can; I so much wish to see you.

Can you see us on our bicycles this weather? It would be a great success. And your dear muddy, dirty dog I was forgetting! I want to see him too.

A thousand tender things and as many clever and voluptuous kisses,

TRIXIE.

And now, Mr. Prompter, please ring down the curtain. This drama is finished.

The actors wash off their paint; the brown holland is put over the boxes. We go home, and all is dark until the next night.

So it is on the mimic stage, but in life there is no ending to the long succession of comedy and tragedy which is played out in many acts, and is never ended.

Death now and then calls at the stage-door, and one of the players: poor, painted, false villain, or roguish clown; tragedy queen, or meretricious dancing girl; is carried away in the black hearse, but the universal spectacle of love and hate goes on all the same.

Thus with my most vile story. I must break off here, but there is no finish to a real book, such as this is.

When the novel is a mere phantasy, it is easy to dispose of the characters. But this tale being a true one, I can only bow and go, making way for some fresh actor, who is waiting in the wings to caper in the light, when I shall have disappeared, whether I will or no; for I am, and so are you, Reader, in the hands of the Great Scene-Shifter.

JULY 1899.–JANUARY 1900.

END OF VOLUME III

Appendices

Appendix A

PLEASURES OF CRUELTY.

ACCOUNT OF A SCENE WITNESSED IN A WOOD, BY A GENTLEMAN, WHO HAPPENED TO BE UNSEEN BY THE ACTORS
(EVIDENTLY FATHER AND DAUGHTER).

FATHER.—"Come, my dear, this is a beautifully quiet spot, let me look at your legs."

DAUGHTER.—"Oh! Papa! Papa! What do you mean, you can always see my feet and ankles?"

FATHER.—"That's nothing, I must see more, and teach you to obey me in everything I order; now, lift up your skirts."

DAUGHTER, all blushes.—"Well then, Papa; there's my legs," drawing up her clothes so as fully to expose beautiful well-filled stockings and the ends of finely embroidered drawers: "Is that what you require?"

FATHER.—"Only a little portion of what I want to see," handling her calves and putting his hand up her drawers, "you have sweetly proportioned legs and beautifully firm flesh, my dear; up higher with your skirts, please."

DAUGHTER, scarlet with shame.—"Oh! Oh! Papa! How can you; there, only a little higher, that's all I can do: it's so indelicate," drawing her skirts half-way up her thighs.

FATHER, in a rage.—"Do as I tell you, Miss, do you think I can't

155

examine my own child without her pretending to tell me it's improper! I will look you all over if I choose to do so, and whip you soundly into the bargain, Miss Prude!"

DAUGHTER, with tears of shame running down her crimson face.— "Oh! Papa, Papa, pity me, I never showed so much to anyone before!" lifting her clothes, so as now to show all her drawers, well up to her waist, but she stands with her legs so close that nothing is visible.

FATHER.—"That's how you dress, is it? It's time I looked after your underclothing a little, your chemise is too long," putting his hand between her legs and pulling out the tail of her undermost garment, "what a pretty little pussey you have, my dear little Miss Bashful, I suppose you won't let your husband even look at or touch that; why how beautifully it's covered with this soft hair!" caressing and tickling the pouting lips with his fingers; "and you're only just over sixteen, you must have been rubbing your belly against something hairy."

DAUGHTER, in still greater confusion, turns away from him to hide her mortification, sobbing hysterically.—"Oh! Oh! Papa, Papa. Have mercy, how can you talk so?"

FATHER, taking out his knife.—"Stand still, Miss Prude, I'm going to make this chemise the proper length, so as to be a pattern of what you ought to wear." Then cuts a great piece off back and front so as to leave her quite exposed where the drawers are a little open, as he purposely leaves them. "You have a fine plump bottom, is it tender? do you feel that?" giving her a loud slap. "Oh! you can feel, can you; does it hurt you much?" as she starts with the sudden smart.

DAUGHTER.—"Oh! Oh! Papa! Pray don't, you humiliate me so!" bursting into fresh hysterical tones.

FATHER.—"Kneel down, and beg my pardon and own that all I do is proper; there, this place will do very well."

DAUGHTER.—"But that's all mud, I can't kneel there!" (Sobbing.)

FATHER.—"Can't again; will you never do as you're told? Down on your knees this instant, or I will kill you."

Daughter, in trembling confusion, kneels in the mud crying and hiding her face in her hands.

FATHER.—"Now, get up, your drawers are only a little soiled," laughing at the great patch of mud on her knees; "take my knife and cut me some of those nice long thin twigs, and ask me to correct you with them."

She complies, being too frightened and confused not to obey; the twigs are handed to her father, who ties them up into a nice little switch; then orders her to kneel on the ground with her bottom towards him; makes her, with her own hands, hold her drawers well open behind for him to inspect her posterior beauties, then makes her pin them back so as they will not close over the exposed rump.

FATHER.—"Now, my dear, you would like me to correct you, would you not, Miss Bashful?"

DAUGHTER.—"Oh! Oh! No. No. Box my ears, anything but that. I've done nothing!"

FATHER.—"You must be made to see your own conduct in the right light: ask me to whip you properly," switching her bottom smartly, and making long red marks at each stroke. "Tell me you wish it or I'll tickle you more and more with this."

DAUGHTER, screaming with pain.—"Oh! Oh! Ah! Papa! I can't bear it, indeed I can't. Oh! Oh! Yes, correct me properly, dear Papa. Oh! Oh! Have mercy," as he cuts harder and harder, drawing little drops of blood from the tender flesh.

FATHER.—"That's right, my dear, you are just beginning to take it in a proper spirit. Oh yes! you can bear it, shriek out, it will do you good," switching away vigorously, and enjoying the wriggling of her rosy-coloured bottom, as each stroke tells its tale: "Confound it! these twigs are not strong enough, they are all breaking to pieces; get up and cut me some better ones, mind you select them well; or I will punish you more and more for it."

The poor girl is almost ready to faint, her bottom smeared with blood from the broken weals; she wants to let down her clothes, but he makes her crawl just as she is to the bushes and cut another birch, enjoying every movement; then when she presents the twigs to him, he makes her kiss them, and tell him, "she hopes he will flog her well for his pleasure and her own good."

FATHER.—"That's right, my dear, I must cut that prudishness out of you; now open your legs well as you kneel, a little more dear," switching her gently at first: "It hurts me as much as it does you, poor dear," cutting harder and raising more weals on her devoted bum.

DAUGHTER.—"Oh! Oh! Papa. Have, have mercy: you're hurting me so! Oh! Oh! I shall die!" as he gives another harder switch, then, "Ah-r-r-r-r-re," as he cuts under between her legs.

FATHER.—"Does that hurt you so much, dear? I think you had better drop your drawers quite down. I must hurt you a little more, for your good; that's right, it will do you good," as she screams frantically for "Mercy, Mercy! Oh! Spare me now, Papa."

DAUGHTER, sobbing and crying in most humiliated distress.—"Oh,

Papa! Oh, Papa! I've done everything; you do hurt so, you are so cruel! Ah-r-r-r-re!" as he gives a sharp under-cut on her pussey.

FATHER.—"That's right; scream loudly; I couldn't help touching up your poor little pussey," cutting again and again, in the same place, and all over her poor naked bottom, till it is quite covered with weals and blood-stained all over.

The poor daughter writhes and wriggles with the pain, her sobs and cries get weaker, till at last she fairly faints.

The sight of her inanimate form seems to bring him back to his natural feeling, for he caresses and kisses her, calling her "his darling victim of a daughter, poor thing, poor thing," etc., and as soon as she revives a little, conducts her from the scene.

The Pleasures of Cruelty. Constantinople (London), 1896, 8vo.

Appendix B

THE DOUBLE LIFE.

(MY ADDITIONS TO THE PREFACE.)

. . . That I was an incestuous father, I admit, but I shall go to my grave happy in the knowledge that I made my daughter's life a happy one. Her last words of love were for her father. She died in my arms and when I lay down my pen in a few moments as the sun sets, I'll take my hat and stick, and slowly climb the hill that leads to the little shady churchyard where Innocent sleeps her last sweet childlike sleep.

I am very old and racked with pains of gout, but I'll rest myself upon a neighboring tomb and gaze at her grave until the light fails, and as I read and read her name cut in the stone, I feel once more as I do at each daily pilgrimage that our incest is forgiven because our great and veracious love had nothing base about it.

When I can no longer climb up to the restingplace of my child, my own daughter, my flesh and blood that was sweetheart, wife, concubine and devoted whore to me her father, I shall be ready to stand before my Maker who will pardon me in his infinite clemency. And you must fain forgive me, reader, for she forgave me long ago and felt no remorse or shame.

May I live to finish this book and join my girl for all eternity.
Amen.

CUTHBERT COCKERTON,
Attorney-at-law.
Brighthelmston, July 1798.

Appendix C

SPRAGUE v. LIHME.
(DIVORCE CASE.) London, 1899.

Mr. Justice Barnes, in directing the jury, said that the case was a
difficult one for them to determine, because of the relations which for
many years had existed between the parties. It was for the petitioner to
satisfy them that the case had been made out.

It was not necessary to give direct evidence of misconduct, because
it was not often that the accused parties were caught in *flagrante
delicto*; but if familiarity, opportunity, and other circumstances were
shown, they might legitimately be asked to draw the inference that
adultery had been committed.

They must not, however, act upon surmise or suspicion, but must
have evidence upon which to draw their inference, at the same time
considering the relationship of the parties which had existed for many
years, because, had it not been for that earlier intimacy, the case might
have assumed a very different aspect.

Appendix D

"In the infidelities that Saint-Fond allows, there is a feeling of debauchery. . . . Saint-Fond enjoys the idea of knowing that you are in
the arms of another; he puts you there himself and has an erection so
to see you; you multiply his delights by the extension you give to your
own, and you will be always more loved by Saint-Fond, when you do to
the utmost that which would arouse the hatred of another."

The heroine replies:

"Saint-Fond will like my tastes, my wit, my humour, and will not be jealous of my body! Oh! how that thought consoles me; for I confess to you, my friend, that continence would be impossible for me. My nature must be satiated at all costs; with my impetuous blood . . . with the imagination you know of, how can I resist these passions which are irritated and inflamed by everything!"—*La Nouvelle Justine ou les Malheurs de la vertu, suivie de l'Histoire de Juliette, sa sœur.* En Hollande, 1797. 10 vols. 18mo. (Pp. 82–83, Vol. 6.)

Appendix E

CESAREE.

This is the simple title of a novel by Edmond Tarbé, a successful author and journalist, turning upon the reciprocal passion of a father and daughter, as embodied in the diary of the former. It is carefully and delicately worked out and the style is perfect. The book was never published. While the first edition was in the press, in 1891, the publishers —the well-known house of Lévy, Paris,—were informed that the subject was one totally unsuited to their *clientèle.* The work of printing was put a stop to, and the author tore up his contract and took the few copies that were finished. These he gave away to his friends and none were ever sold. It is now very rare.

The daughter-heroine, Césarée, is twenty, and her father forty, when they go away on a little trip to Switzerland. They have never lived together, the father having left her when a baby.

The writer describes the pleasure the girl feels at being all alone with her adored father, when they are taken for husband and wife.

The first night they are alone together, they have two bedrooms, communicating, and Césarée begs her Pa to do his writing in her chamber, while she is in bed, reading. He obeys her, and when all is quiet, she gets up and forces him to let her read his diary, where she sees to her delight that he loves her madly. He declares that he fears his passion and she answers:

"There is a barrier which we must never pass. To break it down would be the signal of certain remorse and shame that neither you nor I could resign ourselves to support. But in front of this barrier, we find all liberty of love, and I invite you fearlessly to feasts where our hearts will find satisfactions, which are quite great enough. . . .

"*I am your daughter . . . that is to say, you cannot renew with me the work that brought me into the world. I am your daughter!* . . .

"But if, because I am your daughter, the consummation of our passion is forbidden to us both; on the other hand, because I am your daughter, I belong entirely to your sterile embraces. I am your thing, created by you, animated by you . . .

"Believe in that love and give yourself up to it, father, with complete joy, as I abandon myself to it, proudly and without remorse."

He takes her in his arms and thus describes what he does:

"With a single caress, my hands and my lips at the same time covered her shuddering flesh with one long kiss, embracing her whole soul at once. Passive and silent, as if nearly dead, she thus received in a few ardently-lived moments, the reward of her two years of secret adoration. From the moisture of her outstretched limbs, the perfume that I found twice more, mounted to my brain and penetrated it, in intoxicating emanations. Now I drank it, as it were."

After a variety of charming episodes, poor little Césarée commits suicide and dies a virgin.

Appendix F

AN INFAMOUS FATHER.

Victor Blanvillain, a workman, 38, living at Chatenay, 22, rue des Prés-Hauts, is the father of ten children, of which seven are girls. A few days ago, M. Cuvillier, commissary of police at Sceaux, received an anonymous letter informing him that Blanvillain had inflicted horrible treatment on five of his daughters, of the ages of sixteen, thirteen, twelve, ten, and nine.

After a rapid enquiry, which confirmed the accusation of the letter, the commissary informed the justices in Paris, who ordered a supplementary investigation and charged M. Joly, judge of instruction, to follow up the affair.

This magistrate, after hearing a certain number of witnesses, and having no longer the least doubt of the guilt of Blanvillain, who, besides, had made a partial confession, issued a warrant against the unworthy father.

The workman was at once arrested and taken to the Dépôt; but nevertheless his capture had been made as discreetly as possible, as it was feared that the indignant population of Chatenay might lynch the scoundrel.

Blanvillain's wife is mad with grief, and finds herself with her children in the most cruel position, having nothing to live on but the meagre earnings of her vile husband.

The wretched woman seems in despair and only the advice of the magistrates and the promise of assistance have given her a little energy.

Le Petit Journal, Paris, April 9, 1899.

Appendix G

TETE-A-TETE.

. . . One evening, Monsieur Le Hardeur, who up till then had shown himself almost like a father, frightened me and disgusted me with him to such an extent that I was very nearly calling for the help of the servant-girls of the restaurant where we were dining *tête-à-tête*; or else I should have foolishly jumped out of a window.

. . . It was fearfully hot. I had taken off my hat and slightly opened my surah blouse.

I forgot to eat or drink as I gazed upon the summer sky. . . . I must have been quite lost. I am sure I had the eyes of a little girl examining pretty coloured pictures, one by one.

And I perceived too late that my godfather had emptied two bottles of sparkling Asti, one after the other, and for the last few seconds had been examining me and looking me up and down with the fixed stare of a drunken horse-dealer.

"Hullo there! It's no fun to dine in front of one's napkin," cried he, suddenly. "Do you go in for the beauties of nature?"

I turned round in a fright and I thought he was going to have a fit.

With half-closed eyelids, his cheeks shining and pimply, he stammered out:

"You mustn't leave a poor man all by himself . . . a poor man who has never done anybody any harm; especially as,—as—"

He interrupted himself to breathe noisily, as if invisible hands had tightened his high, starched collar.

"Especially as you are superior to your mamma in every way. 'Pon my word, that madcap Fripette never had such a complexion. Roses in milk. And that head of hair! Silken rings, and so light, so golden, so well planted!"

I imitated in spite of myself his husky tone of voice, and replied with effrontery:

"And what's the next article, sir?"

He was not put out for so little.

"And she has already got hips, the little minx, and love-apples in her basket. First prize for beauty: Mademoiselle Jeannine Margelle? Ninette for her godfather, her excellent little godfather. Drop a nice curtsey to the gentleman, before you get your prize and a kiss."

He had jumped up and thrown himself on me so treacherously that I had not had time to avoid the odious embrace of his arms, and the caress of his wine-bedewed lips.

I struggled against him; I tried to scratch him; I insulted him; vexed, humiliated, trembling with rage and emotion, he let me go at last as if come back to his senses, and half-sobered, growled:

"Confound it! I'm only a juggins, a jay! The jay of jays, to put myself in this state for nothing at all. Yes, I say so, for nothing. Not that you are too young. After all, at seventeen, your confirmation has been over long ago. It's the age when you could take an excursion ticket without fear of accidents."

He took his seat at table again, threw himself back on the chair, quite cheerful, the thumbs in the armholes of his waistcoat of white piqué with blue spots.

"Oh, don't think I'm not inclined to start the game! Unfortunately, it's impossible—the danger signal is up; the line's blocked; I'm condemned for life. People would talk, and there would be too much gossip about the respectable Monsieur Le Hardeur. At the next elections, I should be left alone in my glory. And all that because a lot of people imagine that I worked at your existence; that you are probably my daughter. Yes, Ninette, my own offspring of the left hand. What silly tales get about! And yet there's not a word of truth in it all!"

I was leaning against the window sill, with the impression that I was listening to the ravings of a fool.

"I've compared dates, I've turned over dirty linen like a detective.

There were a pair of us, Flochet and I; two masters, each with the key, slippers and toothbrush. Flochet was only there for show. I had the best of it. But Fripette betrayed us both by the job, hour, day and week, with a fine soldier, an officer of the Cent Gardes, or the Empress's lancers, I don't remember exactly. How could a simple civilian fight, in those days, with the prestige of the sabre, or struggle against the points of waxed moustaches. *Ferrum est quod amant.* You don't understand? No matter, it's Latin for men. So I heard the cry of the cuckoo, and I was a cuckold, as no man has ever been before or since. I am sure of it; I'll show you the letters. Sad recollections; grief; wounds received in action. Q. E. D. that you are the daughter of the handsome soldier and not mine. If it was not that everybody thought the contrary at my club, the little business might have been brought off in the bosom of one's family, but Monsieur Le Hardeur does not possess the right to brave the world's opinion. That's as clear as clean water!"

I was silent; I felt more inclined to cry than to laugh.

Le Journal, Paris, May 17, 1899.

(This episode is from a novel by René Maizeroy, which was begun in the columns of the Parisian daily paper I have stated and was left unfinished.

It was the story of a "cocotte's" bastard daughter, who eventually is destined by her two fathers to practise for the stage and is introduced to a crowd of Lesbians and courtesans. The story broke off at that juncture but was afterwards published under the title of *Amuseuse*, Paris, Nilsonn, 1900, 12mo, illustrated with photographs.)

Appendix H

NOTES FROM THE GAY CITY, by ERIC ARVEL.

(EXTRACT FROM "THE LONDON STOCK EXCHANGE MAGAZINE," JUNE 1899.)

". . . a steady tide of visitors sets in towards the 'City of Pleasure,' the Mecca of the man whose imagination has been fired by the songs and gestures of the Parisian singers and dancers, but who too often on his arrival at the goal of his desire finds everything as flat and dull as the proverbial ditch water, for I know no more prosaic place than Paris under the Republic. The old animation of the boulevards is like the ball at the Opéra during the Carnival—existing simply in the minds of those who have read the memoirs published by men prior to the days of Nestor Roqueplan. The Jardin de Paris, although Oller is always up to date in his attempts to cater for the visitors, is but a very modernised imitation of Cremorne, and the old Jardin Mabille, where Rigolboche and Finette preceded the ladies who delight in such names as 'Grille d'Egout.'

" 'Nini Patte en l'Air,' and 'La Goulue,' has disappeared for want of patronage. Tradition seems to impress English tourists with the legend of Paris; but small wonder that most of them declare on their return that they prefer London to Paris for everything: cooking, drinking, and all the comforts money should purchase when the Briton is on his travels or bound for enjoyment. The summer holidays are the harvest time of those shameless individuals: the touts for all that is bad and vile in a city where men avow deeds so carefully hidden by Pharisees on the other side of the Channel. The police are too busy hunting up small political conspirators to think of arresting thieves, much less these men, who are the purveyors of clandestine places resorted to by foreigners, who often carry their lives in their hands, and owe their safety to the generosity to which they are prompted by the surroundings."

Appendix I

DIVORCE AMONG THE PEOPLE.

". . . And now with regard to girls:

"You know in what conditions of deplorable promiscuity the little people of Paris live. The whole family sleeps in two beds, in the same room.

"As long as the real father is there, we may hope that some remains of instinctive shame will prevent him from showing his children certain sights, from which we turn away our thoughts.

"But what happens when the mother, who cannot live on her own earnings, has started house-keeping with a second husband or a lover? What examples do you think will then be given to the little girls?

"They may think themselves lucky if, one day when the mother has gone out to market, the drunkard, as yet bewildered by the debauch of the preceding evening, does not violate them.

"I know what I am talking about. In the very poor working classes, there is no physical virginity after the age of fourteen."—*Le Bilan du Divorce*, by Hugues Le Roux.

Le Figaro, Paris, April 28, 1899. (Since published in book form.)

Appendix J

THE ALLEGED OFFENCE.

UNDER THE CRIMINAL LAW AMENDMENT ACT.

At the Wimbledon Police-Court, a clerk, 33 years of age, now living at 132, Arngask Road, Catford, but formerly of 153, Hartfield Road, was charged on remand with unlawfully and carnally knowing his step-daughter, Maud Frances Lacey, on various dates between March 1898 and March 1899.

Prisoner has been remanded from time to time for the appearance of his wife. That lady now appeared and denied that she had made any statement to the police beyond saying she was of a nervous and jealous disposition, and very much annoyed at certain things that had occurred between prisoner and her daughter. On many occasions she had caught the pair kissing, once surreptitiously, and this made her extremely jealous, as she thought the girl received attentions which ought to have been paid to herself, and actuated by this she communicated with the police with the idea of getting them separated. Witness gave a direct denial to the most essential points of the girl's evidence.

The girl also went into the box, and denied some of her previous evidence.

Mr. Matthews pointed out that no jury would convict on such evidence.

Mr. Meates said he did not feel disposed to take the responsibility on himself of allowing the case to drop through.

Mr. Matthews, after arguing the legal points of the case at some length, said there was absolutely no corroboration. Prisoner's wife was a jealous woman, who would not suffer her husband to kiss his step-daughter, and that jealousy was her motive for acting as she had was apparent from the fact that she had contradicted all the most vital points of the girl's evidence. If the case was sent for trial it would involve a repetition of a most unsavoury story, which must already have become indelibly impressed on the young girl's mind. Besides, no public advantage would be gained by such a course, and therefore, in the interests of public morality, he ventured to suggest that the case should be dismissed.

Mr. Meates said that a man in the position of father and husband, such as prisoner was, must be able to bring an enormous influence to bear on the witnesses, traces of which there had been all through the hearing. He must, therefore, adhere to what he had already said, and prisoner would be committed for trial at the Central Criminal Court.

"The Illustrated Police Budget," London, May 27, 1899.

Appendix K

"The Bonapartes have been very much in view lately on account of a book, recently published, consisting of reports of Louis XVIII's secret agents in Paris during the Consulate in 1802 and 1803. This period is one of the most interesting in French history. Napoleon was in the very prime of his vigour and genius. His power was felt by the whole of Europe, while at home he was rebuilding what the Revolution had overthrown.

"Napoleon's private character is painted in the blackest colours, in a way that only certain pages of the press with regard to Dreyfus to-day can equal. Hortense Bonaparte, wife of Louis, and stepdaughter of Napoleon, forms the subject of a report, her child being said to be the son of her stepfather. Talleyrand's marriage is related very spiritedly."

"SOCIETY," July 22, 1899.

(See *Relation Secrète des Agents de Louis XVIII.*—Paris, Plon, 1899.)

Appendix L

CONDEMNED TO DEATH.

Montbrison, 18th June.

Bordes, a workman in a foundry, has been condemned to death by the assize-court of the Loire. He murdered his daughter aged ten, and his wife. Bordes had incestuous intimacy with the little girl and unnatural connection with his wife. The assassin lived sixty-five days alone with the corpses of his victims, and it has been plainly shown that he slept on the dead body of his daughter.

The culprit feigned not to know what impulse he had obeyed in killing his wife and child, but the medical testimony was unanimous as to his entire responsibility.

Les Droits de l'Homme, June 19, 1899.

(For the benefit of my readers I may add that this revolting criminal was beheaded on the morning of August 7th., and he died with great courage. He asked for a mass to be performed; confessed his crimes; asked for pardon; had a cup of coffee; lit a cigar, and boldly ascended the scaffold of the guillotine.)

Appendix M

A HORRIBLE CRIME.

(From our own correspondent.)—Charleroi, July 3.

Charles Lechien, a tinker, living at Jumet, was the father of six children, three being girls.

For several years past he had indulged in criminal intimacy with the eldest of his daughters, Marie, nineteen years of age.

Yesterday Lechien met his daughter at the fair of Gesselies, in the company of a young man. This caused him to be terribly jealous.

Last night, all the family were asleep in three beds, in the same room.

Lechien got up and fired three shots of a revolver at his eldest daughter, wounding her in the temple. Marie was killed instantaneously in her sleep and died without making a movement.

Her mother and the other children jumped out of bed and tried to disarm the father, but Lechien had had the time to put two bullets in his head and he then shot his last cartridge at his wife, but missed her.

The pistol now being empty, the murderer, covered in blood, wished to force one of his sons to give him some more cartridges, but he, on the contrary, got the weapon away from him.

Lechien had strength enough left to take to flight; he went and threw himself in the canal of Sars-les-Moines. His corpse was recovered this morning.

Le Petit Journal, Paris, July 4, 1899.

Appendix N

"Jean had been a master at Rocton, my father's school; he had left suddenly, and rumour said because he had been over-attentive to my mother. Jean Messel, my lover, had been, according to the gossip, my mother's lover also. Possibly it was only an idle tale, but as I watched the urbane Mr. Osborne placidly smoking his cigarette, I could not think that he was the man to speak lightly and at random on so serious a subject. Then again, Jean's hitherto inexplicable terror of my father; everything seemed to fit in. It was all very horrible, and my brain reeled as the thoughts rushed through it. I tried hard to disbelieve, but more and more surely the conviction became strong in me that it was true, and that this man, whose kisses had been so sweet upon my lips, had, twenty years ago, kissed the lips of my mother, the mother whose remembrance I cherished, through all my wickedness, beyond anything else on earth. The image of Jean, smiling, debonnaire, and handsome, swam in the misty curtain that hung before my eyes, and a great loathing for him rose up in my heart.

"The vision of the old red schoolhouse at Rocton, and the sundial garden, with its carven hedges, where I used always to imagine my mother walking, was continually with me; but now there was another figure in the garden—Jean, as I imagined him to have been twenty years

ago, as handsome as a man could be. And then his arm came to be
about my mother's waist; but, oh! the picture was too dreadful, and I
ran about the room in despairing efforts to distract my mind."

"The Confessions of Nemesis Hunt."—
"Society," London, August 12, 1899.

Appendix O

At the assizes of Troyes, Carlier, for indecently assaulting his
daughter who he had forced to be his mistress for nearly six years was
condemned to twelve years penal servitude.

Le Journal, Paris, August 12, 1899.

Appendix P

AWFUL STORY OF
A DAUGHTER'S SHAME.

One of the most horrible stories of immorality that could possibly
be conceived was unfolded at the village of Cleasby, before Dr. J. S.
Walton, coroner, Northallerton. It appears that a young woman named
Margaret Eleanor Stott, aged 23, was delivered of twins a fortnight ago,
alleging the paternity of them to her father, a decrepit-looking old man
of 74 years. Whether they were born dead or alive was open to question,
but it seems that they didn't live long, for they were in the first instance placed in a box under the bed, then removed to an outhouse, and
finally the whole circumstances revealed owing to the mother going to
the vicar to ascertain if they could be properly buried in the churchyard. A sister, who should have proved an important witness as to the
disposal of the bodies, and in fact as to whether the children were born
alive, died the previous day. How it was the police were so long in obtaining information is rather strange, seeing that the affair has been the
common gossip of the village for nearly a fortnight; in fact, the strange

doings of the family have frequently been the cause of a good deal of gossip.

After briefly stating the facts to the jury, the coroner called:

Margaret Eleanor Stott, who stated that the children were hers by her father. They were born a fortnight ago that day, and at the birth the only person present was her sister Martha, who had died the day previously, and with whom she was sleeping. Witness had had another child two years ago, and it was still living, but the father of that was a young man at Darlington. Witness sent another sister for Mrs. Turnbull, but she was too busy to come, and no one else was sent for. This last sister referred to was but fourteen years of age, and she was sleeping with her father at the time. There were two rooms in the house, with beds in each of them. The occupants of the house were her father, herself, and two sisters and two boys. The sister who had died was nineteen, whilst the boys were aged four and two respectively. As the newly-born children did not move, her deceased sister picked them up, and put them in a little box under the bed, where they remained a day or two, after which her father buried them. Witness did not see him, but the sister who is dead told her. Witness dug them up last Monday night, and put them in a little house. In the afternoon of the same day Mrs. Smedley warned her that she would get wrong, and she then went to the vicar and asked if she could bury them in the churchyard. In reply to the coroner, she said she did not think the churchyard was the proper place at first. The boy in the house two years of age was hers, whilst the other boy belonged to an unmarried sister, Mary, aged 21.

The Rev. T. Churchyard, vicar of Cleasby, stated that the first witness came to him at seven o'clock last Monday evening, and wanted to bury a "still-born child." Witness asked her a few questions, as he had heard rumours in the village about the girl's father's conduct with her. He communicated with Dr. Johnson, of Darlington, who had attended the family, but he was from home. In the meantime he communicated with the guardian for the village, stating that he could not bury the child, and asked what he was to do. The guardian communicated with the police.

Dr. Walker, of Aldbrough, spoke to having seen the bodies that morning; but they were in such a decomposed state that he could not tell whether they had been born dead or alive.

After Jennie Stott, aged 14, had stated that she did not know the children were buried in the garden.

The jury expressed a desire to hear what the father had to say.

A police constable having requisitioned him, he replied, in answer to the Coroner, that he "knew nothing about 'em, but he was blamed for being the father of the children." Continuing, he said he first heard of it between ten and twelve o'clock on the day they were born. Martha, the deceased daughter, told him that Maggie was confined, and she said there were two children, both dead. He saw them the same morning, when they were put in a box in the bedroom where the daughter was. He next saw them in an outhouse three days afterwards, and in a callous, laughing manner, he exclaimed that he "took a look after them to see that the cats didn't get at them." They were taken through the garden into the house. He had nothing to do with them, and they were never buried by anyone. He certainly never saw anyone bury them. Again assuming a laughing air, he said: "I took blame for them myself; they might be mine. I am blamed for it, but don't know."

The Coroner, intervening, said he was not asking the witness what he was blamed for. He was a disgrace, and a good horsewhipping about his back would do him good. (Witness laughingly assented.) You are a disgrace to be their father, and your conduct here to-day is a disgrace also. I have done with you, you can go.

As the witness seemed in no hurry to go, he was removed from the court, the Coroner observing that the man had become such a sinner that he did not know what sin was.

The Foreman observed that it was generally understood in the village that all the children belonged to the old man.

The Coroner: For over forty years I have fulfilled the duties of coroner over this district, and during that time I have had many singular and serious cases in hand, but never during the whole course of my career have I heard of one to be compared with the rascality of that old villain. It is a wonder that the old women in the village did not take him and put him in the water. He added that he had intended to send a memorial to the Home Office on the subject, and it would be advisable for the jury to back him up. The old man was not worth talking to. He was nothing but a brute, and it was strange that in this country a man could seduce his own children without being punished, and there was no means of getting at him. A law for such offences did exist about 1650, but it had been repealed. He would write to the Home Secretary on the subject.

A verdict was then returned in accordance with the medical evidence to the effect that there was nothing to show whether the children had had a separate existence or not.

Subsequently the old man was brought back and severely lectured by the Coroner, who told him that in the whole course of his career he had never met with a bigger brute, or a more thorough old rascal. If the old women had tossed him into the Tees they would only have done their duty. (Applause.)

"The Illustrated Police Budget," London, August 26, 1899.

Appendix Q

INFAMOUS ACTS.

LA FERTÉ.—Recently we announced the arrest and condemnation of a young girl of fifteen, named Vial, living in the hamlet of Courcelles, charged with indecent exposure. It will be remembered that this girl had shown herself in a complete state of nudity.

The gendarmes, continuing their enquiry, have found against the girl Vial facts of such gravity and of such odious obscenity that we cannot give the details here.

The girl Vial and one of her friends, Jeanne Mahé, used two children nine years old to satisfy their mad passions; they had Lesbian habits, and the evidence of Louis Gabriel Vial and his sister Alice is frightful.

Gabriel Vial is own brother to the condemned girl!

Journal de Seine-et-Marne, September 14, 1899.

Appendix R

Monsieur Coudol has had a lucky escape! Monsieur Coudol, from Nantes, is fifty-six. In 1885, he got legitimately mated, but, inconstant and changeable, he soon abandoned his wife, who obtained a separation.

Monsieur Coudol then came to Paris. He was employed at the Montagnes Russes, then at the Moulin Rouge. Monsieur Coudol likes gaiety.

In this latter establishment lived a female dresser. Pretty? History is dumb on that point. Young? Still blooming, albeit she had a daughter of nineteen.

Monsieur Coudol fell in love with the dresser, madly in love. And when he learnt that the young girl had no father, he offered to legitimize her by marrying her mamma.

The household lived peaceably.

Nevertheless, one fine day, the dresser got tired. Her husband had become insupportable. And did she not engage her affections elsewhere too? But what pretext could be invented to obtain a fine divorce?

Allow me to draw a gauzy veil.

The dresser confided her wish to her daughter.

The daughter made it her duty to help her mother. Together, they organized the indispensable little *flagrant délit*. The legitimized girl consented to play the principal part.

Monsieur Coudol fell into the trap. Two coachmen, taken as witnesses, bore testimony to the affair.

A demand for divorce was registered by Madame Coudol, of Paris, and during the suit the discovery of Madame Coudol, of Nantes, was made.

The bigamist of the Moulin Rouge has just been tried. But he pleaded with such good faith his ignorance of the difference that exists between separation and divorce that he benefited by a verdict of acquittal.

He won't be caught again!

Le Figaro, Paris, October 21, 1899.

Appendix S

"As for the adventure of Mademoiselle Rosine, of whom I spoke to you and which I got from being intimate with Victoire, it is far from being funny. Imagine that she is the daughter of a very rich jeweller. Naturally, we do not know the name, nor even in which quarter is the shop.

"She is just turned eighteen, and the father is a man of forty-four. I tell you the age, you shall see why by and bye. Well then, the jeweller's wife dies and do you know how he arranged matters to replace her?

"Two months after the burial, one fine night, he goes and seeks his daughter Rosine. He quietly sleeps with her. That's a bit thick anyhow, isn't it? Such goings-on are not uncommon among poor people, I know more than one at Grenelle who has been through the same thing, but among middle-class folks who have got money enough to treat themselves to all the women they want! And what sticks in my gizzard more than anything is not that the fathers ask for it, but that the daughters consent to it.

"Now Mademoiselle is so sweet, so amiable, that doubtless she did not wish to let her Papa suffer. Never mind, here they are both nicely trapped. They have placed her here as if in a prison. Nobody comes to see her, and you may well think that orders are given to juggle the child away. A fine bastard who will be able to show off in society!"

Fécondité, by Emile Zola, Paris, Fasquelle, 1899, 12mo. (P. 181).

Appendix T

The Yellow Room

TABLE OF CONTENTS

"There is nothing, I am convinced by several years' experience, so good for a girl as a thorough good flogging administered upon her bare bottom with an elastic birch, she having been compelled to take off her own drawers herself."

EXTRACT FROM A LETTER OF MRS. B. H***N.

CHAPTER I

SIMPLICITY SHOCKED.

"Come in," said Coupeau. "No one will eat you!"

—L'Assommoir.

When the widowed aunt of Miss Alice Darvell, with whom she had been living for several years in Yorkshire, died, her residence was transferred to her nearest relative and guardian's house in Suffolk. And the change from a small house in a bleak and lonely part of the West Riding to a baronet's establishment was hailed with rapture by the handsome and healthy girl of eighteen. The only, or at any rate, the principal, advantage gained by her life with her aunt was one she scarcely appreciated. The life, the bracing air, the country rambles, and the rigorous punctuality of the old lady had allowed Miss Darvell to fully develop all the physical charms which so distinguished her. And not only that, to the fresh complexion, the laughing brown eyes, and the magnificent contour of her form and of her limbs was added a distracting air of reckless ingenuousness, picked up no doubt in her moorland scampers. But become conscious of her charms, she sighed for the pomps and vanities of the world. They were held up to her by her aunt as perils of the deadliest description—a view regarded by Alice with sceptical curiosity. Her solitude increased her imaginative faculty, and the fascination it attached to balls, parties and life generally in the world was greater than their charm actually warrants, as Alice subsequently found out. The only disquiet she had experienced arose from a vague longing which was satisfied by none of the small events in her puritanical life. She was modest even to prudishness; had long worn dresses of such a length as to make them remarkable; had never in her life had a low one on; blushed at the mention of an ankle, and would have fainted at the sight of one. The matter of sex was a perpetual puzzle to her, but she was perfectly unembarrassed in her intercourse with men, and quite unconscious of the desires she excited in them. All she knew of Sir Edward Bosmere of Bosmere Hall was that he was her trustee and guardian; that he was a widower much older than herself, a cousin some degrees removed from her, but that, notwithstanding, she called him "Uncle."

Thither then she went. Sir Edward turned out to be a man of about fifty; very determined in his manner, powerfully built, and of a middle height. But what surprised Alice most was to find herself introduced to a tall, dark girl, who looked about two and twenty, as his housekeeper. She was dressed in exquisite fashion, but Alice thought most indecently, and she, too, called Sir Edward "Uncle."

The first few days were taken up in making acquaintance, but Alice was surprised one morning at breakfast to see Maud grow very pale when told by Sir Edward, that she was to go to the yellow room after breakfast, and that she was to go straight there. This direction was in consequence of some cutlets which were served at the meal being slightly overcooked; and when Alice again saw Maud she was flushed and excited, and appeared to have been crying her eyes out. In some consternation, she inquired what the yellow room was, and the only reply she obtained was that she would find out soon enough. On the same occasion, when Maud had left the breakfast-room, Sir Edward, who had by that time quite taken in Alice, told her he thought she dressed in a very dowdy fashion, and said he had given directions to their maid to provide a more suitable wardrobe for her. The girl was covered with blushes and confusion when he spoke of her dressing like Maud. Now Maud showed a great deal of leg and of other charms; so Alice tried to pull herself together and reply that she really could do no such thing. Sir Edward looked at her in a very peculiar way, and said he felt sure her present mode of dress hid the loveliest neck and limbs in the world. He went on to ask whether she did not admire Maud's style of dress, and if she had noticed her stockings and drawers.

"I have indeed, uncle; but I could never wear anything like them."

"And why not, pray?"

"I should be so ashamed."

"We will soon cure you of that. We punish prudish young women here by shortening their petticoats. How do you like the idea?"

"Not at all; and I will not have anything of the sort done to me."

"I am afraid, miss, you want a whipping."

"I should like" (defiantly) "to know who would dare such a thing."

Sir Edward again looked at her in a peculiar manner, but said nothing more on the subject. Simply observing that he thought it right that young women should learn how to manage a house before they had one of their own and did not know what to do with it, he said she and Maud were to take the management in turn weekly, and that a week from that day she would have to do so.

"In the meantime, my dear, you had better learn as much as you can from Maud; especially not to let them burn cutlets like these." Saying which, he left the room.

At this point the narrative can best be continued by Alice Darvell herself:

"*Wed., July* 3, 188***.*—As soon as uncle had left the breakfast-table, I felt quite disturbed, but on the whole determined to go on as if nothing had happened. A message came a little later by our maid from Maud to say that she could not go out riding as we had arranged. What a terrible woman our "maid" is! Why on earth does uncle have a Scotch-woman of so terrible an aspect for us two girls? She makes you quake if she only looks at you. Well, I made up my mind to go alone; and rode off very soon after..

On my return I met Maud, very red, and looking as though she had been crying dreadfully. She would not tell me what had happened. The rest of the day passed in the usual way. We drove out after lunch, paid some visits, received several at our kettle-drum, dressed for dinner; and while waiting for the gong to sound Maud came to me, and to my horror began talking upon precisely the same subject Sir Edward had been speaking to me about at breakfast.

"Uncle does not approve of your dresses, you little prude, and Janet (the Scotch maid) has another one for you."

"If Janet," said I, "has a dress for me like yours, showing my neck and breasts and back, and my feet, my ankles, my legs—I mean like yours—I declare flatly I won't wear it."

"Don't be a fool, dear. I am mistress this week; you will be next week, as uncle has explained to you, and if you do not get rid of your ridiculous shame you will be soundly punished. You may be thankful if you are only obliged to show your legs up to your knees and your bosom down to your breasts. That is all.'

"I do not care. I have never been punished."

"Very well," said Maud; "have your own way. You will soon know better."

When I got down, there were uncle and Maud, three or four young men, and some very handsome women in low dresses, every one; I was the only one in a high dress. Uncle said something to Maud, who whispered to me that I was to go with her. As soon as we got into the hall, she told me I was to be taken to the yellow room and that I was a goose. I asked her why; she only laughed. Arrived there, she said she was very sorry, but must obey orders. She then strapped my hands firmly behind my back. My struggles were useless in the end, but kept her so long that she said, "I shall take care that you shall have an extra half-dozen for this." I could not think what she meant. It got darker, and still no one came. The yellow room was in an out-of-the-way wing, and I heard the tower clock strike ten. My hands behind me began to hurt, and I began to lose my temper. I wondered how long I was to be kept there, and then who had the right to keep me; and supposed it was called the yellow room because the curtains of the windows, the valances, and the bed-curtains were all yellow damask, and then I wondered what the ottoman, such an enormous one, was doing here, in company with a heavy oak table, a bar swinging from the ceiling, and—what with vexation and impatience I went to sleep.

I was awakened about half-past eleven by carriages driving off. It was pitch dark, and the curtains had been drawn. I know it was about half-past eleven because about half-an-hour later midnight struck. There was a footstep in the corridor, and uncle came in. He said:—

"I am extremely surprised at your insubordination, miss, for which I am about to punish you." What followed I cannot write.

So much for that part of the diary. Later on, by way of penance, as the sequel will show, Miss Alice Darvell was compelled to write out the minutest description of her punishments and her sensations and secret thoughts.

What happened was this; Sir Edward Bosmere at once informed Alice that he would have no more prudish nonsense; that he was going to strip her and flog her soundly, when he had first obtained a promise from her to take off her own drawers—a very important humiliation to which to subject a proud young beauty. She protested in the most vehement manner.

"He had no right to whip her; she would not be whipped by any man or anyone else; he was at once to undo her hands; being kept all the evening in that room without any dinner was quite punishment enough; she did not know why she had been punished; she would not wear horrid dresses which only served to make nakedness conspicuous; and if she was going to be treated in this way, she would go away tomorrow." "As to promising to take off her own drawers, and before him, he must be mad to think of such a thing, and she would die first."

She looked lovely in her fury, and an alteration in the surface of Sir Edward's trousers showed his appreciation of her beauty. He longed to see her naked and all her charms revealed.

"I will not dispute with you, you saucy miss, and your face is too pretty to slap; I will settle accounts with your bottom—yes, your bottom, and a pretty plump white bottom I have no doubt it is. I can promise you, however, it won't be white long. Now lie across that ottoman on your face. What? you won't? Well, across my knee will do as well, and perhaps better."

Putting his arm round her waist, he dragged the girl with him to the sofa, telling her that her shrieks and struggles in that heavily-curtained and thickly carpeted room were of no avail; that even if they were heard no one would pay attention to them, and that the only result would be, if she went on, to double her punishment. He did not, however, at that moment wish to do more than examine the charms that were so jealously concealed, the magnificence of which might be easily guessed from the little that did appear of her figure. He walked her to the sofa and sat down upon it, still holding her by the waist, and then, putting her between his legs, pulled her down across his left one. Her power of resistance was very much lessened by her hands being strapped behehind her, but still she managed to slide down upon her knees in front of him instead of being laid across his lap. He then held her tightly between his knees and proceded to unfasten the neck of her dress, and as the buttons were at the back he was obliged to put his arms round her and draw her so close that he felt her warm pressure upon him. The passion he felt was intensified, and the girl then, for the first time, seemed in a hazy sort of wonder as to whether the treatment she was undergoing was altogether unpleasant, which occupied her to such an extent that she ceased her useless resistance. At length the buttons were all undone to the waist. The dress was pulled down in front as far as the strapped-back arms would allow; sufficient, however, to disclose a neck as white as snow and the upper surfaces of two swelling, firm globes. Sir Edward immediately, placing his left arm under his victim's armpit and round her shoulders, drew her closer to him, spreading his legs wider, and notwithstanding her pretty cries to him to desist, inserted his right hand in her bosom. At last, succeeding in loosening her corset, he was able to caress the scarlet centre of the lovely, palpitating breast whose owner lay in most bewitching disorder in his lap. Her hair had partly fallen; her bosom was exposed by the dress three parts down and the loose corset—her eyes swam, and her colour was heightened.

"Oh, stop! uncle; oh, do, do, do stop! I never felt like this before. Whatever will become of me? I cannot bear the sensation. You have no business to pull me about so."

"Do you not like the sensation, Alice?" asked he, stooping and putting his face into her bosom; "and being kissed like this, and this, and this? And is not this nice?"—taking her red teat between his lips and gently playing with it with his tongue.

"Oh! uncle! whatever are you doing to me?" said the girl, flushing crimson all over, and her eyes opening wide with amazement, while her knees fell wider apart, as she herself fell slightly back upon his right knee.

"Is it nice? Do you like it? Does it give you sensations anywhere else?" asked he, glancing at her waist—and then, a moment after, putting his hand down outside her dress, said, "here, for instance?"

Still a deeper blush of crimson shame, but there was a gleam of rapture after the momentary pressure, followed by the exclamation: "How dare you?"

"How dare I, miss? We shall see. Now you will please lie on your face across my knee. You can rest on the sofa."

"Oh, I suppose"—with some disappointment in the tone—"that you are now going to button up my dress."

"Am I?"

"Then what are you going to do?"

"Make you obey me, and without any more resistance, or you shall have double punishment. Lie down at once, miss."

"Oh, uncle, don't look at my legs! Oh, do not, do not strip me. Oh, if I am to be whipped, whip my hands or shoulders; not there."

"You are a very naughty, obstinate girl, with very much too much prudishness about you. But when you yourself have been forced to expose all you possess in the most unconcealed manner, and have been kept some days in short frocks with no drawers, there will no doubt be an improvement. And, as I said before, I shall flog your bare bottom soundly, Miss Alice; and pretty often if you do not mend. Lash your arms and shoulders, indeed. I shall lash your legs and thighs. Lie down this instant."

The poor girl, seeing resistance useless, said nothing; but the arm put round her back soon cured her inaction. She lay across her uncle's left leg and under his left arm, which he had well round her waist.

"Now," said he, tightening his grasp, "we shall see what we have all along so carefully hidden; eh, miss?" pulling up her dress behind, despite her struggles and reiterated prayers to him to desist.

"No use struggling, miss," he went on, slipping his hand up her legs and proceeding at once to that organ in front which woman delights to have touched.

"Oh, uncle! oh, leave off. How dare you? How dare you outrage me like this? Oh! take your hand away! Oh! oh! oh!"

"So you are a little wet," feeling the hairs moistened by the voluptuous sensations he had caused her by caressing her breasts; "and you hoped that no one would know, no doubt. Now just let me stroke these legs. What a nice" (turning the robe above her waist) "fine pair they are; and" (opening the drawers) "what a pretty, what a perfectly lovely bottom! What a crime to hide it from me. However, you will make amends for that by taking your drawers off presently."

"Never! never while I live! You monster! you wretch! If ever I get out of this room alive I will expose you!"

"My dear, let me try a little gentle persuasion, a novel sensation. If that does not suffice, I can find some more striking argument."

And, again pressing her down upon him, he slipped his hand up, and putting his finger in her virgin orifice in front, he placed his thumb in the rear. Feeling his finger first, she jerked herself upwards, upon which in went his thumb; then, with a little scream, again bouncing forwards, his finger slid in as far as her maidenhead would admit—her hands were all the time still tied. He kept up a severe use of both his finger and thumb for some moments, and she was unable to contain herself, and ultimately obliged to abandon herself to the sensations he provoked. Her legs were stretched out and wide apart; her bottom rose and fell regularly; her lovely neck and shoulders, which were still exposed to his sight, increased his rapture and her dismay; and at last, when the crisis had arrived—pretty nearly at the same moment did it overtake them both—she lay panting and sobbing, almost dead with shame; but for that time subdued.

"Well, dear, how do you like your new experience?"

"Oh, uncle, it is awful, simply awful! I am beside myself."

"When you have rested a moment, will you stand up and take off your drawers before me?"

No answer.

"Answer directly, miss."

With a sudden revulsion of feeling, she bounced out:

"No; I won't! I won't, and you shall not."

Getting up, he went to a chest of drawers, and, opening one, took out a riding-whip. Silently, and notwithstanding her violent resistance, he again got the refractory girl over his knee, with his arm round her, her dress up, and her bottom as bare as her drawers would admit. Across the linen and the bare part he gave her a vigorous cut, making the whip whistle through the air. It fell, leaving a livid mark across the delicate white flesh, and caused a yell of pain. Again he raised it and brought it down—another yell and desperate contortions.

"Oh, uncle, don't! Oh! no more! no more! Oh! I can't bear it. I will be good. I will obey."

Sir Edward paid no attention, and raising the whip, made it whistle a third time through the air. A more piercing shriek.

"It is not enough for you to promise to obey; you must be punished, and cured of your obstinacy. And you called me a wretch and monster"—swish—swish—swish.

"Oh! oh! oh! oh! oh! oh! oh! don't! oh! don't! Oh, you are not!

I say you are not anything but what—oh! oh! put down that whip. Oh! please, dear uncle! You are not a wretch! or monster! I was very naughty to call you so, and I liked what you did to me, only was ashamed to say it. I will take my drawers off before you if you like! I will do *anything*, only don't whip me any more."

"You shall have your dozen, miss"—swish. "So you liked my tickling your clitoris, did you, better than"—swish—"tickling your bottom with this whip, eh?"—swish—swish. "You will expose me if you escape alive, will you?"—swish—swish.

"Oh, stop, stop! You have given me thirteen. For heaven's sake, stop!"

"I have given you a baker's dozen, and"—swish—"there is another because you complained."

Sir Edward was carried away by the passions excited by punishing this lovely girl, and her yell as the whip again cut into her delicate flesh he did not hear, so beside himself was he. Still holding her, he asked the sobbing girl whether she would be good.

"Yes. Indeed, indeed I will."

"There is a very satisfactory magic in this wand. Now, if I unfasten your hands, will you stand up and take your drawers off so that I may birch your bottom for refusing to wear a proper evening dress?"

"Oh, uncle, you have whipped me once, and punished me severely, too, by what you did to me. Why should I be put to more shame?"

"Shame! Nonsense. You should be proud of your charms and glad to show them. What I did should give you pleasure. Anyhow, will you take off your drawers?"

"Oh!" (flushing and in despair) "however can I? I should have to lift my dress quite up, and I should be all exposed. Besides, it is so humiliating."

"Precisely you yourself must bare all your hidden fascinations. And the humiliation is to chastise your prudishness. You must do it. You had much better be a good, obedient girl, as you promised you would be just now."

"Very well. I will then."

"That is a good girl. You shall have a kiss for reward," and, putting his lips on her beautiful mouth, Sir Edward gave her a long and thrilling kiss, and inserted his tongue until it came into contact with hers.

"What a delicious kiss," she said, shuddering with delight; and coyly added: "I shall not so much mind taking off my—my—my drawers" (in a hushed tone, her eyes averted from him) *"now"*

"That is right, dear. Now let me undo your hands. There. Now stand before that mirror and let me arrange the light so that it may fall full upon you. Now I shall sit here."

Miss Alice Darvell walked over to the mirror in a graceful and stately fashion, and started as she saw herself. She turned round and looked shyly at her master, but said nothing. Stooping down, she gathered up her gown and petticoats in her arms and slowly lifted them to her waist. The act revealed a slender and graceful pair of ankles and calves, but the knees were hidden by the garment she was about to remove. After some fumbling with the buttons about her waist—they increased her confusion by not readily unbuttoning, at which she, in a charming little rage, stamped angrily once or twice—the drawers tumbled down.

"Keep up your petticoats," cried Sir Edward," and step out of your drawers. Keep them up," said he, rising, "until I tell you you may let them down. What lovely thighs! what splendid hips! what a lovely, soft, round bottom! Look at it, Alice, in the glass."

"Oh," she said, simply," "I am so glad you think so. I have never looked at myself before."

At which he laughed, and stroked the satin skin with his hand, rubbing her limbs in front and behind and all over her bottom, until at last, when he had gradually stroked her all the way up, he put his hand between the cheeks of her back right through to her cunt, which, and the passage also, he kept gently stroking for some minutes, while she rested against him, uttering inarticulate sounds of delight.

"There," he said at length, "that will do for to-night. You may let your clothes down now. It is so late that the birching shall be postponed until the morning."

"May I take my drawers with me?"

"No, my dear; it will be some time before I shall allow you to wear them again."

"Oh, uncle!"

"Not as long as you are a maiden," added he, significantly.

"Oh, that will be years."

"Will it?" he inquired, innocently.

"Come," he went on, "I will take you to your room. You will in future occupy that one to which I am now going to take you, and not your old one."

"Why, uncle? All my things are in the old one."

"That does not matter, my dear. I must keep you under my eye until you are reduced to abject submission."

The room to which he took her was cheery and warm. Although the month was July, a fire had been lighted, and had evidently been recently stirred. And on a small table near the hearth stood a biscuit box and a small bottle of Dry Monopole. Alice would have preferred a sweeter wine, but was told that was better for her. It was quite plain that either uncle had told someone the precise hour at which he would bring her to the room, or that someone had been watching, for the wine was still frothing in the glass, and therefore must have been poured out but the moment before she entered. Terrible thought— Could anyone have been watching *her* and have seen her nakedness? Her uncle could not have know at what hour he would take her there. She was for an instant paralyzed at the notion; but the next moment, accidentally catching sight of a bare breast and arm, it caused her a certain voluptuous thrill to think she had been seen by someone besides Sir Edward. As she slowly undressed herself, her uncle having gone off and shut the door behind him, it struck her that she would herself, for her own satisfaction, have a peep at all she had been compelled to expose to him. She blushed at her own resolution, and commenced to feel what Miss Rosa Broughton describes as delight-fully immoral, a sensation first taught her by her uncle's hands, and of which all her lifetime until then she had been wholly ignorant, although she had had at times a conviction that some such pleasure exists. She stood before one of the large glasses with several of which her room was furnished, and having let down her wealth of brown hair and divested herself of all but a single garment, she allowed that—her chemise—to slip off her shoulders and arms, and for an instant only gazed at herself in the glass. For an instant only, for, overcome by a flood of shame at her nakedness and at the sense of it, she hurriedly averted her eyes and looked about for her nightdress. That she could not find; and she then recollected that the room was not the same she had previously used, and supposed they must have forgotten to bring her things. No; here was her dressing-gown. She would put it on and go to her old room for her night dress.

She went to the door, and to her utter amazement found that there was no handle inside. She was a prisoner. She looked about, but there was no other door anywhere to be seen.

"Very well," she said to herself; "I shall have to sleep in my chemise."

Taking off her dressing-gown when she was again naked to put on the chemise again made her feel immodest, and as it was cut low in the neck and left her arms bare, she felt more immodest still when she had got it on—a sensation renewed on several occasions when she awoke during the night and was reminded by her bare arms of her plight and of what she had undergone—and was to undergo later in the morning.

Before she got into bed she looked about for the article ladies generally use. There was nothing of the kind in the room, and there was no bell. Then it struck her that the deprivation of her nightdress and of the utensil referred to must have been done deliberately by Sir Edward, and the idea that he had thought of such things so intimately connected with her person gave her a fresh delightful glow of sensuality as she plunged into the cold, silky, linen sheets. The necessary effort to retain her urine, the sense that she was being punished by being made to retain it, and the knowledge that her uncle knew all about it and was so punishing her, excited her to such an extent that she went to bed a very naughty girl indeed.

INITIATION.

"Don't be afraid; a little bleeding does 'em good."

—L'Assommoir.

Awaking next morning about nine o'clock, she caught herself wondering what the whipping would be like, and how it would be administered, and was filled with a delightful sense of shame when she recollected the part of her body which would receive the castigation and the exposure it would inevitably entail. The thought or anticipation of this did not disturb her much. She even contemplated with pleasure the exposure there would be of her legs and thighs, and of that which she did not name to herself, considering the word immodest; but she did trust that her uncle would not flog her very severely.

As she lay thus occupied with these thought there was a tap at the door, and Janet came in with a cup of tea and some bread-and-butter and the announcement:—

"You have just an hour for dressing, miss, for breakfast will be served at half-past ten in the blue sitting-room—the one which overlooks the park. Miss Maud will come to show you where it is."

"Thank you, Janet," said Alice, keeping herself carefully covered. "There are several things I want from my old room—linen and a dress. Will you please bring them?"

"Yes, miss. I have the clothes you are to wear all ready, and will bring them to you."

"What do you mean, Janet?"

Janet did not reply. She grimly thought she would leave the girl to find out for herself.

She returned presently with an armful of clothing, which she deposited on a sofa.

In the meantime Alice had jumped up and donned the dressing-gown. She then again found it necessary to look about for that piece of furniture which is a feature in most bedrooms, but could not find it anywhere. She did not know, however, how to mention the matter to Janet, and while she was wondering how to accomplish it that amiable domestic had left the room. Alice had told her to return in about half an hour to do her hair, and the reply was that her hair was not to be done up that morning—a circumstance which, recalling what was before her, made her blush deeply. Then Janet departed, shutting the door, which only opened from the outside. Alice, consoling herself with the reflection that she could wait at any rate until she was on the way to breakfast, proceeded to wash. In the wall, close to the wash-hand-stand, was a black marble knob, with the word "Bath" upon it in gold letters. It was exactly what she wanted at the moment. Putting her hand upon it, she happened to press slightly, when the panel slid aside and showed a marble-floored room surrounded by looking-glasses, with several large slabs of cork for standing on, and a large bath of green Irish marble in the centre. Proceeding to it, she found that the same plan filled the bath with water as opened the room itself. She soon ascertained that not only was the water perfumed, but deliciously softened. The champagne and the tea made her wish again that she could have got rid of the water she herself contained, but she could not make out how the water ran away or was made to run away from the bath—so that little idea was knocked on the head. While bathing, she caught sight of herself continually in the glasses about her, and fell in love with her round, plump limbs and frame, and wondered why she had never done so before. She also noticed with indignation the red marks across her bottom made by the cruel whip that night, and shuddered as she dried herself with the deliciously woolly and warmed towels, and remembered that she had a flogging to undergo. She came, however, to the conclusion that her disobedience deserved punishment; and felt naughty, as she confessed to herself that she "really deserved to be whipped for it."

Hardly had she so determined than she found her obedience again put to the test. Proceeding to dress, she found the clothes brought far worse than the dress she had refused to wear the evening before. They were fit for a girl of ten, and, indeed, unfit for even her. The chemise was abominably low behind and before, the petticoats were quite short. So was the dress. And the petticoats were so starched that instead of hiding her limbs they would display them. And there were no drawers. What was she to do? Sir Edward was rigid in exacting punctuality at meals and generally. If she waited till Maud came she would be too late, and probably receive a worse flogging; besides, in all probability, Maud would only again laugh at her. So, a little indignantly, she dressed herself in the white silk stockings, which reached just half-way up her thigh, tied them with the rose-coloured garters above her knee; put on the patent leather low-cut shoes, the black and yellow corset, and the white frock with a rose-coloured sash. She tied her hair with a ribbon of the same colour, and then looked at herself. She looked like a great, overgrown schoolgirl, but, she could not help owning to herself, a very lovely one. Her arms were bare, and the frock was so low that she noticed with horror it only just concealed her red teats, looking at her from straight in front, but that if you looked down from her shoulder they were quite visible. And the dress stopped at her knees; no effort could make it longer. And the petticoats would make it stick out so. The only comfort was her hair, which did help to hide her naked back. Dressed at last, but feeling worse than naked, she sat down to wait for Maud, and, to her horror, noticed in a glass opposite that the dress stuck out to such an extent that not only could her leg be seen to the top of the stocking, but that the rosy flesh beyond was quite visible; and after a trial or two she discovered that if she was not very careful how she sat, not only would the whole of both legs be displayed, but her cunt also. She wondered however she could go about, and whether she would have to; and at last the costume so excited her passions that she was compelled to walk up and down, and became so naughty that she did not know how to contain herself or the water she had been unable to get rid of. While fidgetting about the room in this state of agitation, Maud entered, and immediately exclaimed, in the most disingenuous manner:—

"How perfectly lovely you are, Alice, with that blush-rose flush! What a splendid bust! Good gracious! do let me look at them. What lovely straight beautifully-shaped legs" (catching hold of the skirt of the frock). "Oh, do let me see——"

"Oh! don't, Maud! Don't!"

"Very well, dear. But you have not done up your hair. That won't do."

"Janet told me I was not to."

"Yes; I know. But that was a mistake. It hides too much."

"That is just why I like it down."

"And just why I do not, dear. You must let me roll it up for you so that your back and nuque and shoulders may be fully shown. There; now you look a perfect darling. I thought I should find you quite cured of anxiety to hide any charm. Do you not wish now you had take my advice?"

"Yes."

"But," she went on, "it is not of much consequence; for if you had not rebelled, some other excuse would have been made for punishing you."

"Indeed?"

"Yes; and you deserved it, Alice."

As Alice had herself come to this conclusion, and felt her bare legs, she only blushed, and said:—

"Oh, Maud, do you know I have no drawers on; and that when I sit down my legs and all show? Shall I have to go about in this dress? and how long shall I have to wear it?"

"That depends upon how you take your punishment. While you wear it you will certainly have to go about in the house and grounds with it. I suppose you wish you had drawers on?"

"Indeed you may suppose so. Oh, Maud, however can I——"

"We must be going, Alice, or we shall be late."

"Oh, Maud, do tell me, does uncle whip very hard?"

"I should have thought," and Maud's eyes flashed, "you could have answered that question yourself."

"Yes. He hurt me dreadfully with the riding-whip. Have you been birched?"

"Yes. I have."

"Was it very bad?"

"In a few hours you wille be able to judge for yourself."

"How does he birch?"

"Here," said Maud, slyly putting her hand under Alice's petticoats upon her bare bottom.

"Oh, don't, Maud."

"Silly child, you should be obliged to me for the sensation. Do come along to breakfast."

"Oh, Maud, there is something I want to ask you; but how to do it I do not know. Perhaps" (with a deep blush) "the best way is to say they have forgotten to put something in my room."

"I know very well what you mean, Alice. You mean you have no po; and you want to pea. All I can say is that I hope you do not want to very badly, because it is not at all likely that you will be allowed to do so until after your flogging. But, of course, you can ask uncle."

"However could I ask him?" replied Alice, aghast and pale at the notion and the prospect of what she would have to endure. "Does he know?" remembering her thought of the night.

"Yes. Of course he knows; and he does it to punish you, and to help to make you feel naughty. Do you feel naughty, dear?" asked Maud, and, again putting her hand under Alice's petticoats, she began tickling her clitoris.

"Oh, don't! Maud. Oh, pray don't! Oh, you will make me wet myself if you do. Oh, can't you let me go to your room?"

"My dear girl, if I were to let you pea without permission, I should probably be forbidden to do so oftener than twice in the twenty-four hours for a week or a fortnight. And I advise you to say nothing about it to uncle, for if he finds out that you want to very badly, he will probably make you wait another hour. It is a very favourite punishment of his."

"Why?"

"Oh, I don't know; except that it is a severe one. And it is awfully humiliating to a girl to have to ask; but it certainly makes one feel naughty."

"Yes; it does. Do you know, I was nearly doing it in the bath?"

"Lucky for you that you did not. It would certainly have been found out, and you would have caught it. But, Alice, why do you say 'doing it' instead of 'peaing'? When you ask you will have to use plain language."

"Oh, Maud!"

"Yes; and very likely have to do it before uncle. If he finds out you squirm about saying things and calling them by their names, he will make you say the most outrageous things, and write them also. But there is half-past ten chiming. Come along."

When they got to the blue room—on the way to which they passed, to Alice's intense consternation, several servants who gazed immoveably at her—they found Sir Edward there in a velvet coat and kilt. He greeted them cheerily. The view across thu park, in the glades of which the fallow deer could be seen grazing, was, lovely; the sunshine was flooding the room, and the soft, warm summer air wafted in the perfume of the flowers from the beds below (the blue room was on the bedroom floor) through the windows, which were thrown wide open. Alice was so struck by the view that she for a moment forgot to notice how her uncle was gazing at her, until she felt the air on her legs, and it provoked a consciousness at which she blushed.

"How do you like your frock, my dear? It becomes you admirably."

"Does it, uncle?" Looking coyly at him. "I am glad you like it."

"I am glad to see you are a sensible girl after all. We shall make something of you."

"How long am I to wear it, uncle?"

"For a week."

"For a fortnight," struck in Maud, maliciously. "She is to be mistress next week."

Maud knew very well she would find it much worse to be dressed like that when giving orders, and that her orders would not be so well attended to. She revelled in the notion of getting Alice soundly punished.

Sir Edward noticed with a gleam of amusement how fidgetty Alice became towards the end of the meal, and Maud smiled gently to herself. Alice thought that after breakfast she would have a chance. She was disappointed. Sir Edward then said, in a severe tone: "I think, Miss Alice, we have a little business to settle together. Your disobedience cannot be overlooked. You must come with me. Your short skirts will punish your prudishness, but the birch is the best corrector of a bold, disobedient girl's bottom," She grew quite pale, and trembled all over, both with fright and at being spoken to so before Maud, who, reposing calmly in her chair, was steadily gazing at her.

She had got up. When her uncle had finished speaking, he came up to her and took hold of her left ear with his right hand, and saying, "Come along, miss, to be flogged," marched her off to the yellow room.

There, to her consternation, she saw straps and pillows on the oak table. In a perfect fright, she said: "Oh, pray do not strap me up, uncle; pray do not. I will submit."

"Undress yourself," he said, having closed the door; "leave on your stockings only."

"Oh, uncle!"

"You had better obey, miss, or you shall have a double dose. Take off your frock this instant."

"Now your petticoat bodice."

"Now your petticoats. Now your corset and chemise. Now, my proud young beauty, how do you feel?"

He had not seen her to such advantage the evening before. She had then had her long dress on the whole time, and while punishing her he had only uncovered a small portion of her legs. It is true she afterwards had been made to take off her drawers; but the skirt and petticoats gathered about her hips had still concealed much. Now she was naked from the crown of her head to her rose coloured garters. Burning with shame, she put her hands up to her face, and remained standing and silent, while Sir Edward feasted his eyes upon the contemplation of every beautiful curve of the lovely little head poised so beautifully upon a perfect throat; of the dimpled back and beautifully rounded shoulders; of the arms; of the breasts and hips and thighs. It was the most lovely girl he had seen, he said to himself, and then, seating himself, he added aloud:—

"Come here, miss. Kneel down: there, between my knees; clasp your hands, and say after me:—

"Uncle, I have been."

"Uncle, I have been."

"A naughty, disobedient girl,"

"A naughty, disobedient girl."

"And deserve to be soundly birched."

"And deserve to be soundly birched."

"Please, therefore,"

"Please, therefore,"

"Strap me down"

"Oh, no! oh, no! Oh, please don't strap me down!"

"Say what I tell you at once, miss, or it will be worse for you."

"Strap me down"

"To the table,"

"Oh! oh! oh! To the table,"

"With my legs well apart,"

"Oh, dear! I can't. With—with—I can't—with my—oh, uncle!"

"An extra half-dozen for this."

"Oh, uncle!"

"Say at once: With my legs well apart."

"With my—my—oh!—legs" (and she shuddered deliciously and blushed bewilderingly) "well apart."

"And give me"

"And give me"

"Please,"

"Please,"

"Four and a half dozen"

"Oh, uncle! please not so much!" (recollecting the baker's dozen with the riding-whip.)

"You will have more if you do not say it at once."

"Four and a half dozen"

"On my bare bottom."

"Oh! that!—my—I can never say—"

"You must."

"My bare——"

"You had better say it. Stop; I will improve it. You must say: On my girl's bare bottom."

"Oh, uncle!" she said, looking at him; and seeing his eyes gloating upon her and devouring her beauty, and the lust and fire in them, she immediately turned hers away.

"Now, Alice, 'On my girl's bare bottom.' "

"On my girl's bare bottom."

He moved as he said this, and Alice noticed he adjusted something under his kilt.

"Well laid on."

"Well laid on."

"Yes; I will, my dear. I will warm your bottom for you as well as ever any girl ever had her bottom warmed. I will set it on fire for you. You will curse the moment you were disobedient. I will cure you of disobedience and all your silly nonsense. Come along to the table. There, stand at that end"—Alice began to sob—"put the cushion before you, so. Now lie over it, right down on the table. No resistance" (as he fixed the strap round her shoulders she made a slight attempt at remonstrance). The strap went round her and the table, and when once it was buckled she could not, of course, get up. He then buckled on two wristlets, and with two other straps fastened her wrists to the right and left legs of the table; then another broad strap was put round the table and the small of her back. This was pretty tight, as were also those that at the knees and ankles fastened her legs, wide apart, to the legs of the table. She was like a spread eagle, and her bottom, the tender skin between its cheeks, her cunt, and her legs were most completely exposed.

"Now, my dear, you will remain in that position half an hour and contemplate your offences, and then you shall have as sound a flogging as I ever gave a girl."

"Oh, uncle, before you flog me, do let me do something. Maud told me I should have to tell you, but I do not know how to. I will come back directly and be strapped down again if you will only let me. And, oh! please do not leave me in this dreadful position for half an hour."

"You must say what it is that you want."

"Oh, uncle"—feeling it was neck or nothing—"do let me go and pea before I am flogged. I want to, oh, so dreadfully. I have not been able to all the morning, nor all night."

"So you want to very dreadfully, do you, miss?" and going up to her he put his hand between her legs from behind, and severely tickled the opening through which the stream was burning to rush. It was all that Alice could do to retain it.

"Oh, don't! Oh! If you do I shall wet myself. I shall not be able to help it. Oh, uncle, pray, pray don't! Oh, pray let me go!"

"No, miss, I certainly shall not. It is a part of your punishment. There was an unnatural coldness about these parts of yours which this will help to warm up. Have you not felt more naughty since you have had all that hot water inside you?"

"Yes; I have."

"And you are beginning to see how ridiculous prudishness is. Now, just you think about your conduct and your disobedience until I return to whip you, and remember you owe your present shameful position to them."

Saying this, Sir Edward left the room. Poor Alice, left to herself, all naked save for her stockings; her arms stretched out above her head and tightly strapped; her legs divided and fastened wide apart; the most secret portions of her frame made the most conspicuous in order that they might be punished by a man—did feel her position acutely. She considered it and felt it to be most shameful. Her cheeks burned with a hot, red glow. But all concealment was absolutely impossible; the haughty beauty felt herself prostrate before and at the mercy of her master, and experienced again an exquisite sensual thrill at the thought that she really deserved to have her bottom whipped by her uncle.

Presently Maud came into the room in a low-necked dress, with a large bouquet.

"Well, Alice," she said, "I hope you enjoy your position and the prospect before you."

"Oh, Maud; go away. I can't bear you to see me in this position. I won't be punished before you."

"Silly goose! Young ladies strapped down naked, and stretched out for punishment like spread eagles, are not entitled to say shall or shan't. What a lovely skin and back, Alice. Alas! before long that pretty, plump, white bottom will present a very altered appearance. How many are you to have?"

"I was made to ask for four dozen and a half, well laid on."

"And you may depend upon it, you will have them, my dear, most mercilessly laid on"—stroking her legs and thighs, which caused Alice to catch her breath and to coo in a murmuring way from the pleasure Maud's hand gave her. Maud asked her whether she had tried to induce her uncle to let her go somewhere.

"Yes," replied Alice; "I did. But he would not."

"And I suppose you want to very badly," went on Maud, maliciously placing her fingers on the very spot.

"Yes; I do. Oh, don't, Maud, or you'll make me!"

"Now mind, Alice, whatever you do, hold out till your birching is over. If you do not I warn you that you will catch it."

"I think it is a very, very cruel, horrid punishment," said Alice, whimpering.

"It is severe, I know, and it is far better not to be prudish than to incur it. But here comes uncle."

"Now, you bold, disobedient girl, I hope you feel ashamed of yourself," said Sir Edward, entering the room and shutting the door. "Maud will witness your punishment as a warning to her what she will receive if she is disobedient."

Going up to the wardrobe, he selected three well-pickled birches, which had evidently never been used, for there were numbers of buds on them. They were elastic and well spread, and made a most ominous switching sound as, one by one, Sir Edward switched them through the air at which Alice shuddered and Maud's eyes gleamed.

"Oh, pray, pray, uncle, do not be very severe. Remember it is almost my first whipping. It is awful!"

Maud had changed the dress she had worn at breakfast and, as already mentioned, now had on one cut very low in the body; her arms were bare and her skirts short. Between her breasts was placed a bouquet of roses.

"Hold these," said Sir Edward, giving her the rods.

He then put his left arm round Alice, and said: "Now, you saucy, disobedient miss, your bottom will expiate your offences, and by way of preface"—smack, smack with his right hand, smack, smack, smack. "Ah, it is already becoming a little rosy."

"Oh, uncle! Oh, how you hurt! Oh, how your hand stings! Oh! oh! oh!"

"Yes. A bold girl's bottom must be well stung. It teaches her obedience and submission"—smack—"what a lovely, soft bottom!"—smack, smack, smack.

Maud's eyes gleamed and her face flustered, as Alice, wriggling about as much as the straps allowed, cried softly to herself. When her uncle had warmed her sufficiently, he removed his arm and moved about two feet away from the girl, whose confusion at the invasion of her charms by the rough hand of a man increased her loveliness tenfold. Maud held one birch in her right hand. She, too, looked divine. Her dark eyes flashing, her lovely bosom heaving, she handed it, retaining the other two in her left hand, to her uncle. Alice could not see that as she gave him the birch, as soon as her hand was free she slipped it under her uncle's kilt from the back, and the instant increase of his passion and excitement left no doubt as to the use she was making of it. Sir Edward stood at the left side of his refractory ward. He drew the birch, lecturing her as he did so, three or four times upwards and downwards from back to front and from front to back between the cheeks of the girl's bottom, producing a voluptuous movement of the lovely thighs and little exclamations of delight.

"Oh! oh! oh! don't do that! Oh! oh! how dreadful! Oh, please, uncle!" trying to turn round, which, of course, the straps prevented. He next proceeded to birch her gently all over, the strokes increasing in vigour, but being always confined to the bottom.

"Oh, uncle, you hurt! Oh! how the horrid thing stings! Oh! it is worse than your hand! Oh! stop! Have I not had enough?"

"We will begin now, miss," said he, having given her a cut severe enough to provoke a slight cry of real pain; "and Maud will count."

Lifting up the rod at right angles to the table on which she was bound down, he brought it down with a tremendous swish through the air across the upper parts of her hips.

"One," said the mellow voice of Maud—her right hand and a portion of her arm hidden under her uncle's kilt, the movements of its muscles under the delicate skin and the wriggles of the Baronet showing that Maud had hold of and was kneading a sensitive portion of his frame. The bottom grew crimson where the stroke had fallen, and the culprit emitted a yell and gasped for breath. With the regularity of a steamhammer, he again raised the rod well above his shoulder, and again making it whistle through the air, he again gave her a very severe stroke.

"Two," said Maud quietly.

A shriek. "Oh! stop! Oh! stop! Oh! *stop!*"

Swish. "Three," calmly observed Maud.

"Oh! you will kill me. *Oh!* I can't—I can't——"

Swish. "Four, uncle."

"Oh, ah! Oh, I can't bear it! Oh, I will be good! Oh, Maud, ask him to stop——"

Swish. "Five"

Maud had given her uncle an extra pull when Alice had appealed to her, and this stroke was harder in consequence. Spots of blood began to appear where the ends of the birch and its buds fell, especially on the outside of the off thigh. The yell which followed number five was more piercing, and choking sobs ensued; but Sir Edward, merely observing that she would run a very good chance of extra punisment if she made so much noise, without heeding her tears or contortions or choking, mercelessly and relentlessly gave her six, seven, eight, and nine, each being counted by Maud's gentle voice.

"Now, miss, that you have had one-sixth of your punishment——"

"One-sixth! Oh! oh! oh! I can't bear more! Oh, I can't bear more! Oh, let me off! You will kill me! Oh, let me off! I will—I will I *will* indeed be good——"

"I suppose you begin to regret your disobedience."

"Oh, don't punish me any more," cried the girl, wriggling and struggling to get free—of course ineffectually, but looking perfectly lovely in her pain.

"Yes! You must receive the whole number. It is not enough to promise to obey now; you should have thought of this before. You are now having your bottom punished, not only to make you better in future, but for your past offences."

And Sir Edward walked round to the right side of his niece, and there, in the same place, but from right to left, gave her nine very severe cuts. Alice yelled and screamed and roared and rolled about as much as she possibly could, perfectly reckless as to what she showed.

The next nine were given lengthwise between her legs. Her bottom being well up, and the legs well apart, the strokes fell upon the tender skin between them, and the long, lithe ends of the rod curled round her cunt, causing her excruciating agony.

"There is nothing like a good birching for a girl." Swish.

"One," said Maud, moving voluptuously.

"Oh! oh! yah! Oh! my bottom! Oh! my legs! Oh! how it hurts! Oh! oh! oh!"

"They are all the better for the pain!" Swish

"Two," said Maud.

"Oh! oh! oh! Oh, don't strike me there!" as the birch curled round her cunt.

"And the exposure. I do not think you will disobey." Swish.

"Three," said Maud, apparently beside herself, her eyes swimming.

"Oh! oh! oh! yah! Oh! I shall die! I shall *faint!* Oh! dear uncle! I will—please forgive me—I will never disobey. I will do *anything;* ANYTHING; ANYTHING!"

"I daresay you will, miss; but I shall not let you off;"—swish—"there's another for your cunt."

"Four," said Maud.

"Oh! Oh! not there! Oh! I am beside myself! I shall go *mad!* I shall *die* or go *mad!*"

"You will not do anything of the sort, and you must bear your punishment." Swiish.

"Five," counted Maud.

The cries gradually lessened, and the culprit seemed to become entranced, whereupon the uncle, at whom Maud looked significantly, directed the remaining four strokes to the insides of the thighs, leaving the palpitating red rose between them free from further blows, *for the present.*

Alice's moans were then succeeded by piercing shrieks, but her uncle, perfectly deaf to them, continued the flogging. When the third nine, given lengthwise, had been completed, Sir Edward put down the birch he had used and took a second from Maud. During the pause, his niece, with sobs and tears, earnestly implored him to let her off. For all reply, he again took up his station at her left side, and saying: "No, miss; I shall certainly not unstrap you; you have been far too naughty. I will punish you, and your lovely legs and bottom, to the fullest extent of the sentence, and teach you to be good, you bold hussey, and give you a lesson you will not forget in a hurry"—gave her nine more sound cuts; but this time, instead of their being administered on the upper part of her bottom, perpendicularly, they were given almost horizontally on its lower part, where it joins the thigh. Fresh yells and shrieks, all of no avail, were uttered by the unhappy girl, who in her agony lifted up her head, her shoulders being fastened down with the strap, and prayed her uncle, by heaven, to spare her. But the relentless rod still continued to cut into her tender and now bleeding flesh, as she was told "she would receive no mercy."

Maud's even voice continued to number the strokes, and Maud herself seemed aflame, and the sight of the agony her uncle was inflicting seemed to excite her sensuality in an extraordinary degree. Her lips were moist; her eyes swam; the eyelids drooped; and all the indications of a very lovesick girl appeared in her. The bleeding bottom, the tightly-strapped limbs, the piercing cries, and the relentlessly inflicted punishment excited her strongest passions. She could have torn Alice limb from limb; and she encouraged her uncle, by rolling his balls and pulling and squeezing his prick, to continue the punishment in the severest manner.

She gloated over the numbers as she called them out.

Sir Edward, too, seemed beside himself. His eyes were as two flames; he watched every motion of Alice's body; gloated upon all she displayed; could have made his teeth meet in her delicate flesh, which he lacerated with the rod yet more severly as his organ, already excited to an enormous size, was still further enlarged by Maud's hand.

At length, Alice's lower bottom having been well waled from right to left, as well as from left to right, there remained but the nine strokes to be given lengthwise.

For these, Sir Edward took the third birch from Maud, who by this time was standing with her legs wide apart, uttering little sounds and breathing little sighs of almost uncontrollable desire.

The unhappy culprit's yells had somewhat lessened, for the flowing blood had relieved the pain; and it had also been so severe that her sensitiveness to it had much diminished. But now, feeling the rod curling round her cunt, which, being all open and wet, was more than ever exposed, she yelled in a perfectly delirious manner.

After some few of these strokes had been given, her uncle asking her whether he was a wretch and a monster, as she had called him last night, she replied with vehement denials:—

"No! oh, no! oh! oh! oh! oh, no! Not a monster! Not a wretch! My own dear uncle, whom I love! Oh! oh! oh! My bottom burns! Oh! oh! It is on fire!"

"Will you be a good, obedient girl miss?"

"Yes! Yes! *Yes!* Oh! indeed—"

"And thank me for whipping you?"

"Yes; indeed I do."

"Whip well in, uncle," said Maud quietly, in her rich voice.

And he did so. Alice shrieked; flooded the floor with urine, and fainted!

Maud, beside herself, threw herself backwards on the long and broad divan—her breast, her legs (without drawers) wide extended. Sir

Edward, throwing down the birch, threw himself upon her with fury. He inserted his enormous affair into her burning cunt, and he fucked her so violently that she almost fainted from delight.

When Alice came round, Sir Edward rose from Maud's breast, and then Maud said, in clear tones:—

"Uncle, I told Alice yesterday evening, when she kept me so long before I could succeed in tying her hands, that I would take care it secured her an extra half-dozen."

"Oh, uncle! I beg Maud's pardon. Oh! after all I have gone through, let me off that half-dozen. Oh, *dear* Maud! do ask uncle to let me off. Oh, do! If I am birched any more I shall go mad! I shall —I shall indeed!"

Maud, still lying backwards on the couch, supported by a big, square pillow, said nothing. Her hands were clasped behind her head.

But Sir Edward said: "No miss; you can never be let off! You must have the half-dozen. It will be a lesson to you." And taking up the birch, he gave her six severe strokes, distributed evenly all over her bottom.

As they were being administered, Maud's left hand stole down to her waist and found its way between her legs.

While Alice was smothering her sobs and cries after her last half-dozen, Sir Edward again threw himself upon Maud and enjoyed her.

About ten minutes or a quarter of an hour later he proceeded to unstrap Alice.

She could not stand without Maud's help. The cushion and carpet were soaked with her urine and stained with her blood.

"You will to-morrow have a dozen on the trapeze, miss, for disgracing yourself in this beastly manner; you will write out fifty times, 'I pea'd like a mare before my uncle'; and for the next fortnight you will only pea twice in the twenty-four hours. And now come and kiss the rod and say: 'Thank you, my dear uncle, for the flogging you have given me.' "

Quite docilely she knelt down before him, kissed the rod he held to her lips, and repeated the words.

"Will you be a good, obedient girl in future?"

"Yes, dear uncle; indeed I will!"

"Tha's a good thing. There is, you see, nothing like a good, sound flogging for a girl. Were the rod more in use how very much better women we should have. Now go with Maud and get some refreshment. I have various engagements, and shall not be in till dinner. After lunch you had better have a sleep." And so saying, he packed the two girls off to Alice's room, shut the yellow room door, and ringing for a footman, gave orders that the estate steward and horses should be in attendance at the front door in half an hour.

Maud and Alice went to the latter's room. By Maud's advice, Alice, who was so sore that she could scarcely move, got into bed and had some strong broth and Burgundy, and presently fell asleep. Maud spent her afternoon at an open window reclining in a lounge chair, pretending to read a novel, but in reality revelling in the reminiscences of the morning and meditating upon its delights—and wondering when she would get whipped next herself—until she was disturbed by some afternoon visitors.

CHAPTER III

MYSTERY

> "My passions, however, are very strong; but my Soul
> and Body are hostile sisters, and the unhappy pair, like every
> imaginable couple, lawful or unlawful, live in a perpetual
> state of war."

> —MADEMOISELLE DE MAUPIN

Alice's slumbers were profound. For four or five hours she continued in the deepest sleep; but as consciousness gradually returned to her she dreamt: and dreamt, as she had never done before, of love. Her innocence was gone; and she would awake an experienced girl. Her dreams were of the softest pleasures; they were prompted by that new and wonderful sensation, under the influence of which she still was, which had been roused once for all while she lay ignominiously extended under her uncle's eye and received the cruel lashes of the birch upon the most secret and divine organ of her exquisite body. They, it is true, profaned the Temple; but they summoned to life the Divinity there enshrined. Her sexual instincts were aroused; she became conscious of her femininity. She felt the influence of Man; and a longing and insatiable desire to possess him. She now knew why she was beautiful, and in her dreams she pictured herself with soft delight —her velvety skin; her soft, plump, round arms; her throbbing bosom, and the ravishing sinuosities of her back—as being embraced by her uncle; she felt his weight on the front of her thighs; she imagined his tongue again between her lips. Her body glowed; her charms ripened; her mind, casting away the prudish veils with which it had so long been encumbered, already contemplated life in another and rosier light, and prepared her to bloom into that lovely and beautiful woman she was so soon to become.

Innocence! (so called) and virginity! in you we do not believe. Flowers, not of virtue, but of a dunghill; the conceptions and impure fruit of Shame, begotten upon Superstition—this is the pedigree we give to you. Ye are fostered by those who fatten upon the fears of the ignorant and weak-minded. Poor human creature, trembling upon the threshold of nature's holiest of holies; terror-stricken at the revelation of her most tremendous mystery about to be made you; you are swooped upon by the priest and called upon to deny your own nature! Your young and budding desires are described to you as sin, such as will condemn you hereafter to endless flame! Impurity is imputed to passion the most natural and the chastest which can possess the soul! and, outraged by the obscene imputation, it recoils in horror upon itself; but if initiated, if forearmed with knowledge, it crushes and stamps the foul tempter under foot, exclaiming: "Monster! the obscenity is in thee. Avaunt!"

Yes; we would have it enacted that all young creatures who had not by one and twenty years of age become women should be made so by compulsory union with a lover; and as the measure could not have a retrospective effect, all old maids—incomplete human creatures, mentally and physically, that they are—should be given three months and the services gratuitously of the most energetic advertising agency in the matrimonial market, and if they did not within that period form some true union and become the fulfilment and completement of some man (for no man is perfect until he includes woman), and, moreover, produce to the court incontestable proofs of the destruction of their maidenhead, that they should perish ignominiously as unnatural deformities. And so infatuated are many of these old deformities that we believe some would perish, although no doubt most would prefer forcible violation; and therefore those who, at the end of the three months, failed to produce the required evidence in court should be given one more chance. They should be placed in charge of a robust curate or other officer of the court, and this charge should be called marriage; the union to endure during the joint lives of the parties; and if at the end of the year the husband swore that all his efforts to storm his old virgin's citadel had failed, the marriage should be declared null; the old woman transfixed by the usher with a weapon to be duly provided for the purpose, and fitted to carry it out, and then strangled; and the curate or other officer provided forthwith with another beauty.

You will say this marriage of yours is a punishment; and we reply, perhaps marriage always is, but in this case that it ought to be so, as the men concerned—all of them—should be those, and those only, who have been indicted and convicted before a court composed of young women, of not having found and enjoyed a mistress before the completion of their twenty-fifth year. We apprehend that the class would not be very numerous, and "marriage" would therefore receive a salutary limitation.

But listen! Alice is rubbing her eyes and puzzling herself with reasons why she should be so possessed by the idea of, and longing for, her uncle, who had used her so cruelly. His being somehow or other overshadowed her, and she seemed to long to be absorbed in it. The strictest analysis of her craving only reduced it as far as a wish that he should take her in his arms and do with her what he wished—what that would be she knew not, but instinctively felt it would be something tremendous, which would entirely alter her whole subjective existence. He had seen her naked; he had reduced her, naked, to absolute submission to his will; he had inflicted upon her the cruellest pain; and the direct medium of the infliction of this pain had been the most secret portion of her body. Yet she delighted in the notion that *he* had seen her (with the exception solely of her stockings) completely nude; she enjoyed the idea that his hand had inflicted the stripes of which she still felt the effects; her breath came more quickly and she trembled with joy when she called to mind that it was to him she had been compelled to display, with the greatest possible humiliation to her, the most intimate recesses of her person and her most jealously-concealed charms without any reserve whatsoever.

She was much puzzled, and her perplexity was accentuated as she moved and felt how tender and how sore her bottom still was.

"Shall I ever be able to sit down again?" she wondered.

Then she recollected the catastrophe that had taken place the moment before she had swooned in that inexplicable ecstasy, and her cheeks flushed and grew hot with shame. And they flushed again and grew still hotter the second time when she recollected that she had to write out fifty times, "I pea'd like a mare before my uncle."

What a little beast she was, and how well she deserved flogging! How just and proper it was that for the next fortnight she should be allowed to relieve herself but twice in the twentyfour hours. The inconvenience would be a very proper lesson for so naughty a girl as she was.

In the midst of these reflections, in came Maud with some egg-flip.

"I would not let them disturb you for luncheon, dear, as I am sure uncle would wish you to be fresh in the evening; and, besides, you must have needed the rest dreadfully. How did you like your whipping?"

"Oh, Maud, it was dreadful! How cruelly severe uncle is."

"I suppose it has made you hate him?"

"No; that is the strangest thing about it. Last night I thought my hatred of him could not be sufficiently intense; but I now feel that I am completely mastered by him, and find that I am glad that it is so!"

"Dear Alice, that was my own experience."

"Has he whipped you, Maud?"

"Yes, dear; and sometimes I purposely do something in order to get myself flogged."

"How curious! When did he whip you first?"

"Oh, long ago. I must give you a full account of it another time. Did you faint with pain?"

"No. I seemed in heaven."

"You do not seem very much exhausted; but you had better eat this cake and egg-flip—it is better for you than tea—and let me look at that poor bottom and see what can be done for it."

So Maud sat down upon the bed, and Alice, to her own astonishment, now nothing loth, laid on her face while Maud removed all the bedclothes from her waist downwards, and, as they chatted, gently anointed her bottom with Vinolia cream, and gave her many a pleasant sensation by the adroit use she made of her hands and fingers.

Alice explained that she now felt a much more experienced girl, and much surprised at a former coyness, which she thought must have appeared extremely ridiculous.

She wondered that anyone could be prudish.

"Yes," said Maud, "It is want of education"—smiling—"and as for modesty, I verily believe innocent girls are only just one little bit less nasty than the very British old maid herself," ended Maud, with a delicious laugh.

"And you, Alice," she went on, "how absurd you were when first you came, blushing at every second word, buttoning your dress up to your throat, wearing it on the ground, and almost screaming at the mere mention of an ankle."

"Oh, Maud, you do not know what I went through in the yellow room. When uncle turned up my petticoats and whipped me, and made me take off my own drawers before him—oh! oh! oh! the mere thought of it is fearful—and then when he put me across his knee and put his finger and thumb——"

"Where?" asked Maud.

"Oh, one in frond and the other behind"—hiding her face with her hands.

"Like that?" said Maud.

"Yes. Just like that. Oh, Maud! oh, how nice! Well, dear, the wonder is that I am alive."

"The sweetest has to come yet, Alice dear. You said you were glad that uncle had mastered you. Do you not long for him?"

"Oh, Maud, I cannot tell you how I do. In such a strange way. I feel I could devour him!"

"Well, dear, all in good time. At any rate, you will not wish to conceal your charms now."

"Oh, no. I take quite a healthy delight in displaying them. I think a long dress quite immodest, because it must be a sign of a mind itching with nasty thoughts."

"Unless, indeed," she continued, after a moment's thoughtfullness, "it is because the natural growth has been checked."

"Oh, Alice, I am so glad that you are such a sensible girl. What splendid times we shall have together. I was never before so fully convinced how right uncle is in his opinion that there is nothing like a sound flogging for a girl. But although we have such a good opinion of ourselves, there are heaps of people who would condemn us with faint praise, and say we were only engagingly immoral. Uncle told me once it was because we were free and emancipated and capable of freely enjoying pleasure which the silly geese—although it is such a *natural* pleasure—think they are bound to deny themselves. There, Alice dear,' ceasing her rubbing, which she had so caressingly done; "is the poor bottom better?"

"Yes, thank you, Maud dear, ever so much. I feel so surprised at being able to lie so unconcernedly before you."

"You see, Alice, you are emancipated—almost. Now you had better have a warm bath, and mind that you use the soap scented with attar of roses. Make a good lather, and bathe yourself all over with it. And then, my dear, you are to put on a low chemise of black silk trimmed with yellow, a yellow corset, black silk petticoats, yellow stockings and shoes, and a net dress with great big yellow spots all over it. It won't come below your knees, dear," said Maud, significantly, at which Alice gave a joyous laugh. "In your bosom you are to place some yellow roses which the gardener has been ordered to bring in on purpose for you."

"And," went on Maud, interrupting Alice, "you are to have your hair twisted up in one great coil and fastened with this arrow, which, you see, is studded with cairn gorms; and round your throat," opening a casket on the dressing table, "you are to put this necklace" (a magnificent one of cairn gorms set in brilliants). "By the bye, you are to tie your stockings with black, not yellow garters, and mind that the first petticoat you put on is that which is lined with yellow silk. Now mind, Alice, and do not make a mistake."

"Oh! how lovely!" cried Alice. "How good you are to me you dear Maud, to take such an interest in me. I shall be dressed all in black and yellow. Why? I wonder."

"Because," mockingly answered Maud, "black and yellow are the devil's colours, and you have his beauty."

"Now, Maud, you are laughing at me. I wonder what you will wear?"

"Oh, something not so striking, dear. You see, it is your turn to-night. You are to be the heroine of to-night. And before I go to dress, I must say goodbye to you, Alice, for I shall not have another opportunity of doing so during the evening, and to-morrow I shall not see you girl again."

"What on earth do you mean, Maud?" asked Alice, experiencing an unaccountable sensation of which she did not understand the significance. "You are not going away, surely?" in alarm.

"Oh, no, you dear goose," replied Maud. "I only meant that I should not see you a girl to-morrow because in all probability you will then be a woman," and the room rang with the musical and merry peal of laughter Maud gave.

"You speak in riddles, dear. I wish you would explain, and not tease me so."

"Not I," said Maud. "Write to Miss Ada Ballin, of the *Ladies' Pictorial*, duly enclosing a coupon, and she will tell you the difference between a girl and a woman; or, by the bye, as it is not the sort of matter the editor (who ought to be circumcised) would allow an explanation of publicly, you had better send her a fee for a private reply; or, better still," she went on maliciously, "ask her for the address of a medical man competent to set forth the mystery personally to you, and," said Maud, in shrieks of laughter at her own wit, "Miss Ada Ballin will certainly send it, if you enclose a stamped, addressed envelope so that it may be sent you privately, as it would be a violation of professional etiquette to publish it; and misses are said to hate violation of every sort. Come! Come! Alice," seeing that Alice began to pout, thinking that Maud was laughing at her, "do not be offended at my nonsense. You will know all about it by to-morrow yourself. Dear me, there's the dressing bell. Only an hour to dinner. Whoever would have thought it was so late?"

"Why not stop and dress here?"

"No; not to-night, dear. One word more, Alice. I heard that you are, for the next fortnight, only to go somewhere twice every day. Now, dear, take my advice and do it late as you can after dinner, and in the morning after you have left the yellow room, if you have to go there. And I know you have to to-morrow."

"Yes; I have; but I do not dread it so much. But I am not going to be birched; am I?"

"No, dear. You are going to have a dozen on the trapeze, which is in some respects worse. I can't stop to explain, though, because, if I do, I shall be late, and then I should be birched."

"Oh, Maud! Very well, dear, I will take your advice, with thanks."

"I am sure you will find it good. Here's Janet. I must run off."

(A fire upon a summer's night is an agreeable thing.) Between it and Alice there at once appeared to be something in common. She and the fire were the only two black and gold things in the rosy apartment. The fierce flame struck Alice as being a very adequate expression of the love she felt seething in her veins. She felt intoxicated with passion and desire, and capable of the most immoral deeds, the more shocking the better.

This naughty lust was soon to have at least some gratification. Maud had seated herself at the piano—an exquisite instrument in a Louis Seize case—and had played softly some snatches of Schubert's airs, and Alice had been reclining some minutes on a rose-coloured couch—a beautiful spot of black and yellow, kept in countenance by the fire—showing two long yellow legs, when Sir Edward noticed that every time she altered her position she endeavoured, with a slightly tinged cheek, to pull her frock down. Of course he had been gazing at the shapely limbs and trying to avail himself of every motion, which could not fail to disclose more—the frock being very short—to see above her knee. He thought once that he had succeeded in catching a glimpse of the pink flesh above the yellow stocking.

Alice, sensible of her uncle's steadfast observation, was more and more overwhelmed with the most bewitching confusion; her coy and timid glances, her fruitless efforts to hide herself, only serving to make her the more attractive.

Maud looked on with amusement from the music-stool, where she sat pouring liquid melody from her pretty fingers, and mutely wondering whatever had come over Alice, and whatever had become of the healthy delight in displaying her charms of which she had boasted before dinner. Maud felt very curious to know how it would end.

"Alice," at length said her uncle, with a movement of impatience, "have you begun to write out that sentence I told you to write out fifty times?"

"Oh, no, uncle! I have not."

"Well, my dear, you had better set to work. It will suggest wholesome reflections."

So Alice got up and got some ruled paper, an inkstand, and a quill pen; then, seating herself at a Chippendale table, began to fiddle with the pen and ink.

Her uncle continued to watch her intently. Maud had ceased to play, and had thrown herself carelessly on the couch which Alice had just left. Maud's dress, too, was quite low and very short; but in the most artless way she flung herself backwards upon the sofa and clasped her hands behind her head, thus showing her arms, neck, bust, and breast to the fullest advantage; and pulling her left foot up to her thigh, made a rest with the left knee for the right leg, which she placed across it, thus fully displaying her legs in their open-work stockings and her thighs encased in loose flesh-coloured silk drawers tied with crimson ribbons. Her attitude and abandon were not lost upon Sir Edward.

Alice's sensations were dreadful. How could she, there, under her uncle's eye, write that she had "pea'd"? And not only "pea'd", but with shame and anger she recollected the sentence ran, "like a mare!" —like an animal; like a beast; as she had seen them in the street. And all "before her uncle." Whatever would become of her if she had to write this terrible sentence; to put so awful a confession into her own handwriting; to confide such a secret fifty times over with her own hand to paper? If it was ever found out she would be ruined—her reputation would be gone—no one would have anything to say to her —she would have to fly to the mountains and the caves. She had not realized until it came to actually writing it out how difficult, how terrible, how impossible it was for her to do it. If her uncle knew, surely he would not insist. He could not wish her to humiliate herself to such an extent; to ruin and destroy herself with her own handwriting; neither could he have realized what it would be for her to write such a thing. While these thoughts were passing through her mind, she kept unconsciously pulling and dragging at her frock. If only she could cover herself up. So much of her legs showed; and the long yellow stockings made them so conspicuous under her black frock. Although they were above her knee, unless she kept her legs close together she could not help showing her black garters. And her arms and her neck and her breast were all bare. She began to feel almost sulky.

"Well, Alice," at length said her uncle; "when are you going to begin?"

"Oh, uncle! it is dreadful to have to say such a thing in my own handwriting—I am sure you have never thought how dreadful."

"You must chronicle in your own handwriting what you did, miss. Writing what you did is not so bad as doing it. And you will not only write it, but you shall sign it with your name, so that everyone may know what a naughty girl you were."

"Oh, uncle! oh, uncle! I can't. You will burn it when it is done; won't you?"

"No; certainly not. It shall be kept as a proof of how naughty you can be."

And as she kept tugging at her frock and not writing, her uncle said:—

"Maud, will you fetch the dress-suspender? It will keep her dress out of her way."

Maud discharged her errand with alacrity. In less than three minutes she had returned with a band of black silk, from which hung four long, black silk ribbons. Making Alice stand up, Maud slipped her arms under her petticoats and put the band round Alice's waist next her skin, buckling it behind, and edged it up as high as the corset, which Janet had not left loose, would allow. The four ribbons hung down far below the frock, two at the right and two at the left hip— one ribbon in front, the other at the back.

Maud then walked Alice over into the full blaze of the fire. Putting her arms round her and bending down, she took the ribbons at Alice's left side one in each hand, and then pulled them up and joined them on Alice's right shoulder in a bow. The effect, of course, was to bundle half Alice's petticoats and dress up about her waist, disclosing her left leg from the end of the stocking naked. Maud, with little ceremony, then turned her round, and, taking the ribbons at her right side, tied them across her left shoulder, thus removing the other half of Alice's covering and displaying the right leg. She then carefully arranged the frock and petticoats, smoothing them out, tightening the ribbons, and settling the bows. And by the time she had finished, from the black band round her waist nearly to her garters, Alice was in front and behind perfectly naked—her breast and arms and thighs and navel and buttocks. The lower petticoat was, it will be remembered, lined with yellow, and the inside was turned out. It and the stockings and the two black bands intensified her nakedness. She would sooner have been, she felt, stripped entirely of every shred of clothing than have had on those garments huddled about her waist, and those stockings, which, she instinctively knew, only heightened the exhibition of her form and directed the gaze to all she most wished to conceal.

"Now, miss," said her uncle, "this will save you the trouble of vain and silly efforts to conceal yourself."

"Oh, uncle! uncle! how can you disgrace me so?"

"Disgrace you, my dear? What nonsense! You are not deformed. You are perfectly exquisite. With," he continued, passing his hand over her, "a skin like satin."

Feeling his hand, Alice experienced a delicious thrill, which her uncle noticing, recommended her to sit down and write out her imposition—a task which was now a hundred times more difficult. However could she, seated in a garb which only displayed her nakedness in the most glaring manner, write such words?

"Alice," said he, "you are again becoming refractory."

Putting his arm round her, he sat down and put her face downwards across his left knee. "You must have your bottom smacked. That will bring you to your senses." (Smack—smack—smack—smack—smack—smack.)

"Oh, uncle! don't! Oh!"—struggling—"I will write anything!"—smack—"oh! how you sting!"—smack—smack—"oh! oh! oh! Your hand is so hard."

Then, slipping his hand between her legs, he tickled her clitoris until she cooed and declared she would take a delight in saying and writing and doing the "most shocking things."

"Very well, miss! Then go and write out what I told you; sign it; and bring it to me when it is finished."

So Alice seated herself—the straw seat of the chair pricking her bottom—resolved, however, to brazen out her nakedness, and wrote with a trembling hand: "I pea'd like a mare before my uncle; I pea'd like a mare before my uncle; I pea'd like a mare before my uncle." Before she had half completed her task, she was so excited and to such an extent under the influence of sensual and voluptuous feelings that she could not remain still; and she felt the delicate hair in front about her cunt grow moist Before she had completed the fiftieth line she was almost beside herself.

At last, for the fiftieth time, she wrote:—

"I pea'd like a mare before my uncle."

And with a shudder, signed it, "Alice Darvell."

During her task Maud had looked at what she was writing over her shoulder, and Alice glowed with shame. So had her uncle; but

Alice was surprised to find she rather liked his seeing her disgrace, and felt inclined to nestle close up to him.

Now Maud had gone to bed, and she was to take her task to her uncle.

He was seated in a great chair near the fire, looking very wide awake indeed. He might have been expected to have been dozing. But there was too lovely a girl in the room for that. He looked wide awake indeed, and there was a fierce sparkle in his eye as his beautiful ward, in her long yellow stockings and low dress, her petticoats turned up to her shoulders, and blushing deeply, approached him with her accomplished penance.

She handed it to him.

"So you did, Alice," said he, "so you did," sitting bolt upright, "pea like a mare before me, and here is, I see," turning over a page or two, "your own signature to the confession."

"Oh, uncle, it is true; but do not let anyone know. I know I disgraced myself and behaved like a beast; but I am so sorry."

"But you deserved your punishment."

"Yes; I know I did. Only too well."

He drew her down upon his knee, and placed his right arm round her waist, while he tickled her legs and her groin and her abdomen, and lastly her clitoris, with his hand and fingers.

He let her, when she was almost overcome by the violence of her sensations, slip down between his knees, and as she was seeking how most effectually to caress him, he directed her hands to his penis and his testicles. In a moment of frenzy she tore open his trousers, lifted his shirt, and saw the excited organ, the goal and Ultima Thule of feminine delight. He pressed down her head, and, despite the resistance she at first made, the inflamed and distended virility was very quickly placed between the burning lips of her mouth. Its taste and the transport she was in induced her to suck it violently. On her knees before her uncle, tickling, sucking, licking his penis, then looking in his face and recommencing, the sweet girl's hands again very quickly found their way to his balls.

At last, excited beyond his selfcontrol, gazing through his halfclosed lids at the splendid form of his niece at his feet—her bare back and shoulders—the breast which, sloping downwards from her position, he yet could see—her bare arms—the hands twiddling and manipulating and kneading with affection and appreciation his balls; his legs far apart, himself thrown back gasping in his arm chair; his own most sensitive and highly excited organ in the dear girl's hot mouth, tickled with the tip of her dear tongue, and pinched with her dear, pretty, cruel ivory teeth—Sir Edward could contain himself no longer and, grasping Alice's head with both his hands, he pushed his weapon well into her mouth and spent down her throat. He lay back in a swoon of delight, and the girl, as wet as she could be, leant her head against his knee, almost choked by the violence of the delightful emission, and stunned by the mystery revealed to her. How she loved him! How she dandled that sweet fellow! How she fondled him! What surreptitious licks she gave him! She could have eaten her uncle.

In about twenty minutes he had recovered sufficiently to speak, and she sat with her head resting against the inside of his right leg, looking up into his face; her own legs stretched out underneath his left one—she was sitting on the floor.

"Alice, you bold, bad girl, to pea like a mare. I hope you feel punished now."

"Oh no, uncle, it was delightful. Does it give you pleasure? I will suck you again," taking his penis, to his great excitement, again in her warm little palm, "if you wish."

"My dear, do you want to pea?"

"Yes; before I go to bed."

"Then here is the key. Run along and go to bed."

"Oh, I would rather stay with you."

"Although I have whipped you and birched you and smacked you and made you disgrace yourself?"

"Yes, dear uncle. It has done me good. Don't send me away."

"Go, Alice, to bed. I will come to you there."

"Oh, you dear uncle, how nice. Oh, do let down my things for me before I go. Some of the servants may see me."

"And," she continued, after an instant's pause, with a blush, and looking down, "I want to be for you alone."

Touched by her devotion, her uncle loosed the ribbons; let fall, as far as they would, her frock and petticoats; and giving her a kiss, and not forgetting to use his hand under her clothes in a manner which caused her again to cry out with delight, allowed her to trip off to her bedroom. But not without the remark that she had induced him to do that which did not add to her appearance; for the rich, full, and well-developed girlish form had been simply resplendent with loveliness in the garments huddled about her waist; the petticoat lining of yellow silk relieved by the black bands from her waist to her shoulder crossing each other, and bits of her black frock, with its large yellow spots, appearing here and there. And as the eye travelled downwards from the pink flesh of the swelling breasts to the smooth pink thighs, it noted with rapture that the clothes concealed only what needed not concealment, and revealed with the greatest effect what did; and, still descending, dwelt entranced upon the well-turned limbs, whose outlines and curves the tight stockings so clearly defined.

Sir Edward, who had made her stand facing him, and also with her back to him, was much puzzled, although so warm a devotee of the Venus Callipyge, whether he preferred the back view of her lovely legs, thighs, bottom, back, nuque, and queenly little head, with its suggestion of fierce and cruel delight; or the front, showing the mount and grotto of Venus, the tender breasts, the dimpled chin and sparkling eyes, with the imaginations of soft pleasures and melting trances which the sloping and divided thighs suggested and invited.

The first thing which Alice noticed upon reaching her room was the little supper-table laid for two; and the next that there were black silk sheets on her bed. The sight of the supper—the chocolate, the tempting cakes and biscuits, the rich wines in gold mounted jugs, the Nuremburg glasses, the bonbons, the crystallized fruit, the delicate omelette—delighted her; but the black sheets had a somewhat funereal and depressing effect.

"What can Maud have been thinking of, my dear, to put *black* sheets on the bed; and to-night of all nights in the year?" asked Sir Edward, angrily, the instant he entered the apartment, and hastily returning to the sitting-room, he rang and ordered Janet up. She was directed to send Miss Maud to "my niece's room, and in a quarter of an hour to put *pink* silk sheets on the bed there."

Then Sir Edward returned, and giving Alice some sparkling white wine, which with sweet biscuits she said she would like better than anything else, he helped himself to a bumper of red—standing—expecting Maud's appearance. Alice was seated in a cosy chair, toasting her toes.

Presently Maud arrived in a lovely déshabille, her rich dark hair tumbling about her shoulders, the dressing-gown not at all concealing the richly-embroidered robe de nuit beneath it, and the two garments clinging closely to her form, setting off her lovely svelte figure to perfection. Her little feet were encased in low scarlet slippers embroidered with gold, so low cut as to show the whole of the white instep.

Her manner was hurried and startled, but this pretty dismay increased her attractions.

"Maud," asked her uncle, "what do you mean by having had black sheets put on this bed, when I distinctly said they were to be pink?"

"Indeed, indeed, uncle, you said black."

"How dare you contradict me, miss, and so add to your offence? You have been of late very careless indeed. You shall be soundly punished. Go straight to the yellow room," he went on to the trembling girl. "I will follow you in a few moments and flog you in a way that you will recollect. Eighteen stripes with my riding-whip and a dozen with the cat-o'-nine-tails."

"Oh, uncle," she gasped.

"Go along, miss."

Alice, to her surprise, although she had some little feeling of distress for Maud, felt quite naughty at the idea of her punishment; and, noticing her uncle's excitement, concluded instinctively that he also felt similar sensations. She was, consequently, bold enough, without rising, to stretch out her hand and to press outside his clothes the gentleman underneath with whom she had already formed so intimate an acquaintance, asking as she did so whether he was going to be very severe.

"Yes," he replied, moving to and fro (notwithstanding which she kept her hand well pressed on him). "I shall lash her bottom until it bleeds and she yells for mercy."

"O, uncle!" said Alice, quivering with a strange thrill.

"Go to the room, Alice. I shall follow in a moment."

Poor Maud was in tears, and Alice, much affected at this sight, attempted to condole with her.

"The riding-whip is terribly severe; however I shall bear it I can't tell; and then that terrible cat afterwards; it will drive me mad."

"Oh, Maud, I am so sorry."

"And I made *no* mistake. He *said* black sheets. The fact is, your beauty has infuriated him, and he wants to tear me to pieces."

Sir Edward returned without trousers, wearing a kilt.

"Now come over here, you careless hussey," and indicating two rings in the floor quite three feet apart, he made her stretch her legs wide, so as to place her feet near the rings, to which Alice was made to strap them by the ankles. "I will cure you of your carelessness and nattention to orders. Your delicate flesh will feel this rod's cuts for days. Off with your dressing-gown; off with your night-dress." Alice was dazzled by her nakedness, the ripeness of her charms, the whiteness of her skin, the plump, soft, round bottom, across which Sir Edward laid a few playful cuts, making the girl call out, for, fixed as she was, she could not struggle.

Alice then, by her uncle's direction, placed before Maud a trestle, the top of which was stuffed and covered with leather, and which reached just to her middle. Across this she was made to lie, and two rings on the other side were drawn down and fixed her elbows, so that her head was almost on the floor, and her bottom, with its skin tight, well up in the air. Her legs, of course, were well apart. The cruelty of the attitude inflamed Alice.

"Give me the whip," said her uncle. As she handed the heavy weapon to him, he added, "stand close to me while I flog her, and," slipping his hand up her petticoats on to her inflamed and moist organ, "keep your hand upon me while I do so."

Alice gave a little spring as he touched her. Her own animal feelings told her what was required of her.

Maud was crying softly.

"Now, miss," as the whip cut through the air, "it is your turn" —swish—a great red wale across the bottom and a writhe of agony— "you careless"—swish—"wicked"—swish—"disobedient"—swish— "obstinate girl."

"Oh, uncle! oh! oh! oh! oh! I am sorry, oh, forgive——"—swish —"no, miss"—swish—"no forgiveness. Black sheets, indeed"—swish —swish—swish—"I will cure you, my beauty."

Maud did her best to stifle her groans, but it was clear that she was almost demented with the exquisite torture the whip caused her every time it cut with relentless vigour into her bleeding flesh. Sir

Edward did not spare her. The rod fell each time with unmitigated energy.

"Spare the rod and spoil you, miss. Better spoil your bold, big bottom than that," he observed, as he pursued the punishment. The more cruel it became the greater Alice found grew her uncle's and her own excitement, until at last she scarcely knew how to contain herself. At the ninth stripe, Sir Edward crossed over to Maud's right to give the remaining nine the other way across.

Swish—swish—swish—fell the heavy whip, the victim's moans and prayers absolutely unheeded.

"A girl must have her bare bottom whipped"—swish—"occasionally; there is nothing"—swish—"so excellent for her"—swish—"it teaches her to mind what is told her"—swish—"it knocks all false shame"—swish—"out of her; there is no mock modesty left about a young—lady after"—swish—"she has had her bottom under the lash."

Alice trembled when she saw the cat-o'-nine-tails, made of hard, tightly twisted whip-cords, each tail bearing several knots, and when she looked at the bleeding bottom she grew sick and pale. But when her uncle began to lecture Maud as he caressingly drew the terrible scourge through his fingers, and to tell her that for a hardened girl such as she was a whip was insufficient punishment, and that she must also be subjected to the cat's claws, Alice began to revive, and she noticed that, while Sir Edward again approached boiling point, Maud gave as much lascivious movement as her tight bonds permitted.

But the first three strokes, given from left to right, evoked piercing yells and shrieks; the next three, given across the other way, cries and howls of the wildest despair, followed by low sobs. The blood flowed freely and was spattered about the room. Alice felt some on her face and arms.

"You will not forget again, I know," said Sir Edward, as he wielded the terrible instrument. "You careless, naughty girl, how grateful you should be to me for taking the trouble to chastise you thus. The cat has quite irresistible arguments, has she not?"

The last six were given lengthwise, first along the legs, then round the bottom, and lastly on the cunt. Maud's roars and yells were redoubled; but in an ecstasy of delight she lost her senses at the last blow.

Alice, too, was mad with excitement. Rushing off, as directed, to her room, she, as her uncle had also bid her do, tore off all her clothing and dived into the pink sheets, rolling about with the passion the sight of the whipping had stimulated to an uncontrollable degree.

Sir Edward, having summoned Janet to attend Maud, hastened to follow Alice.

Divesting himself of all his clothing, he tore the bedclothes off the naked girl who lay on her back, inviting him to her arms, and to the embrace of which she was still ignorant, by the posture nature dictated to her, and looking against the pink sheet a perfect rose of loveliness. Sir Edward sprang upon her in a rush and surge of passion which bore him onwards with the irresistible force a flowing sea. In a moment he, notwithstanding her cries, was between her already separated legs, clasping her to him, while he directed, with his one free hand, his inflamed and enormous penis to her virgin cunt. Already it had passed the lips and was forcing its way onwards, impelled, by the reiterated plunges of Sir Edward, before Alice could realize what was happening. At last she turns a little pale, and her eyes open wide and stare slightly in alarm, while, finding that her motion increases the assault and the slight stretching of her cunt, she remains still. But the next moment, remembering what had occurred when *it* was in her mouth, it struck her that the same throbbing and shooting and deliciously warm and wet emission might be repeated in the lower and more secret part of her body, and that if, as she hoped and prayed it might be, it was, she would expire of joy. These ideas caused a delightfull tremor and a few movements of the buttocks, which increased Sir Edward's pleasure and enabled him to make some progress. But at length the swelling of his organ and his march into the interior began to hurt, and she became almost anxious to withdraw from the amorous encounter. His arms, however, held her tight. She could not get him from between her legs, and she was being pierced in the tenderest portion of her body by a man's great thing, like a horse's. Oh, how naughty she felt! And yet how it hurt! How dreadful it was that he should be able to probe her with it and detect all her sensations by means of it, while on the other hand, she was made sensible *there,* and by means of *it,* of all he felt.

"Oh! uncle! Oh! dear, dear uncle! Oh! oh! oh! oh! Wait one minute! Oh! not so hard! Oh, dear, don't push any further—oh, it is so nice; but it hurts! Oh, do stop! don't press so hard! Oh! oh! oh! Oh! please don't! oh! it hurts! Oh! I shall die! You are tearing me open! you are indeed! Oh! oh! oh!"

"If you don't"—push—push—"hold me tight and push against me, Alice, I will—yes, that's better—flog your bottom until it bleeds and the blood runs down to your heels, you bold girl. No, you shan't get away. I will get right into you. Don't," said he, clawing her bottom with his hands and pinching its cheeks severely, "slip back. Push forward."

"Oh! I shall die! Oh! oh! oh!" as she felt she pinches, and jerked forward, enabling Sir Edward to make considerable advance, "Oh! I shall faint; I shall die! Oh, stop! Oh!" as she continued her involuntary motion upwards and downwards, "you hurt excruciatingly."

He folded her more closely to him, and, altogether disregarding her loud cries, proceeded to divest her of her maidenhead, telling her that if she did not fight bravely he would punish her till she thought she was being flayed alive; that he would tear her bottom for her with hooks; and he slipped a hand down behind her, and got the middle finger well into her arse.

After this, victory was assured. A few more shrieks and spasms of mingled pleasure and pain, when Sir Edward, who had forced himself up to the hymen and had made two or three shrewd thrusts at it, evoking loud gasps and cries from his lovely ward, drew a long sigh, and with a final determined push sunk down on her bosom, while she, emitting one sharp cry, found her suffering changed into a transport of delight. She clasped her uncle with frenzy to her breast, and throbbed and shook in perfect unison with him, while giving little cries of rapture and panting—with half-closed lids, from under which rolled a diamond tear or two—for the breath of which her ecstasy had robbed her.

Several moments pased, the silence interrupted only by inarticulate sounds of gratification. Sir Edward's mouth was glued to hers, and his tongue found its way between its ruby lips and sought hers. Overcoming her coyness, the lovely girl allowed him to find it, and no sooner had they touched than an electric thrill shot through her; Sir Edward's penis, which had never been removed, again began to swell; he recommenced his (and she her) upward and downward movements and again the delightful crisis occurred—this time without the intense pain Alice had at first experienced, and with very much greater appreciation of the shock, which thrilled her from head to foot and seemed to penetrate and permeate the innermost recesses of her being.

Never had she experienced, or even in her fondest moments conceived, the possibility of such transports. She had longed for the possession of her uncle; she had longed to eat him, to become absorbed in him; and she now found the appetite gratified to the fullest extent, in a manner incredibly sweet. To feel his weight upon the front of her thighs—to feel him between her legs, her legs making each of his a captive; the most secret and sensitive and essentially masculine organ of his body inside that part of hers of which she could not think without a blush; and the mutual excitement, the knowledge and consciousness each had of the other's most intimate sensations, threw her into an ecstasy. How delicious it was to be a girl; how she enjoyed the contemplation of her charms; how supremely, overpoweringly delightful it was to have a lover in her embrace to appreciate and enjoy them! How delicious was love!

Sir Edward, gratified at length, rose and congratulated Alice upon her newborn womanhood; kissed her, and thanked her for the intense pleasure she had given him.

After some refreshment, as he bade her good-night, the love-sick girl once more twined her arms about him, while slipping her legs on to the edge of the bed, she lay across it and managed to get him between them; then, drawing him down to her bosom, cried, "Once more, dear uncle; once more before you go."

"You naughty girl," he answered, slightly excited; "well, I will if you ask me."

"Oh, please, do, uncle. Please do it again."

"Do what again?"

"Oh! It. You know, What—what—what," hiding her face sweetly, "you have done to me twice already."

"Don't you know what it is called?"

"No. I haven't the slightest idea.'

"It is called 'fucking.' Now, if you want it done again, you must ask to be fucked," said he, his instrument assuming giant proportions.

"Oh, dear, I do want it ever so; but however I can ask for it— please uncle—will—will you, please—please—f—f—fu—fuck me once more before you go?" and she lay back and extended her legs before him in the divinest fashion.

In a moment he was between them; his prick inserted; his lips again upon hers; and in a few moments more they were again simultaneously overcome by that ecstasy of supernatural exquisiteness of which unbridled passion has alone attempted to fathom the depths, and that without reaching them.

Exhausted mentally and physically by her experiences and the exercises of the evening, Alice, as she felt the lessening throbs of her uncle's engine, found she was losing herself and consciousness in drowsiness. Her uncle placed her in a comfortable posture upon the great pillow, and throwing the sheet over her, heard her murmured words of thanks and love as she fell asleep with a smile upon her face. Janet came and tucked her up comfortably. And she slept profoundly.

Chapter V

PUNISHMENT.

Whipping grown girls is a pastime rare
Few males, if called on, could refuse to share.

—Romance of Chastisement.

Alice lay awake next morning listening to the birds, in a sweet trance as the recollection on which she dwelt of what she had passed through the night before. She felt completely changed, and could she have seen the dark stains upon the crimson sheet under her, she would have known that she really was so.

She met Maud in the breakfast-room and was warmly greeted by her.

"Well, love; well, Alice?" cried she, clasping both her hands in her own and gazing into her face with a glance in which there was deep meaning.

"Oh, Maud!" ejaculated Alice, blushing, and then, to turn the subject, "how are you, dear, after that terrible flogging? I could almost have cried at what you suffered at one moment, and yet I could have made uncle tear you in pieces the next."

"Yes," said Maud; "I have experienced the feeling. The result was that you and your uncle enjoyed yourselves the more. Now, wasn't it?"

After breakfast Alice remembered that she had to go straight to the yellow room. She did so without much dread, feeling that she could not have worse to go through than she had already suffered; although one or two chance expressions of Maud had made her doubtful of this conclusion; and the cold sternness of her uncle startled and alarmed her after his warmth and tenderness of the preceding evening. When he met her and wished her good morning in the breakfast-room he was apparently absolutely unconscious, and certainly totally forgetful, of what had passed.

Alice went with Maud arm-in-arm to the yellow room, wondering what the trapeze would be like.

Her uncle soon followed her and locked the door. He had a long carriage-whip and some sheets of paper which she recognised in his hand.

"You are Miss Alice Darvell, and this is your handwriting and signature?" asked he severely, showing the papers to her.

"Oh yes, uncle; they are," answered the girl, trembling with fright.

"You pea'd like a mare before your uncle, eh, miss?"

"I—I—I couldn't help it."

"Did you?"

"Y—ye—yes!"

"Well, you shall be flogged like a mare. Strip yourself."

"Oh, uncle!"

"Strip yourself absolutely naked, or," he said, raising the whip and lightly slashing it about her legs, for her frock only came down to her knees, "you shall have double."

She jumped as she felt the lash sting her calves, and drew up her legs one after another.

Then, seeing her uncle's arm again raised, she began to quickly undo her bodice and slip off her frock; her petticoats and corset soon followed, and, lastly, slipping off her chemise, she stood naked except for her long stockings, and covered with a most bewildering air of shame, not knowing whether to cover her face or not, or how to dispose of her hands and arms.

"Take off your shoes and stockings," said her uncle.

She had to do so seated in her nakedness, and the action added extremely to confusion.

Sir Edward then went to a bracket or flat piece of wood screwed on the wall, on which were two hooks fixed back to back and some distance apart; round them was fastened a thick crimson silk cord. As he unwound it, Alice saw that it communicated with a pulley in the ceiling over which it hung, and dangling from which was a bar of wood about two-and-a-half feet long—the cord dividing about three feet above it and being fastened to each of its ends.

"Now, Maud," said Sir Edward, "put her in position and fix her wrists."

Maud walked up to Alice and led her beneath the pulley. Sir Edward allowed the bar to descend to a level with the top of her shoulders. Maud then took the naked girl's right wrist and fastened it by a strap ready prepared to one end of the bar, so that the back of the hand was against it. And then she did the same with the left hand.

"Ready?" asked Sir Edward.

"Ready," answered Maud.

Whereupon he pulled the cord, availing himself of the hooks to get a purchase, until Alice's arms were stretched high above her head, and her whole body was well drawn up, the balls of her feet only resting on the floor.

"Oh, uncle! oh, uncle! oh, please! oh! not so high! oh! my arms will be dislocated! oh! it hurts my wrists!" and, involuntarily moving, she found very little would swing her off her feet.

Sir Edward, finding her sufficiently drawn up, fixed the cord, and, taking the whip in his right hand, played with the lash with his left as he gloated upon the exquisite naked girl—her extended arms, her shoulders, her breasts, her stomach, her navel, her abdomen, her back, her thighs, her buttocks, her legs, all displayed and glowing with shame and beauty.

At last, raising his whip, as he stood at her left, he said:—

"So we 'pea'd like a mare before uncle,' and are now going to be flogged like a mare."

Alice, in silent terror, drew up first one leg and then the other, showing off the exquisitely moulded limbs, and giving more than a glimpse of other charms.

"And," went on her uncle, "on the very part guilty of the offence." Whisp—whisple.

He had raised the whip, swinging out the lash, and brought it down with full force across the front of the girl's thighs, the lash striking her fair on the cunt. For a moment she was speechless, but the next emitted a piercing yell as she threw her head back and struggled to be free.

Sir Edward's arm was now across him.

Whisp, whisple went the whip as he gave the return stroke severely across her bottom, making her dance with anguish and leaving a red wale.

Whisp, whisple went the whip with merciless precision back again.

Alice's gymnastics were of the most frantic description. She jumped and threw out her legs and swung to and fro, showing every atom of her form, in utter recklessness of what she showed or of what she concealed.

When three strokes had been administered backwards and forwards from the left side, Sir Edward went round to the right—there her bottom received the forward and her front the back strokes, and well laid on they were. Sir Edward delighted in the infliction of a punishment which left his victim no reserve or concealment whatever, and he made the whip cut into the flesh.

Alice, almost suffocated with her cries and sobs, writhed for several minutes after the last stroke. At last her agony became less intense and her sobs fewer.

A high stool was then put before her and on it a po.

It was pushed close up to her, and Sir Edward inserted his hand from behind and tickled and frigged her cunt, saying:

"Yesterday you pea'd to please yourself. To-day you shall do so to please me."

Alice, beside herself, knew not what to do. She had not relieved herself since the night before. At last, with a shudder, a copious flood burst out, partly over her uncle's hand, and she gave a groan as she realized the manner in which she had been made to disgrace herself.

Her uncle then loosened the rope sufficiently to let her heels rest on the ground, and calling Maud to the sofa, which was immediately in front of Alice, he threw her back on it, while she quickly unfastened and pulled down his trousers, exposing his back view entirely to Alice. Maud, too, whose petticoats were up to her waist, threw wide her legs, and Sir Edward, prostrating himself upon her, fucked her violently before Alice.

Never was Alice so conscious of her nakedness as then.

Never, apparently, did Maud enjoy the pleasure of a good fucking more than she did in the presence of that naked and tied-up girl.

And never did Sir Edward acquit himself with greater prowess.

Alice's movements, as she saw her uncle's exertions in Maud's arms, and his strong, sinewy, bare and hairy legs, and his testicles hanging down, and heard his deep breathing and Maud's gasps and sighs—began again, but this time from pleasure instead of pain. She could not, however, as she longed to, get her hands to her cunt, and could only imitate the motions of the impassioned pair before her by a sympathetic movement to and fro—which expressed, but did not assuage her desires—and by little exclamations of longing.

At length the crisis was reached, and Sir Edward sank into Maud's embrace, while Alice could see, and imagined almost that she could *hear,* the throb, throb, throb that was sending thrill after thrill through Maud, and was causing her such a transport of delight that she seemed about to faint from it.

And then he untied her, and was about to leave them, when Alice said, in a most bewitching way:—

"Could you not 'fuck' (a deep blush) me—just once, dear uncle?"

Het half-closed eyes, her splendid form, her nakedness, reawakened her uncle's love and reinvigorated his bestowal of those sensible proofs of it in which ladies so delight. He replied:

"Maud has made me work pretty hard, my dear; but," putting one hand upon her shoulder as she faced him, "as you honour me with such a command, I should be but a *fainéant* and ungallant knight were I not to execute it—or at any rate to make an effort to do so," added he, leading the beautiful girl, nothing loth, to the couch whereon he had enjoyed Maud and gently pushing her backwards, amid her cries and exclamations and involuntary but pretty reluctance, inserted himself into her embrace. She inundated him once, and Maud, perceiving it, slipped her hand between his thighs. This help, good at need, soon worked the cavalier up to a proper appreciation of the situation in which he lay, and to a due expression of his sense of it; to the lady's intense gratification especially, as her forces were sufficient to enable her to, a second time—and this time at exactly the right instant—

Tumble down,
And break her crown

and, fortunately, *not* "come tumbling after" Jack, as Jill does in the story.

Although her uncle gave her these marks of affection, yet he did not relent in severity. She was kept without drawers the whole fortnight—a severe punishment! And the stiff white petticoats kept what skirts she had well off her legs, so that when she was seated could not fail to be seen.

And, indeed, after the lashing on the trapeze, she was not allowed to resume that day any garments at all.

She had been given a notebook in which she was compelled to make an entry of every fault and the punishment she was to receive for it.

In her room, on that particular day, aghast at her own nakedness, and thinking herself alone, she had taken up a pair of drawers which, by accident or design, were left there—she had gone to get ready for luncheon—and put them on, when suddenly Sir Edward entered the room.

"What do you mean, miss, by putting on those things? Did I not tell you you were to remain naked the whole of to-day?"

"I only put them on for a moment. I felt so ashamed of being naked."

"Take out your book and write:—For being ashamed of being naked, and for disobedience to my uncle, I am to ask him to give me two dozen with the tawse across his knee after supper this evening, and I am to remain stark naked for three days."

"Oh! oh! oh! Forgive me, dear uncle. I won't be ashamed any more. I won't disobey you any more. I won't indeed."

But it was no use.

At luncheon she had to sit down naked. All the afternoon she had to go about so. If only she might have had one scrap of clothing on! At dinner she could not dress, absolutely naked again; not even shoes or slippers permitted. And that to last three days more! All the evening naked; and as she thought of it she rolled over on to the pillow of the couch and hid her face; but, notwithstanding, felt naked still.

After supper came those terrible two dozen with the tawse. The tawse is a Scotch instrument of punishment, and in special favour with Scotch ladies, who know how to lay it on soundly. It is made of a hard and seasoned piece of leather about two feet long, narrow in the handle and at the other end about four inches broad, cut into narrow strips from about six to nine inches in length.

Alice had never seen, much less felt one.

She was commanded to bring it to her uncle, and had to go for it naked—not even a fan was allowed! How could she conceal the least of her emotions? Oh, this nakedness was an awful, awful thing!

She brought it, and opened her book and knelt down and said:

"Please, uncle, give me two dozen with the tawse for being ashamed and trying to cover my nakedness, and for my disobedience."

"Across my knee."

"Across—your—knee."

"Very well. Get up. Stand sideways close up to me. Now," taking the tawse in his right hand and putting his left arm round her waist, "lean right down, your head on the carpet, miss," and holding her legs with his left one, he slowly and deliberately laid on her sore bottom two dozen well-applied stripes. Then letting her go, she rolled sprawling on the carpet with pain and exhaustion.

The three days' nakedness were rigorously enforced.

They entirely overcame and quenched every spark of shame that was left about her, and she was much the more charming. Her silly simplicity, her country ignorance, were replaced by an artless coquetry and a self-possession which took away the breath and struck those in her presence with irresistible admiration.

Other punishments, too, she had to endure, some of them of a fantastic character.

The fortnight passed rapidly; but the last week, during which she was mistress, was a trying one for her. The servants scarcely heeded a baby in short frocks, with bare legs except for her long stockings, and became careless.

Many a smacking she received across her uncle's knee in the dining-room, or wherever they might happen to be, for some short-coming; often was she sent away hungry from the table and locked up in a black hole for hours because she had not ordered this or that, or someone had done what he disapproved of. And after supper every evening, and all night if he was in the humour, she was required to be at his disposal and to give him pleasure in every form his endless ingenuity could invent.

At the end of the week, when her drawers were restored to her, she scarcely cared for them; but had not worn them long when the recollection of having been so much without them gave her the sweetest sense of shame possible.

CHAPTER VI

THE END.

Quoth she, "Before you tumbled me
You promised me to wed."

—OLD SONG

So life continued for a long while at Bosmere Hall. The summer ripened into autumn; winter followed, and then spring, when, on good authority, it is said the thoughts turn to love.

The hunting had delighted Alice, notwithstanding that she had been once or twice soundly birched by her uncle in the open air for some error of the *ménage*, and made to ride home without trousers.

She came, however, to like these punishments; but one day she thought she had seriously offended him, for he declared his intention of marrying her to his heir. She would have preferred him.

The heir and she met at a ball. He was a charming young man. Alice's bashfulness had long departed. She recognized some likeness to her uncle—she knew his wishes. She waltzed five or six times with her cousin, who was intoxicated with her beauty and her short dress, her openwork stockings with the clocks at the side, the tiny little dancing shoes; the rosy flesh, and the perfume of love in every breath she exhaled.

They went together to supper, and afterwards retired to a distant conservatory. Soon his arm was about her, while his other hand was busily engaged, to her delight, underneath her petticoats. The honeyed phrases and sweet nothings that so please lovers followed, and they were to be married in three months. The period rapidly passed.

On her wedding day her uncle presented her with a hundred thousand pounds personal property of his own, which became her own, apart from her husband and the inheritance and settlements, and also with the famous cairn gorms.

Alice smiled and wept as brides will on her departure to spend Easter with her husband at Rome.

She taught him much, and, on the other hand, learned one or two things from him. But what surprised her most of all was that, whilst she often thought with ridicule and contempt of the days spent with her old aunt in Yorkshire, she always regarded with joy and satisfaction those spent at Bosmere Hall with her uncle and Maud, and felt she would ever consider them as the happiest of her life.

SUBURBAN SOULS
BOOK TWO

I am at the top of the sinners' class and my only excuse is that somehow I manage to be intensely wicked on an honourable, chivalrous basis of my own. You shall find out my style of villainy as you read on . . .

Book Two of SUBURBAN SOULS completes the erotic masterpiece of Jacky S. It is published together with twenty appendices including *The Pleasure of Cruelty*, *Condemned to Death* and the complete text of the notorious erotic novel, *The Yellow Room*, which is referred to in *Suburban Souls* as having been edited by Jacky S. himself.

Also in this series: